'Hitchcockian chills and thrills a 34 survival and deception.' *O, The* and *magazine*

'Swanson specializes in writing mesmerizing thrillers that subvert readers' expectations. The author works his particular magic once again with *Every Vow You Break* . . . Swanson's shape-shifting saga is reminiscent, by turns, of such foreboding films as *Vertigo* [and] *Fatal Attraction*.' *Wall Street Journal*

'Swanson has a bent for revenge and murder. Fans will not be disappointed.' *USA Today*

'Will give you major *Fatal Attraction* vibes . . . A tantalizing plot, steamy scenes, and passionate relationships.' *PopSugar*

'The further we go into [Swanson's] devilishly twisty tales, the more hooks he sets . . . Bride-to-be Abigail had a booze-fueled one-night stand . . . and is now being stalked by the man with whom she dallied. *Fatal Attraction*, right? Well, maybe, but we quickly see there's more to it than that.' *Booklist*

'Swanson delivers another stellar thriller full of adrenaline-inducing surprises and a plot that turns on a dime.' *BookBub*

Peter Swanson's novels include *The Girl With a Clock for a Heart*, nominated for an *LA Times* book award, *The Kind Worth Killing*, a Richard & Judy pick and the iBooks store's thriller of the year in 2015, and, most recently, *Rules for Perfect Murders*. He lives with his wife and cat in Somerville, Massachusetts.

EVERY VOW YOU BREAK

PETER SWANSON

faber

First published in the UK 2021
by Faber & Faber Limited
Bloomsbury House, 74–77 Great Russell Street
London WC1B 3DA

First published in the USA in 2021
by William Morrow, an imprint of HarperCollins Publishers,
195 Broadway, New York, NY 10007

This paperback edition first published in 2022

Typeset by Typo•glyphix, Burton-upon-Trent, DE14 3HE
Printed and bound by CPI Group (UK) Ltd, Croydon, CR0 4YY

A CIP record for this book
is available from the British Library

ISBN 978-0-571-35851-9

2 4 6 8 10 9 7 5 3 1

For Charlene, once again

EVERY VOW YOU BREAK

She first spotted him at Bobbie's Coffee Shop on Twenty-Second Street. He was at a window seat, idly looking at his phone, a white mug in front of him. Abigail was on her way to the office for her half day, dodging pedestrians on the sidewalk, thinking about the wedding, wondering if maybe she should have invited her cousin Donald and his wife, whose name she always forgot.

Her feet kept moving but it was as though her heart had skipped a beat. It was definitely him, same wiry frame, same beard, same high cheekbones. Even through the glare coming off the plate-glass window, she recognized him right away. And she also knew that he'd come to New York City because of her. He must have.

When she made it to her office and settled down at her desk, her heart still thudding, she took a moment to consider all the possibilities. First of all, why was she so sure he was here to find her? She lived in New York, not some small town that no one visited. He could be here on vacation, here to visit friends, here for work. And even if he had come here to find her, how much did he even know about her? They hadn't given each other their real names. She still only knew him as Scottie, and he knew her as Madeleine. She told herself there was nothing to worry about and tried to concentrate on work.

But walking home, the nights getting darker earlier these days, she took a different route, staying off the busy avenues.

She had no plans for that evening—Bruce was attending a work dinner—and she made herself an omelet, flipped through the channels, found one that was showing *The Ring*, the American remake with Naomi Watts. She'd watched it as a kid at a slumber party, and all the girls there had been traumatized except for Abigail, who'd fallen asleep in a brand-new world, one that had movies in it that seemed designed just for her.

After the credits had rolled, she sent a text to Bruce saying she was going to bed, then quickly checked her emails, ignoring one from Zoe titled emergency wedding question and opening an email from an address she didn't recognize titled simply, Hi.

Dear Madeleine, I am sorry to write you like this so soon before your wedding, but I can't stop thinking about you. If you don't share similar feelings, then tell me and I promise to never bother you again. But if you do feel the same way, then maybe it's not too late to cancel the wedding. The exact halfway point between New York City and San Francisco is Wood River, Nebraska. Maybe they have a Travelodge we can meet at? Just hopeful, Scottie

She read the message through twice, an ache moving from the base of her throat down to her stomach. The email would have been bad enough, but she'd seen him earlier. In her neighborhood. Or had she? If he was really here, then why didn't he say so in the email?

He doesn't want to entirely freak you out.

He was here, and he was looking for her. Maybe he'd figure if she responded positively to the email, he'd say something like, *Guess what, I'm actually in New York. Didn't want to tell you because I thought you might be thinking I was stalking you. Ha ha.*

And maybe it was as simple as all that. He was here in New York for some reason besides coming to find her and decided to send the email. All she had to do was tell him that she was still getting married, and she'd never hear from him again. But another part of her was telling her that it was more serious than that, that he'd somehow fallen for her, and now he was stalking her. What other word described it?

Also: How had he gotten her email address?

Even without her real name he could have figured it out, right? Maybe he knew someone at the hotel who had procured it for him. Or maybe she'd said something to give away the identity of Bruce—he was a fairly public figure, after all. Either way, the fact that he now had her email address meant he knew her name, and she didn't know his. His email address was simply bluestreakwp@yahoo.com, which gave no indication of his identity, unlike hers, abigailbaskin90@gmail.com, which gave up not only her name, but the goddamn year of her birth. She googled "blue streak" on the off chance she'd luck out, but there were too many things: a movie, a kind of fish, and several companies, even one in San Francisco, but it was for a catering place that looked as though it had gone out of business.

She considered her options. Simply not answering him felt like the right thing, but somehow she knew he'd try again. Reluctantly she decided to send a reply, something as impersonal as she could make it, letting him know that his feelings were one-sided. She began to construct the email. Should it be dismissive? She didn't think so. The last thing she wanted to do was piss this guy off. The message should be nice yet firm, unmistakably a brush-off. She also wanted the email to underplay what had happened between them in California, just in case someone else read it. There was no reason for her to confirm what had transpired. She grimaced to herself, realizing that she was acting like a criminal. She wrote:

Scottie, it was so nice meeting you. Yes, my wedding is still on. Three days away, and I can't wait. Thanks for thinking of me, and take care.

She read it over about ten times, finally deciding that it struck the perfect middle ground between being nice and making sure that he got the message. She took out the "so," worried that it might sound a little too positive, and hit send.

Twelve hours later there was no reply.

She told herself that was the last she'd hear from the stranger she'd slept with on her bachelorette weekend.

"How many men have you slept with?"

"Excuse me?" she said. "That's none of your business."

"But it's part of what we're talking about, right?" he asked, leaning back slightly, reaching for his glass of wine.

They'd been talking about marriage, or, more specifically, Abigail's upcoming marriage—three weeks away, exactly—and how she could only admit to being ninety-nine percent sure—"ninety-nine-point-ninety-nine, really" —that she was doing the right thing.

"It's not *necessarily* part of what we're talking about," she said, reaching for her own glass of wine, even though it was empty. He picked up the bottle to refill it.

"Well, that's like saying that sex isn't part of marriage," he said.

"Have you met my parents?" she said. It was more of a joke than an actual observation. Her parents were separated; their version of a separation, anyway, which meant that her dad had moved into the small studio apartment above the garage.

"My guess is you have very little idea about what your parents get up to, or don't get up to, in the bedroom."

He'd filled her glass too high, but the wine—a Pinot Noir—was delicious, and she took a long swallow. *Slow down*, she told herself, although she was also telling herself that it was a bachelorette party (it was *her* bachelorette party) and even though all her friends had disappeared somewhere in the haze of the previous hours, she was still entitled to drink some wine with the blue-eyed bearded guy wearing the vintage flannel shirt and the wedding ring. He was very Californian, she thought, with his bright white teeth, and some kind of braided leather bracelet with a green stone pendant, but she wasn't holding that against him. They were *in* California, after all, on a terraced patio surrounded by an olive grove. Abigail moved her Adirondack chair a little closer to the dying fire.

"That's probably for the best," she said.

"What is?"

"Not knowing what my parents get up to in the bedroom."

The man said, "That's a good idea." Abigail didn't know exactly what he was talking about but then he stood, lifted his own chair, and moved it closer to the fire-pit. "We're the only ones left out here," he said.

"You're just noticing that now?" she said.

"I can't take my eyes off of you," he said, but in a mocking tone.

"I don't even know your name, do I?" Abigail said, worried, as soon as she'd said it, that he'd already told her.

"If I tell you, will you answer a question?"

"Sure. Why not?"

"You already know the question."

"How many men have I slept with?"

"Right. How many men have you slept with?"

2

Abigail Baskin lost her virginity to a visiting actor at her parents' summer theater in Boxgrove, a small town in western Massachusetts. She was seventeen years old, and the actor said that he was twenty-two. A few years later, however, she'd looked him up on IMDb after he'd gotten a couple of small roles on television, and discovered that he'd probably been closer to twenty-six. Not that it mattered much. She'd been ready, and he'd been beautiful.

In fact, the moment that she'd seen him she knew that her longtime plans to lose her virginity to Todd Heron were out the window. She and Todd had been together since they were both fourteen years old, and Abigail had read enough adult contemporary fiction to know that Todd and she had already settled into a teenage version of a passionless marriage. They were best friends, made each other laugh, and had steadily progressed from a year of kissing to the occasional bout of sexual activity that included the proverbial "everything but." These bouts usually ended in a conversation in which both parties agreed that the timing wasn't right, or that the location, usually Todd's parents' semifinished basement, wasn't, or that it wasn't romantic enough. They began to plan scenarios in which they could each lose their virginity in an actual bed, and with the opportunity to fall asleep together afterward, no parents around. But Todd's parents, his dad the chief of Boxgrove's rarely used fire department, his mom a bookkeeper at the Congregational church, were never not around. And Abigail's parents, who ran the Boxgrove Summer Theatre, were always around as well, working constantly, even during the months when there were no productions. They said they didn't have the time to travel, but Abigail had begun to suspect that they also didn't have the money.

The summer that Abigail turned seventeen she and Todd had resigned themselves to the status quo, Todd working long hours—early mornings—at the local golf course, and Abigail working long hours—the evening ones—as a hostess at the Boxgrove Inn. Their relationship became a series of texts in the rare hours they were both free. And when Abigail wasn't hostessing, she was helping out, as she always did, at her parents' theater. Lawrence and Amelia Baskin were putting on five productions that summer, up from their usual three, including a revival of Ira Levin's *Deathtrap*. Zachary Mason had come up from New York—all the actors came up from New York—to play Clifford Anderson. Abigail, despite many crushes on television stars and film actors, hadn't realized just how much she had a specific physical type until the moment she first saw Zachary. He was tall and thin, with high cheekbones and mussed hair. He reminded Abigail of

Alain Delon in *Purple Noon*, her current movie obsession, and when she first saw him, as she was getting the room ready for the table read, her stomach flip-flopped like she was a heroine in a cheesy romance. It must have shown on her face, because Zachary looked at her and actually laughed, then introduced himself while helping her set up the room. A little bit of the sudden infatuation immediately went away when she realized just how much he was like all the other aspiring actors that came here for the summer. He wore skinny jeans and had a tasseled scarf wrapped twice around his neck even though it was July, and Abigail could make out a tattoo on the inside of his forearm that looked, without her being able to read all of the words, to be some Shakespearean text.

"Ah, the daughter," he said.

"They haven't thought of me as their daughter for a long time. I'm their unpaid intern."

"Well, you look just like your dad." It was the first time Abigail had heard this, since most people told her she looked like her mom, maybe because her mom, like Abigail, was tall and had dark hair. But Abigail did feel she looked just like her father. She had his large forehead, his downturned eyes, his short upper lip.

"Is that a good thing?" Abigail asked.

"Are you fishing for a real compliment?"

"Of course I am."

There was activity in the hallway outside the conference room, a bustling of bodies and a few conversations starting up, and Zachary leaned in quickly to Abigail and said, "You are very pretty, but you're probably only sixteen and I'm twenty-two, and I'm going to leave it at that."

"I'm seventeen," Abigail said as the room began to fill.

Deathtrap ran two weeks. It turned out to be one of the better productions of the summer; Abigail saw it twice, and was relieved that Zachary was not only good, but almost great. It didn't hurt that he was playing opposite Martin Pilkingham, the soap actor who performed at least one role for Boxgrove every summer. Zachary and Martin had great chemistry. A critic from the city actually came up in order to review the play; "A Revival in the Berkshires Warrants the Drive" was the headline.

Halfway through the production Abigail was sitting on her front porch, in the swinging chair, rereading *Red Dragon*, when Zachary wandered by along the sidewalk. She checked her phone, realizing it was later than she thought, and shouted out a hello that made him turn in obvious surprise. *At least he wasn't purposefully walking by my house in hopes of seeing me*, she thought, as she came down the front porch steps. Although why that would make a difference, she didn't know. They walked together at least two miles that night, the night getting cooler, Zachary talking about all the parts he'd almost gotten in TV shows and commercials. When he dropped her off, Abigail swung quickly into his arms and kissed him. He kissed back, and with his arms lifted her almost entirely off her feet.

"I don't know," he said, his voice hoarse.

"I do," Abigail said, and half ran to her front door, not wanting to give him a chance to talk them out of what was happening.

The wrap party, like all of Boxgrove's wrap parties, was held in the basement tavern at the Boxgrove Inn. Abigail got there early to help Marie, the bartender, set up the platters of snacks, and in return, Marie poured Abigail what looked like just a Sprite, but with vodka in it. The night before, after the second-to-last performance, Zachary and Abigail had fooled around once again, in his dressing room. At one point, Abigail thought they were going to have sex, and she broached the topic of condoms.

"You want to do this right here, right now, in my dressing room?" he'd asked. He already knew Abigail was a virgin because they'd discussed it.

"I don't care where we do it, I just want it to be with you," Abigail said.

"Let's talk just a little bit more about this, okay?" Zachary said. "Are you a hundred percent sure? I'm going back to New York in three days, and you and I—"

"You want written consent?" Abigail said, and laughed. Sexual harassment was all over the news, and she appreciated Zachary wanting to make sure, but she was ready.

"I'm considering it," he said, but laughed as well.

After the wrap party Abigail had been planning on going home with her parents, then doubling back to meet

Zachary in his room at the inn, but both her parents had left the party on the early side. "I'm exhausted, honestly, Abigail," her mother had said. "But you stay here. You're young." Abigail, who didn't want to get too close to her parents in case they smelled the vodka on her breath, waved goodbye as they climbed the stairs to the street level. Then she returned to the booth where Martin Pilkingham was holding court and drinking scotch. She'd known him her whole life, and he felt more like an uncle to her than her actual uncles.

Toward closing time, the bar mostly empty, Zachary, gripping a pint of Guinness, pulled Abigail into a dark corner of the pub. She could smell the alcohol on his breath as he touched her face. "It feels so wrong, but it feels so right," he said.

It was his hand on her face, and not the words, that made what he'd said sound like he'd memorized a script, that caused her knees to go temporarily weak. He took her arm and they walked through the winding hallways of the inn to his room.

She never saw Zachary again, except in an episode of *Law & Order: Special Victims Unit*, and a terrible indie horror film called *The Ghosting*. The day after the wrap party Abigail went for a run with her friend Zoe and told her all about it. But what she really wanted to do was tell Todd; he was her friend, after all, and it seemed wrong that she couldn't tell him about this momentous occasion.

She made a date with Todd to get lunch the following day, after his shift at the golf course, and she broke up with him, telling him she thought they should be single for their senior year of high school. He seemed somehow relieved.

3

I've slept with four men," Abigail said to the bearded guy whose name she still didn't know. "And one woman. Does that count?"

"Sure," he said.

"Not a huge number, I know," she said.

"Probably about average." He was pulling on a cardigan sweater, and Abigail wished she had her own extra layer. There were still embers in the firepit but any heat it gave off had diminished a while ago. Still, it was too perfect to consider going inside; the sky was a cluster of stars, and the air smelled of the lavender that bordered the patio. "I always heard," he continued, "that when a man tells you how many women he's slept with you should halve that number, and when a woman tells you how many men she's slept with you should double it."

"So you think I've slept with eight men?"

"And two women."

"Right. And two women."

"No, I don't think that. I think you're telling the truth."

"I am, actually. I have nothing to lose. I'll never see you again."

"That's probably true. A little sad, though."

Abigail shifted forward in her cushioned Adirondack chair, to get closer to the ineffective fire.

"You're cold?" the man said.

"A little bit. Not enough to go inside, though."

"Want my sweater?"

Abigail found herself saying, "Yes. If you're honestly offering."

Before she was done talking, he'd pulled the sweater off and was handing it over to her. She noticed how thin and muscular he was under the tight-fitting flannel shirt. She pulled her arms through the still-warm sweater. One of the smoldering logs in the firepit popped loudly. Her phone buzzed again in her jeans. It was Kyra, checking in. U okay?

She wrote back: Fine. About to go to sleep. CU at breakfast?

There was a hotel right on the vineyard, twelve rooms, and that's where the members of Abigail's bachelorette party were staying. She had her own suite; Kyra was staying with Rachel, and Zoe was staying with her sister, Pam, who'd come down from Seattle.

"Why are you here, again?" Abigail asked, realizing as soon as she'd said it that she'd already asked him that question, maybe twice. She ran her tongue along her teeth, always a good test to see just how drunk she was.

"I'm at a 'still a bachelor' party for my friend Ron," he said, making air quotes. "His engagement just broke off, and I'm here celebrating with him. He passed out about five hours ago."

"Right. You told me that. And you're from San Francisco and you're an actor. See, I remember everything."

"I'm an amateur actor, at a community theater, but I'm really a carpenter. That's how I make my money."

"Furniture-making," Abigail said triumphantly.

"That's right," he said.

"Stick with that," Abigail said. "There's no future in the theater." She'd almost said *furniture in the theater*. She really was drunk.

"Why do you say that?"

"My parents ran a regional theater for twenty years, and it nearly broke them. It *did* break them, I mean . . . financially, for sure, and also emotionally. They went out of business two years ago and now they'll be in debt for the rest of their lives. My father works at an AMC Theatre, and even though they still sort of live together, both of them tell me that they're separating."

"I'm sorry."

"We'll see if it takes," Abigail said, aware that she sounded flippant, despite the fact she felt anything but. She'd been to her parents' house recently, and they did seem to be living separate lives, her father having moved out, and her mother putting all her energy toward starting an art gallery with her best friend Patricia.

"But twenty years isn't nothing. Running a business or being in a marriage. They did something they loved, or that I assume they loved, and they created art. It's not . . . all about success or money."

"No, it was never about money with them, but then it became all about the money, only because they didn't have any. And maybe I'm just getting cynical, but I think of all those plays they produced each summer, and they're just gone now, just some photographs and maybe a few hazy memories. It all added up to nothing. It makes me sad."

"So, what do you do?"

"I'm in publishing, another dying industry."

"I don't know about that."

"I work for an independent press that primarily publishes poetry, so, in my case, it's definitely dying."

"Probably," he said. Then added, "Are you a poetry fan?"

Abigail laughed, probably because of the construction of that phrase, as though poetry had fans in the same way that sports teams did, or television series. "I read poetry," she said. "If that's what you're asking. And not just for my job."

"Who do you read?"

Whom do you read, she said in her head. Out loud, she said, "Lately I've been into Jenny Zhang. But Poe is my favorite."

The man looked upward, as though trying to remember something, then said, "'For the moon never beams without making me dream of the beautiful Annabel Lee.'"

Abigail laughed. "Oh, look at you, quoting poetry in the firelight." She didn't mention that he'd gotten the quote wrong.

"I got lucky. That's one of the few poems I know."

"Well, trust me. Any opportunity you get to quote a poem, you've got to take it these days. It's a dying art."

"Says the person who works at a poetry publisher."

"I'm hanging on for dear life. It's a good place to work, actually."

The man smiled, more of a smirk. He really was handsome, despite the new agey bracelet and the whitened teeth. "When I asked you what you did for a living, I thought you were going to say you were a hedge fund manager or something, the way you talked about your parents."

"What do you mean?"

"Oh, only that you seemed cynical about trying to make a living in the arts. I figured you'd have gone into something more stable."

"No, that's my fiancé. He's not a hedge fund manager, but he invests in start-up companies. He can finance my career in the arts, for what it's worth."

"Is that why you're marrying him?"

An ember had floated out from the firepit and landed on Abigail's sweater. The man's sweater, actually, Abigail thought. She swatted at it, hoping it wouldn't leave a mark.

"What did you ask?"

"I asked if you're marrying your fiancé because he's wealthy, and now that I'm repeating that, I realize it's none of my business."

"No, that's okay. And also no, that's not why I'm marrying Bruce, but I do think I'm probably marrying him because of the personality traits that make him rich."

"What do you mean by that?"

"Before I was with Bruce I was with this guy for a long time. He was a writer, a poet. We had a lot in common, I guess, but it was exhausting. He was constantly asking me to read things he'd written or sharing things he'd read. He had this notion of a creative life together, that we'd be broke, and happy, and constantly drunk, and misunderstood. And I got sick of it. Bruce is simple, but in a really good way. All his validation comes from his work, and his work is essentially bankrolling creative people. It's just so nice to go see a movie with him, and not have him react with rage, or jealousy, or monologue at me about the hidden themes of what we've just seen."

"So you're saying he's boring."

"Who, Bruce? Yes, and it's awesome."

"So, the writer guy, what was his name?"

"His name was Ben."

"So what number was Ben?"

"What do you mean?"

"Was he number two of the men you slept with?"

Ben Perez and Abigail were in the same incoming class at Wesleyan, both English majors, but they didn't meet until they shared a class called Waugh, Greene, Spark during the second semester of sophomore year.

After that first class they walked to the dining hall as though they'd done it a hundred times, ate together, and that night went to see *Black Narcissus* at the Center for Film Studies on campus. They stayed up late in Ben's single dormitory room, the window cracked, sharing a pack of Camel Blues and a bottle of cheap burgundy, listening to Nino Rota soundtracks. Abigail was instantly infatuated, and that whole first day and night with Ben was filled with the terrifying and thrilling feeling that she'd just met the person who might be the most important person in her life. Her freshman year she'd dated a senior named Mark Copley, who was both Wesleyan's top tennis player and the editor of its lit magazine. Their relationship was a strictly weekend affair—Friday night parties after which Abigail would spend the night at Mark's off-campus apartment. Sometimes she'd stay for the weekend, but not always. Abigail, who tended to relate all the occurrences in her life to books or movies, saw her relationship with Mark as two sophisticated partners living lives both separate and together. She thought of Tomas and Sabina in *The Unbearable Lightness of Being*, how the regulated infrequency of their time spent together was what kept it alive. Still, Abigail wound up being hurt when Mark never introduced her to his parents over graduation weekend, and she wasn't surprised when he told her that now that he was no longer in college, he thought they should stop seeing each other.

"You don't want to waste your next three years of college with a college graduate. I'll cramp your style," he said.

"I think you mean I'll cramp your style," Abigail replied.

"That, too," he said.

So it actually felt good that immediately after meeting Ben, Abigail was plunged into an intense romance, the two of them joined at the hip, living, it seemed, in each other's mind. They saw the same movies, read the same books. He wanted to write poetry, and Abigail, although she didn't admit it to anyone but Ben, dreamt of being a novelist. They were together for the next three years of college, and then moved to New York City immediately after graduation, getting an apartment downtown not a whole lot bigger than a one-car garage. Ben changed after college, although it took two years for Abigail to really notice. At school, he'd been content to be a student, to be learning from others, honing his craft, absorbing the world. But once they were settled in New York, Abigail getting a job at Bonespar Press and Ben working at the Strand Book Store, he became obsessed with making it as a poet, befriending a circle of slam and spoken-word poets (even though he claimed to despise those particular genres), and spending more time sending out poems to literary magazines than actually writing them. When he got rejections, he sulked for days, and when he got accepted his mood would improve, but for diminishing lengths of time. He spent hours on the internet getting into fights on comment boards, and he drank constantly. Abigail joined him, but only at night. They would meet friends at Pete's Tavern, and Ben would argue with anyone about anything, something he'd always done, but it was starting to exhaust Abigail. They brought the arguments home with them from the bar, and sometimes, hungover and exhausted the following morning, Abigail couldn't even remember what they'd been fighting about. It was always something minor, like the time Abigail told Ben that she loved *Shakespeare in Love* and he'd been so upset that he disappeared for an entire night.

Three years after college, Abigail was ready to leave Ben, trying to figure out the best way to do it, when, by chance, she spotted him coming out of McSorley's Tavern, his arm draped around a mutual friend of theirs, Ruth, a jewelry maker living in Brooklyn. Abigail felt a surge of betrayal and anger, like a sudden punch to her stomach, but that feeling lasted for less than an hour. He'd given her a way out and she took it. Still, untangling their relationship, both logistically and emotionally, took nearly a year. It was the same year that the Boxgrove Theatre went out of business, and her parents, who had always represented, at least to Abigail, pillars of competent adulthood, suddenly seemed like a pair of frightened children. Abigail went home every weekend to help them deal with the enormous amount of stuff—the props and costuming—they'd acquired in twenty years, but also to provide emotional support. It wasn't just that they were crushed by the failure of their business, they were crushed by what they both perceived as the failure of their lives. And they were in debt, mainly because of the loans they'd taken out in order to send Abigail to Wesleyan. All of this—the dissolution of her relationship with Ben, her parents' failures—made Abigail feel hollowed out, purposeless.

She decided to move home, to help them, emotionally and financially, through their transition into new lives, but they refused.

"Please don't let us drag you down, Abigail," her mother said. "Go live your life. We're totally fine."

But it was her father she was more worried about. He'd aged about ten years since the collapse of the theater. One night, after her mom had gone to bed, Abigail and her father had stayed up to watch *Two for the Road* on Turner Classic Movies. He drank steadily through the movie, finishing off the red wine from dinner, and afterward told Abigail that they'd already canceled their premium cable subscription, that it was going away at the end of the month, and he was trying to watch as many old movies on TCM as possible.

Something about that particular detail made Abigail so sad that she had to get up and tell her father she was going to the bathroom, just so he wouldn't see her cry.

When she came back out, she said to her father, now watching *Charade*, "I talked to Mom about this, and she wasn't thrilled by the idea, but I'm thinking of coming home for a while. I know that I could get a job at—"

"No, no, Abby. Your mother and I discussed this. Not a chance. It's totally enough that you come back on weekends, and you have that great job—"

"It's not that great a job."

"It's in publishing. You're in the greatest city in the world. Please. We are one hundred percent fine."

"Okay," Abigail said. "I hear you both, loud and clear."

4

Back in New York, unmoored by her breakup with Ben and feeling powerless to help her parents, Abigail moved into a three-bedroom apartment with two strangers and took an extra job as a nanny for a family on the Upper East Side to just be able to pay her share of the rent. She kept thinking about her father's words to her, that she had a job in publishing in the greatest city in the world, and somehow those facts, instead of making her happy, made her feel sad and worthless. She was where she'd wanted to be, but she felt like an impostor, a small-town girl playing grown-up in the city.

She started spending time with her college friend Rebecca, who was heavily subsidized by her parents and had her own place near Gramercy Park. Abigail knew that some of Rebecca's fondness for her was attraction, and out of curiosity, and a requisite amount of attraction herself, Abigail got drunk one night with coworkers, then showed up at Rebecca's apartment at just past midnight. It was a sexual encounter so awkward that both of them seemed to know, instantly, that they'd killed their friendship. And they kind of had, even though they continued to text and meet for drinks and coffee. But by this point Abigail had decided that, despite her parents' protests, what she really needed to do was move back to Boxgrove, stay with them, or Zoe, for a while, and get a job waitressing so she could help them with some of their bills. It wasn't just that she wanted to do it, she was also somehow longing to do it. Moving home would give her purpose.

She was just about to enact this plan when she met Bruce Lamb. She was on her lunch break at a coffee shop, looking at job listings in western Massachusetts, when he sat down at the next table. Abigail glanced at him briefly, just as he was glancing at her, and they smiled at each other, the quick, noncommittal smiles of city people. Abigail remembered thinking that even though the decent-looking thirty-year-old man was wearing faded jeans and a rumpled blazer she could tell that those jeans and that blazer probably cost more than two months of her rent. She went back to job-hunting.

When the man finished his goat-cheese salad he stood, cleared his dishes, then came over to Abigail's table. "Excuse me," he said.

She looked up at him, raising an eyebrow.

"Can I take you to dinner tonight?" he asked.

Abigail laughed, but then she said, "Okay," surprising herself a little by the swiftness and surety of her answer.

"Do you live around here?"

"Close enough," Abigail said.

He named a restaurant with a French-sounding name, and they agreed on eight o'clock.

After he left, Abigail thought that at least she'd be getting an expensive dinner in the city bought by a perfect stranger before she left. It could be her New York story.

Dinner was actually nice. She'd thought that, considering the way he'd asked her out, he'd be a player, but he was actually down-to-earth. Almost innocent. He'd just moved to New York from Silicon Valley, where he'd been living ("not really living, just coding") for the past ten years. He'd started two companies and sold them both, and he was sick of being the idea man and decided to be the moneyman instead, starting up an angel investor business. "I didn't want to do it in Silicon Valley and I'd always dreamt of living in New York."

On their third date she told him about her plan to leave the city and move back in with her parents, and she told him about the guilt she felt because of the college loans, and how beaten down her parents were, and how she was sick of the city, anyway. The words came out in a rush, her voice cracking on the word "helpless," and another voice in her head was imagining that Bruce was right now searching for the EXIT sign.

But after she was finished talking, he said, "I'll pay your college loans."

"What?"

"I'll pay them. How much are they?"

28

"That's not the point. I can't have you paying my college loans."

"Look. I give money to charities all the time. I have more money right now at my age than I'll ever in a million years be able to spend. You're a good person. I assume your parents are good people. Let me pay the loans. You can still move back home. I'm not trying to get you to stay in New York."

"It's crazy. We don't even really know each other."

"Look," Bruce said, and took a deep breath through his nostrils. They were at an upscale gastro pub, sitting at the corner of the bar, a plate of truffled deviled eggs between them, and they both had to talk a little louder than they normally would to be heard. "When I lived in Silicon Valley, I gave pitches all the time, and the standard line among my colleagues about giving pitches was to practice them, to know exactly what you were going to say, and to stick to the script. I used to do the opposite. I'd go into pitch meetings and just speak from my heart, describe my product exactly as it was. I never practiced. I never worried about how I'd come off. I just went in with total honesty, and it made the whole thing so much easier."

"What does this have to do with you wanting to pay my loans?"

"I think because when I told you I wanted to do that, I wasn't being entirely honest. So, here it is, I'm about to be totally honest. I don't believe in love at first sight, but something very close to that happened when I saw you in the coffee shop. I wanted—no, I needed—to get to know you, so I took a shot. And now here we are three dates later and I know, with certainty, that I want to spend the rest of my life with you. No, let me finish. You're the most interesting woman I've ever met. You love poetry and horror movies, and dress like a 1950s housewife. You're far smarter than I can ever hope to be, and you're kind and selfless. Plus I think we fit, and I know that we could make it work. I feel, in a way, that you are now my purpose for living. I don't expect you to have the same feelings. I would be pleased, obviously, if you shared some of them, but that's not why I'm telling you this. I just want to be open. I think we should be together. I also think that if you're about to tell me that I'm scaring the shit out of you, and that you never want to see me again, that I still want to pay your student loans, because you're a good person and you shouldn't have to worry about something that I can take care of so easily. Consider it your payment for sitting through this embarrassing speech."

"It's not embarrassing," Abigail said, although she was having trouble meeting his eyes.

He must have noticed, because some of the color left his face, and he said, "Oh, I fucked up."

"No, no, no. You didn't. It's just that honesty is . . ."

"It's embarrassing."

"I guess so, yes."

30

"Should we just forget I ever said what I just said?"

"No, not at all. I like you, too, and I want to keep seeing you. To be honest, I don't have the confidence about our relationship that you seem to have, but maybe I'm just in a fragile place right now. How about I stay in New York a little longer than I planned, we continue to see one another, and I will consider letting you pay off some of my student loans, but I don't want you to bring it up again until I do?"

He looked relieved, some of the color returning to his cheeks, and said, "Deal."

After that conversation, Abigail let herself relax with this new, strange man. There was something childlike and inexperienced about him, despite his success and his wealth. He loved horror movies like she did, but he'd never seen anything before the turn of the century, and Abigail introduced him to the greatness that was 1970s horror. She showed him pockets of New York City that he'd never have discovered, and together they took a weekend trip to Philadelphia to go to her favorite museum, the Mütter, a place famous for its displays of vintage medical instruments and numerous skulls and skeletons. It turned out he had a macabre streak similar to hers, or at least an interest. He did love many of the old movies she showed him, and he admitted that when he'd first seen her in that coffee shop one of the things that had attracted him was how she'd looked like a woman from a different time.

"What was I wearing? I can't remember," she said.

And he told her in detail, about how she'd been wearing a black dress with a high white collar, and how her hair was held back by her polka-dot headband. She didn't tell him that that was the headband she wore when she hadn't washed her hair in a couple of days.

She did worry that she only enjoyed being with Bruce because of his willingness to be introduced to new things by her, and that, over time, it wouldn't be enough. But he introduced her to things as well. Great restaurants, for one. An appreciation for cocktails. He even took her to the opera—they went to see *Macbeth*—and it was an almost transformative experience for Abigail.

And there were qualities about Bruce that she really did love. He was a vulnerable person, despite all his successes. In some ways, he reminded her of her own father, always questioning his life, always looking for reassurance. There was something passive about him, and it led to her feeling stronger in his presence. She didn't know if this was a good thing or a bad thing, but she did know that it was a dynamic that she was comfortable with.

Down deep, she knew that Bruce was more in love with her than she was with him. But wasn't that the case with every couple? There was always one person in each relationship who cared a little more than the other. And wasn't it better to be the person who cared less?

One year after they'd started dating they were engaged, the student loans were paid off, and Bruce was already pressuring Abigail to let him invest in bringing back the Boxgrove Theatre.

"You'll lose money," she told him.

"Then it's a write-off for my taxes. Either way, I win."

"I don't even know if my parents would want to save the Boxgrove. It was a lot of work for them. It's probably what eventually wrecked their marriage."

"Ask them and find out."

"How about we do it after we're married?"

This was in June, and they had set the wedding date for the beginning of October. "Whatever you want to do for the wedding is fine with me," Bruce told her. "If you want something huge, let's do it. If you want to get married at the registry, I'm happy to do that as well. But I want to plan the honeymoon."

"Oh yeah?" Abigail imagined some sort of grand tour of Europe.

"I have a place in mind."

"Yeah?"

"That's all I'm going to tell you."

"Well, you'll have to tell me a little more than that. Like what kind of clothes I'll need to pack."

"Fair enough. But that's all I'm telling you."

"I'm intrigued."

"It's kind of life-changing," Bruce said, and she wondered exactly what that meant. She truly did not know. It was hard to know what would impress him. She'd brought him to a classic New York diner that had blown him away, and it turned out he'd never actually been in a diner before. Before he was rich, he'd lived almost exclusively on take-out Korean food while he coded at home, and after he was rich, his new friends had introduced him to top-end restaurants. He'd skipped the in-between restaurants and the dive bars and the lean years. He was also both innocent and experienced when it came to relationships. He'd had a longtime girlfriend from his freshman year at college—his only year at college, as it turned out—who'd broken his heart by leaving him for one of his early business partners. He was vague about any relationships he'd had since then, and Abigail sometimes suspected that maybe he'd been to prostitutes with other Silicon Valley types. (There'd been a trip to Thailand after his first big sale.) But in bed he was conservative, and while it was nice, Abigail sometimes missed the sex with Ben, usually drunken, frenzied, and filled with talk. Bruce made a lot of sincere eye contact when they made love, and sometimes it was a little too much for her, but that was who he was. He was sincere. And if the price to pay for a lifetime with a guy like that was a little too much reverence in the bedroom, then Abigail thought she could put up with it.

The bachelorette party was his idea. He was having his own bachelor party back in California, flying all his friends to an island in the Puget Sound. ("This place run by Chip Ramsay. You'll meet him—he's legendary.") "Legendary" and "life-changing" were two of Bruce's

34

favorite adjectives, a fault she chalked up to too many years on the West Coast. Abigail told him that she thought she'd just have a night out with friends in New York for her bachelorette party, but he told her they should do a weekend away, and he offered to pay, of course. She mentioned that she'd always wanted to go to Northern California, and an hour of web-browsing later he'd found the perfect place, Piety Hills, a Spanish-style vineyard that boasted its own hotel and restaurant. He booked it, and paid for the rooms, although she talked him into getting just three rooms for the five of them. "We can share," she'd said.

She was grateful, plus a little bit annoyed, that he'd gotten so involved with the planning. And she was equally annoyed when they arrived at Piety Hills and were told that there would be a special dinner for all of them—a seven-course meal—in the wine cellar, already paid for. It was generous, and sweet, but it wasn't what she had pictured, exactly, for her bachelorette night. She told her friends this during dinner.

"I don't know, Ab," Zoe said. "This is pretty amazing."

"I guess I was just picturing us all in the bar upstairs, getting a little rowdy."

"We can do that after dinner," Zoe's sister, Pam, said. "They're open late."

"Okay. I feel better. It's just that sometimes Bruce is . . . too attentive, I guess."

"Yeah, that must suck."

"I know, I know. I'm not complaining."

After dinner they all did go to the bar, drinking several more bottles of the amazing wine, and eventually spilling out onto the patio area, with its firepit and a sky full of stars. Abigail, who'd been tired earlier, found herself fairly drunk and wide awake by midnight, then time suddenly sped up and her friends had disappeared one by one, and the fire was dying down, and she was wearing a stranger's sweater.

5

"Frankly," she said, staring at the half inch of wine at the bottom of her glass, "it's getting a little creepy how much you seem to care about my sex life."

The man held up both hands. "Okay, I'll stop. I *am* being creepy. I just . . . you seem a little hesitant about this impending marriage, and as someone who's not in a particularly happy marriage myself, I guess I'm projecting a little."

"Because you wished you'd slept with more women when you were single."

"I've slept with plenty of women. I think my problem was that I hadn't been in a serious emotional relationship with another person before I got married. I don't think either of us had been. And when we couldn't have kids, it just took too much out of us, and now it just feels joyless."

"Do you think you'll get divorced?"

"Probably. I think she's already involved with someone else, this guy she works with, although I'm guessing it's more of an emotional affair right now. Honestly, when I think about it, I worry more about who's going to get the dog. And I worry about my parents, because they both love her, love my wife. More than me, I think."

"But if you're not happy . . ."

"Right," he said, straightening his back but staying seated. "Enough about this, though. Let's get back to you." He held up his glass. "To the bride-to-be. May you have better luck than the rest of us."

Abigail took the last sip of her wine. "Your hand is trembling," she said. "Are you cold?"

"I'm fucking freezing to death," he said, smiling.

"Oh my God. Take your sweater back."

He reached across and placed his hand on Abigail's arm to stop her from taking the sweater off. "No, then you'll be cold."

"Let's go inside, then."

"I'd rather stay cold. If we get up and go inside, you're suddenly going to realize how late it is, and how tired you are, and then you're going to go to your room and I'll never see you again."

"How late is it?" Abigail asked, looking at her wrist where she normally wore her Fitbit before realizing she'd taken it off for the night.

"I'm not telling you," the man said, digging into the front pocket of his pants, pulling out a crumpled pack of cigarettes. He extracted one, putting it between his lips, and said, "I hope you don't mind. I limit myself to one a day, usually around this time of night."

"How do you do that? I only smoked in college, but I was up to a pack a day in less than a month."

"You want one now?" He held out the blue pack of cigarettes, a French brand, and Abigail took one.

"Why not?" she said.

"They're unfiltered, so go easy. I figure if I'm only going to have one a day it might as well pack a punch."

He lit her cigarette first, then his, using matches that had been tucked inside the pack.

Abigail slid back along her seat and blew a plume of smoke into the night. The taste of smoke in her mouth made her feel younger than she was, younger and drunker. The whole evening was reminding her of something, and she realized that it felt like that first night she'd spent with Ben Perez in college, like she'd met a stranger and suddenly anything was possible. And even though she didn't want to admit it, she didn't want the night to end, either. She liked this guy. Or at least she liked the feeling of being with this guy. She liked his insistent questions, and his honesty. And she liked his sweater. It was a yellow cardigan with corduroy elbow patches. It smelled old, but in a nice way—mothballs and aftershave.

Tilting her head back, she stared across at the man. "You never told me your name. Remember, it was part of the deal. I tell you my entire sexual history and you tell me your name."

"Maybe, at this point, we shouldn't tell each other our names."

"We could make them up," Abigail said.

"Sure. How about I make up your name and you make up mine?" He tapped his cigarette, and ash dropped onto the patio. She wondered if smoking was even allowed at this vineyard.

"Okay. You go first."

"Um, I'll call you Madeleine."

Abigail thought about it for a moment. "I can live with that, I guess. Why Madeleine?"

"I don't know. It just popped into my head, like it's the name that you should have. I'll call you Maddy for short. What's my name?"

"Scottie," Abigail said.

"Scottie? Why Scottie? It makes me sound like a dog."

"It's a movie reference," Abigail said. "If I'm Madeleine, then you're Scottie."

The man pursed his lips, then said, "*Vertigo*."

Abigail smiled. "Yes."

"If I recall, that particular relationship didn't end very well."

"Look, you started this, Scottie, when you named me Madeleine, so don't blame me."

"You're too young," the man said, "to know about movies like *Vertigo*."

Abigail took a long drag on her cigarette, her throat burning, then picked a shred of tobacco from her tongue. "My father gave me my movie education, and my mother gave me my book education. I was an only child, so I was also their project."

"What are you going to do with all those skills after you get married?"

"Oh, let's not talk about that right now."

"Is that because it's a boring subject or because you're not going to work after you get married?"

"Why do you say that?"

The man stretched an arm above his head and rotated his wrist.

"Because your fiancé is rich."

"Him being rich has nothing to do with whether I'll keep working. And, no, it's not the reason I'm marrying him, but it is a part of him that I find attractive. I won't lie. It will be very nice to never have to think about money again, because, honestly, that's all that my parents seemed to do before they separated, and I worry it's wrecking them. You're really overly concerned that I'm marrying the wrong guy." During this short speech, another internal speech was going through Abigail's head, one in which she told herself that she sounded haughty and defensive. She stared at the cigarette in her hand, realized it was making her dizzy, and flicked it into the fire.

"Point taken," the man said. "I'm only overly concerned because of jealousy. But you've convinced me. He sounds like a catch. I just think that, knowing you for all of two hours, you're an amazing person, and I don't think you should sell yourself short for someone less than amazing. It is the rest of your life, after all."

That phrase "the rest of your life" had actually been going through Abigail's head a little bit during the course of the weekend, a thread of worry that Bruce's over-protectiveness, his undying love for her, was going to wear thin over time.

The man stood up. "And with that final obnoxious comment I think I'm going to quit while I'm still ahead." He dropped the cigarette onto the patio and ground it out under his foot. She thought he was going to leave it there, but he picked it up and put it in his jeans pocket.

Abigail stood as well. "It was only a little obnoxious."

"If I have one more glass of wine, I'm going to beg you not to marry him, and to run away with me."

Abigail laughed. "When it rains, it pours. Oh, your sweater."

She pulled it off, the fabric crackling a little with static electricity, and handed it back to him. Then the man held out his hand, as if to shake hers, and said, "Madeleine, nice meeting you."

She shook his hand and their eyes met, and a part of her took two steps back and watched this stranger and herself in their circle of firelight. It felt like watching the last spontaneous romantic moment of her life. There was a hitch in her breath, and for an awful moment she thought she was going to cry. "How about a hug?" she asked, and he pulled her in toward him, and because she was cold, she let the hug go on too long. He smelled of smoke, but not in a bad way.

Abigail thought: *Don't do it. Don't kiss this man.*

After they separated, he said, "Do you believe there are little pockets of time and space that exist outside of the rest of our lives? Like maybe this is one of them, and anything that happens right now doesn't count? It will just be forgotten, a secret only between us."

A phrase ran through Abigail's head. *One last fling.* Rachel had said it to her earlier that evening, just after Abigail had first spotted the man in the flannel shirt across the U-shaped bar in the restaurant. Rachel had noticed her staring, and said, "One last fling?"

"Excuse me?" Abigail had said.

"It's a thing: one last fling before the ring."

"What do you mean, it's a thing?"

"I don't know, Abigail, don't get mad at me. I was just kidding."

Don't do it, you'll regret it.

And those words kept running through her head as she stepped into the stranger's arms again and kissed him, telling herself that was all that was going to happen. That she was allowed a kiss, one drunken kiss, before getting married.

But the kiss was just too good, and she told herself that maybe this *was* a little pocket of time. A pocket of time without names and without consequences. The world spun, and he was a good kisser, and when his hand touched her neck, an involuntary shudder went through her body.

Later, a few hours later, another phrase ran through Abigail's mind as she lay, awake and sober, in the king-sized bed of his room. *Reader*, she thought, *I slept with him.*

6

"I want to hear all about the meal," Bruce said, after they'd hugged and kissed, and as she slid into the seat across from him at a midtown Mexican restaurant.

"God, that meal," she said. "It was amazing."

"Tell me about it."

Abigail had been nervous about seeing Bruce for the first time since the trip to California, and now she was so relieved that they were actually talking, and that he hadn't instantly been able to see the infidelity written all over her face, that the details of the meal went entirely out of her head.

"Let me think for a moment," she said, and then was saved by the waitress appearing to take their drink orders. When he asked her again, the memory of that meal came back to her, and she described it course by course. He seemed so pleased hearing the details that Abigail relaxed some more, even though her guilt ratcheted up a little bit. It was going to be all right, she thought. She'd gotten away with it.

A week earlier, after skulking from Scottie's room (she still thought of him by the name she'd made up), she'd tried to fall asleep in her own hotel bed, but only managed about two hours of fitful, edgy half sleep. Every time she thought she was going to trip over the edge into unconsciousness, images of what had just occurred erupted in her mind. Before she knew it, morning had arrived, and she sent a text to all the bachelorettes that she was sleeping in and skipping the brunch buffet, then she sent a separate text to Zoe, asking her to swing by her room when she got a chance. Five minutes later, Zoe, looking as though she'd gotten ten hours of deep sleep, arrived with a plate of croissants. When the door was shut behind her, Abigail told her everything that had happened.

"Jesus," Zoe said. "That's not like you."

"I know. I don't know what happened. I was drunk, but I wasn't that drunk. I think . . . maybe I'm telling myself something. Maybe I don't want to marry Bruce."

"This is what I think," Zoe said. "Don't make any rash decisions now. Wait a few days. See what it feels like to see Bruce again. See if you keep thinking about this guy—"

"It wasn't about him. It was romantic, but he's married, and he's not even my type—"

"And you don't know his name."

"Oh God," Abigail said, and laughed, the act of moving her facial muscles painful. "I don't even know his name."

"Just don't beat yourself up. Wait a few days and see how you feel. Maybe it did mean something, and then you can talk to Bruce."

"It would destroy him."

46

"Don't worry about that right now. If you need to break it off, he doesn't have to know about what happened here."

"Okay," Abigail said, and took a deep breath. Zoe, despite the complications of her own life, always gave great advice. Abigail held a croissant in her hand but hadn't taken a bite. She took a small one now, flakes falling down onto her lap.

"One question," Zoe said. "Condom?"

"Yes, we used a condom."

"Good. He had it with him?"

"Well, it wasn't mine. So, yes. You think it's creepy that a married guy on a trip brings a condom, right?"

"I didn't say that."

"God, it is creepy, isn't it? Did I get totally played?"

"Shh, relax. Did you have fun?"

"It was actually pretty nice."

Better than pretty nice, Abigail told herself, but didn't say it out loud.

"Maybe that's all this is. You had a fling before getting married, and no one ever needs to know about it besides me. These things happen. Better now than in a year."

"Okay. Don't tell anyone, please."

"Fuck you. Who would I tell?"

"I know. I just had to say it out loud."

"I'm not telling anyone. Don't beat yourself up about it. It happened."

Abigail took her advice and tried not to make any decisions until she saw her fiancé. And now they were eating a normal lunch, and Bruce was so pleased to see her. She was still guilty, but maybe she'd been making too much of a big deal about it. She'd be faithful in their marriage, and this was one last moment of singlehood. For all she knew, he'd done the same thing on his bachelor trip.

Maybe because she was so relieved that the lunch was going well, Abigail drank two margaritas. Then, over coffee, and while they were splitting a slice of key lime pie, she said, without thinking too much about it, "I never heard the details of your bachelor weekend. Anything I should know about?"

He smiled, his eyes half closing. "Why? Do you have a confession to make about your trip?"

"No. I'm asking about yours. Was it a strictly guy thing, or did you all go to some strip club?"

"Puget Sound strip clubs *are* the best. You didn't know that?"

"Yeah, you should have seen the Piety Hills Chippendales show. Very impressive."

His smile was gone, and he said, "Even though we're not married yet, I consider myself betrothed to you. I have since we first kissed. I know you didn't feel the same way about me in the beginning, but I hope that you do now."

"God, yes. Sorry. I was just kidding you."

"Are you sure nothing happened in California?"

She could feel her cheeks flushing, and she hoped he thought it was simply the alcohol she'd drunk. "Zoe got a little handsy when she was zipping up my dress."

Finally, he smiled. "Sorry I got serious. I wish I was the type of guy who didn't worry about these things, but I'm just not. I believe in loyalty."

"I do, too."

After lunch she walked slowly to her apartment, starting to feel better, and realizing just how much tension she'd been holding in her body the past few days. When she got home, she felt herself missing Bruce already and called him.

"Hi," he said, concern in his voice.

"Hey."

"You forget something at the restaurant?"

"No. I just wanted to keep talking to you. Is that okay?"

"Of course it is. Although I think you're drunk."

"Get used to it. Once we're married it's going to be two-margarita lunches every day."

"Hmm," he said, and she could hear someone talking to him in what sounded like a cavernous room.

"Where are you?"

"Walking into my building. David, the doorman, wants to know how my lunch was. He was the one who recommended the place."

"Tell him it was great."

She heard muffled talking in the background, and when Bruce got back on the line she said, "You should go. I was just calling to hear your voice one more time."

"I'm glad. I like it. We can keep talking. It's a long ride in the elevator."

"This is what I wanted to ask you, actually. Where do you see us in ten years?"

"Where do I see *us*?"

"Yeah. Besides being married, obviously. You're a planner, so I'm sure you've thought about it. I just wanted to know how you envisioned our lives together down the line."

"Are you asking me about starting a family?"

"No, no. God. Just, how do you see us?"

There was silence on the phone, although Abigail could hear background noise, muted voices, the sound of Bruce moving through space.

"I see us as happy," he said at last. "Whatever I'm doing, I'll be successful and engaged and on the cutting edge of the new technology. For you, I picture you as a successful writer. In ten years, we'll be at your book launch together. And all our friends and family will be there. Your parents will be back together, and maybe they'll be running the theater again, and it'll be successful this time. Basically, that's what I see. Success and happiness."

"You're an optimistic man, Bruce," she said.

"I am. You know that about me already, or at least I hope you do. All my life I've pictured myself as successful, and because I can picture it, that's how I make it happen. It's not that hard, actually. It's just visualization. Mental energy. And that's what I see for us. We're going to take over the world, babe."

"Okay. Now you've gone too far."

Bruce laughed. "Sorry for being who I am . . . but it's all I've got. I gotta go now. Can we table this conversation and pick it up later?"

She was going to give him a hard time for the corporate lingo, but instead said, "I love you, Bruce. And I love your optimism."

"Love you, too, Abigail."

She drank a tall glass of water, then lay down on her couch and thought about what Bruce had said. When Abigail had been in high school, she'd imagined herself living in New York City with a good job. When she'd achieved that goal, it hadn't made her happy, or at least it hadn't made her happier. If Bruce's prediction came true, about how successful they'd be in ten years, would she still feel the emptiness that constantly nestled inside her? Maybe it was just the loneliness of being an only child, something she'd never shake. Maybe it was something more—an inherited dissatisfaction—and she'd be one of those rich women who have affairs out of boredom and start drinking wine at three in the afternoon.

Or maybe, and this was her hope, Bruce's optimism—his clear-eyed view of himself and the world—would somehow rub off on her. It was a hopeful thought, and she chose, in the dusty light of the afternoon, to believe it. She also believed, and she'd felt this for a while, that the fact that they were different was a good thing. Two bitter, creative people don't really go together, not for a long and happy marriage anyway. Bruce would balance her out, keep her grounded.

She texted Zoe:

the wedding is on.

Before she got a text back, she decided that lying down was a bad idea. She got up and watered her plants and thought some more about Bruce and how he saw the world. It was so different from how she saw it. Even though she'd grown up in the warmth of a happy family, with a roof over her head, there had always been a dark side to her, someone who considered the world vaguely threatening. She expected the worst, knew it could all come crashing down. Had she picked that up from her parents? She supposed she had. Her father, even though he was a dreamer, was quick to fold when the going got rough. Every time the Boxgrove Theatre was putting on a new play he'd be filled with anticipation, excited by the possibility that, creatively, they were on the cusp of perfection. But he'd also been filled with anxiety, worried that what they were putting on would be a total disaster. In reality, it was never either of those extremes. But the fact that they never produced a play that was truly remarkable—at least in his own estimation—continued to vex him, and after every season he would slip into a depressive episode that lasted throughout the month of September.

Abigail's mother was different. To her, the theater was a financial enterprise first and a creative enterprise second. If they made money, she'd be happy enough. But the theater hardly ever made money.

Thinking of them now, she suddenly wanted to hear one of their voices. Abigail called the landline, her father picking up after three rings.

"Hi, Daddy," she said.

"Who's this?" he responded. It was an old joke.

"Mom must be out."

"She is. Why'd you ask, because I picked up the phone?"

"I guess so. I expected her. Are you living back in the house?"

"No, I'm still above the garage. Your mother is out, so I'm sneaking back in to look for my copy of *Shakespeare's Imagery*. You know, the Spurgeon book. You don't happen to remember where it is, do you?"

"No."

"I know that the last time I saw it, it was next to the sofa in the study, but it's not there now. Your mother probably moved it somewhere."

"Dad, I was thinking of coming home for a weekend before the wedding, spend some time with the two of you." Abigail was surprised even as she said the words.

"Everything okay?"

"Yes, of course it is. Just thought it would be nice. What's going on this weekend?"

"I work Saturday at the movie theater," he said, stretching the word "theater" into three highly stressed syllables, "but that will give you some time with just your mother. No, please come. We'd love to see you. What about Bruce?"

"Bruce and I will be spending the rest of our lives together. Besides, he's cramming as much work into his weekends as possible before the wedding and the honeymoon. It'll be great to see you both."

"Come up. I'd love it. We'd love it."

7

She took the train to Northampton, where Zoe picked her up. It was late afternoon, the second weekend of September, but the first weekend that actually felt like September. The sun was high and bright but there was a bite to the air. Zoe convinced Abigail that they should grab one quick drink in town before heading to Boxgrove.

"How was it seeing Bruce?" she asked Abigail, after they'd both ordered Negronis at the Tunnel Bar, a cocktail place built into an old railway tunnel.

"It was fine. Great. He's very excited about the wedding."

"He give you details about his bachelor weekend?"

"You mean, did I give him details about my bachelorette weekend?" Abigail said.

Zoe smiled, leaning back because their drinks were being delivered. "I guess," she said.

"Yeah, I told him all about it. He said it was no big deal."

"Really?" Zoe leaned forward again, incredulous.

"No."

"Oh. But it was okay?"

"It was good to see him. I'm hoping to forget certain details of that weekend. I'm hoping you do, too."

Zoe turned her fingers in front of her lips and mimed throwing away the key.

At six-thirty Zoe dropped Abigail off at her parents' house. Walking from the curb to the front door, Abigail could see her parents through the bay windows of the living room, her father studying the bar and her mother moving back and forth in the open-plan kitchen area. She'd wondered if they were going to put on a united front during her visit, and it seemed that she had her answer.

She opened the door to the smell of roast chicken.

After dinner, Abigail's mother went to bed first. It had been a perfectly pleasant evening, during which the most controversial topic was where to sit creepy cousin Roger at the wedding reception.

"Port?" her father said, now that Amelia was gone.

"Sure. Why not?"

He poured two glasses, then resettled on the plaid recliner that had always been his favorite chair.

"You and Mom are very chummy," Abigail said.

"We get along still, so long as we don't talk about certain topics, and so long as I remain in the guesthouse."

"That doesn't sound like a typical separation. I mean, you two might be able to find a way back to each other." She tried to keep the hope out of her voice.

He frowned. "I don't know. As far as your mother is concerned, we're over. The reason I'm just in the guesthouse is because I don't have the money to get my own place. We're not mad at each other, but we just burned out, I think. It was all those years running a business together. We turned into business partners instead of husband and wife, and now that the business is poof, so is the marriage."

He leaned back, his shoulders sloping, and Abigail caught a glimpse of what he was going to look like in his extreme old age.

Abigail almost began the conversation about Bruce resurrecting the Boxgrove Theatre with his own money, but it didn't seem the right time. She'd decided before the weekend that that was a conversation for after the wedding. Instead, she said, "Have you thought about couples counseling?"

He shrugged. "It all costs money, and I don't think it would make a difference. Abby, I think you should be focused on your own nuptials and not your mother and me. We're not a project for you."

"Ha."

"You remember the campaign?"

"Of course I do."

It was her father's favorite story from her childhood. When Abigail was eleven, she'd overheard her parents talking about how ticket sales were down that summer. Without telling them, she'd created an ad campaign, handwriting flyers to advertise each of that summer's shows, and handing them out from a table she set up on their front lawn. She'd worn a beret she'd found in the theater's costume department because it looked "right for the occasion," she'd said.

"You were such a fighter. I couldn't believe it."

"Did it do any good? You think I sold a single ticket?"

"I know you did. Pam Hutchinson from across the street told us she bought a ticket because of you. Unfortunately, it was for *Lips Together, Teeth Apart* and she never looked at us the same way again."

"And I sold a ticket—two tickets, I think—to *The Winter's Tale*."

"You have a good memory."

They both sat silent for a moment, Abigail wondering if she did have a good memory, or if it was just the repeated telling of the story that had lodged it in her mind. Her dad said, "We didn't know where you'd come from. I mean, your mother and I were ambitious to a certain degree, but neither of us was a salesperson. You were a firecracker. We always used to say, 'At least we don't have to worry about her. Abby'll be fine.' And you are."

"Dad, are you a little drunk?"

"A little bit. Just sentimental now that I'm in the winter of my years."

Lying in her old bedroom that night, staring up at the stick-on stars that she'd put up on her ceiling years ago, Abigail kept thinking about what her father had said about her being a firecracker. The proof was right on her ceiling, where she'd spelled out her own name in the midst of the galaxy. Had she been that self-centered, or was it just confidence about her place in the world? She had had confidence for most of middle school and some of high school. She remembered being fearless, always up for a fight. That was how she and Zoe had become such good friends, despite how different they were in so many ways. Max Rafferty had spread a rumor about Zoe giving him a hand job after the seventh-grade dance, and the next day Abigail had snuck up behind Max while he was in line at the cafeteria, tugging down his pants, snagging his underwear along for the ride. She'd been friends with Zoe then, but not best friends. After that, they were inseparable.

And that wasn't the only time she'd gotten revenge.

Freshman year of high school Abigail heard that a former friend, Kaitlyn Austin, had been going around saying that Abigail's parents were the town perverts and that they loved to put on disgusting plays. This was after a production of *Spring Awakening* that had caused a brief ripple through the more conservative elements of the Boxgrove community. Kaitlyn Austin told everyone that she'd heard that the Baskins only put on the musical so that they could cast young actors to have sex with. She said that every year there were orgies at the Boxgrove Theatre, an idea so ludicrous that Abigail was initially more amused than pissed off. But the rumors spread through their small regional high school.

It was around this time, too, that Abigail had discovered thrift store shopping, dressing one day in a poodle skirt from the 1950s, and the next in a fringed leather jacket. Kaitlyn began calling Abigail "the freak," and it was a nickname that stuck around for at least a year. Part of her didn't even care that much about being called a name, but it was the fact that the name had originated with Kaitlyn that stung. Abigail became consumed with the idea of getting revenge. She did, eventually, but not until senior year. Knowing that Kaitlyn and her family were away for the Columbus Day weekend, she'd walked across town just before midnight and broken into their house through a window they'd left open. She'd gone straight to Kaitlyn's room and searched it, stealing a stack of her diaries. On the way out, she'd slashed all the tires on Kaitlyn's Subaru. She could still remember the feel of the knife puncturing the rubber, the hiss of air as the tires slumped.

That night, she'd felt sickened with herself but a little elated. And she'd never told anyone, not even Zoe.

Abigail, remembering the type of person she'd been in adolescence, wondered if she'd changed, if somewhere along the line she'd become more passive. She wasn't sure. She knew that she could have moved back to Boxgrove after college, but instead she'd gone to New York and gotten a job in publishing. That was more than any of her high school friends could say. But, despite the fact that she was still in the city, she did feel as though something in her had altered. Maybe it was her upcoming marriage to Bruce. Because he was so rich, because he had been the one to initiate the relationship, and because he was so single-minded in his pursuits, he made her feel like she was second fiddle to his ambitions. No, that wasn't true, necessarily. He made her feel as though he'd invited her onto his boat, and now that boat was careening down a river, and she was just a passenger. But what was wrong with that? And one thing that she'd be gaining from the marriage was financial security, which meant free time, which meant she could finish her novel. And writing a novel would be her own thing, nothing to do with Bruce.

She was beginning to get tired and shifted onto her side. Somehow the image of a boat stayed in her mind as she slipped into sleep, gliding effortlessly along a churning river, the rush of water in her ears.

She spent the next day with her mother. They had lunch in town at the Boxgrove Inn, then drove to a boutique clothing store in the next town over to look for a dress for her mom to wear to the wedding.

It was only when they got back home, each collapsing with a cup of tea in the living room, that Abigail asked her mother about the separation.

"Ugh," Amelia said. "I don't hate your father. Obviously, you know that. How could I? It's just that . . . it's just that we spent so long trying to get the theater to work, and that was where all our energy went. I just don't have anything left to give him, and he knows that, too."

"But you still care for him?"

"I do. Of course I do. Here's the thing, Abby. When I

think about my life—the rest of my life, I mean—if I stay with your father then I know exactly what it's going to be like. But if we split up, if we each get another chance, then something else might happen. Something exciting."

"You mean you might meet someone new?"

"It's not just that, although I have thought about that. It's just that I need space to be me, to change a little, to allow something to happen. It's your father who'll meet someone new, probably."

"Why do you say that?"

"Let's just say he falls in love too easily."

Abigail sat up. "Has dad had affairs?"

"I don't know," Amelia said, lowering her voice even though they were alone in the house. "I wouldn't call them affairs, but most summers when we were putting on shows, he'd fall in love with one of the actresses who came up. He was not good at hiding it. From me *or* from them. You remember Audra Johnson?"

"Sure."

"I don't think they actually had a sexual affair, but they definitely had an emotional one. It was a hard summer."

"I'm learning so much," Abigail said. Then she added, "You never . . . ?"

"Me? No. I think, for me, being married, and being in business together, I was all in, all the time. That's why I want a break now. Those twenty years, it was so much work, and now it just feels like . . . I wonder if it was worth it."

"Mom," Abigail said. "It was totally worth it. Think about what you accomplished, all the plays you put on, all the actors you employed, all the people who were entertained, who were intellectually stimulated. You made art." Abigail was aware, even as she was saying the words, that she was parroting what the man from the bachelorette weekend had said to her. She felt a flush of feeling for that man whose name she never even knew.

"No, I know," Amelia said, and put her mug down on the side table. "I keep thinking the same thing. Just because something ends doesn't mean it didn't have value. Your father and I . . ."

After a pause, Abigail realized her mother wasn't going to finish the sentence and said, "I guess marriage is hard."

"Maybe not for everyone, honey. Maybe not for you. We really like Bruce, you know that?"

"I know you do."

"And we can't wait for the wedding."

"You won't cry, will you?"

"I'll try not to cry too much. Can't vouch for your father. What do you want for dinner tonight? If I were here alone, I'd probably eat cereal." She'd moved to the edge of the sofa, her hands on her knees, suddenly practical.

"Cereal sounds great."

Abigail waited for her mother to rise and go to the kitchen, but she stayed seated for a moment, then said, "You know, Abby, we'll always be a family, the three of us. That will never change."

"I know, Mom," Abigail said.

That night Abigail woke just before dawn, struggling up from a bad dream that slipped away as soon as she tried to recollect it. Her chest hurt, and there was perspiration in her hairline. She lay still for a little while, wondering if she'd be able to fall back to sleep, but her body tingled, as if she'd had too much coffee. She watched the bedroom window fill with gray light and thought about her parents. They'd never seemed so vulnerable to her as they did this weekend. Even so, it was clear to her that Bruce's plan to fund the Boxgrove Theatre again was a nonstarter. Or seemed to be. Her mother wasn't interested in going down that road again, and she wasn't sure that her dad would have the energy, either.

Her train was leaving Northampton at ten that morning, and for a few minutes Abigail wasn't sure she wanted to go back to New York. She didn't necessarily want to spend any more nights in her childhood home consoling her parents. But she suddenly imagined life if she lived here in Boxgrove, maybe in a cute studio apartment near the town center, the rent cheap enough that she wouldn't have to work full-time, and she would have time to write. She'd get coffee at the Rockwell Diner and go to the tavern at the inn on Friday nights, where she'd probably know everyone in the place. She thought of Bruce, and for a surreal ten seconds couldn't picture his face. Then it came to her, and with it, her fantasy about returning home disappeared.

8

Bruce, after Abigail returned to the city, suggested that Abigail and he should spend the remaining nights before the wedding in their own apartments. At first Abigail thought it was an unnecessary restriction, but she soon grew to like the arrangement. There were only two weeks left before the wedding, and there was something old-fashioned and romantic that, after eating dinner together, Bruce would accompany her back to her apartment and they would kiss under the streetlamp as a way of saying good night. Bruce also suggested that they watch a film together—Abigail in her apartment, he in his, and they could talk about it later. They'd watched *The Omen* and *Carrie* (Abigail's picks) that way, then watched *The Descent* and *Kiss the Girls* (Bruce's picks). After a brief bout of hot September days, the weather had cooled, and the city was bearable again. Those post-dinner walks home, her arm casually looped through Bruce's, discussing what film to watch that night, made Abigail feel as though she were falling in love with not just Bruce, but New York City all over again.

The wedding was all planned. They were getting married in a refurbished barn in the Hudson Valley, home to a Michelin-starred restaurant and a boutique hotel. Just ninety guests, sixty of them coming from Abigail's friends and family. In some ways, planning the wedding had been relatively easy, with Bruce accepting all of Abigail's decisions. It didn't hurt that money was not a consideration. Even so, Abigail made sure that, except for the rustic opulence of the actual location, the wedding itself would not be over-the-top. No caviar service at the reception, no specially made designer dress. Also, no DJ who might play Ed Sheeran. She found an interesting band that specialized in covers of 1960s French pop.

Bruce had several friends coming to the wedding, but very little family, just his father, plus his father's sister and her family. Bruce's mother was alive, but they were estranged. "She knows I'm getting married, but, honestly, weddings are not her thing. Marriage was not her thing," he said. Both of Abigail's parents came from fairly large families and there was going to be a glut of cousins coming from near and far. Despite their circumstances, Lawrence and Amelia Baskin remained excited for the wedding, looking forward to seeing extended family, probably looking forward to a weekend that would take their minds off the failure of both their theater and their marriage.

Abigail was keeping her job at Bonespar Press but cutting her hours in half, figuring that she and Bruce didn't need the money, and that she could use the extra time to start real work on her novel. It was a psychological thriller about twin girls being raised in a rotting brownstone in the city, their parents both artists who refused to leave the house. Of the twins, one wants to stay in the house forever, and one wants to leave. That was all Abigail had so far, definitely not enough to mention it to any of her friends, including Bruce. But she'd written the first ninety or so pages, and didn't hate it, and now she just wanted to see where the story would take her.

She'd also negotiated with Bonespar Press for two months' unpaid leave that began a week before the wedding. She had spent two days training the temp employee who would be covering for her while she was gone, and then she'd gone out for celebratory drinks with her coworkers on the last day before her leave. They'd gone to Abigail's favorite East Village bar, and it was there that she ran into her ex Ben Perez, who came in at midnight by himself. For one brief moment Abigail thought that he had come there to confront her, but then she saw the surprise on his face and she realized that it was just coincidence. They said hello; he was drunk and kept telling her that he'd just been out with a bunch of writer friends and he was stopping in for one last drink before heading home. Abigail bought him a bourbon sour and told him she was getting married. "Yeah, I know all about it," he said. "I run into your friends all the time."

"Who do you run into?"

"Kyra, for one. She said you're marrying a gazillionaire, and that she thinks you're doing it just for the money."

"She *said* that?"

"Something like that."

It had occurred to Abigail that when you marry someone so conspicuously wealthy people are going to talk, but, still, hearing that Kyra had said something so catty made her chest hurt.

"I'm not marrying him because he's rich," she said, instantly annoyed that she was defending herself to Ben.

"I didn't say it. She did."

Her work friends were beginning to put on coats and settle up bills, and Abigail, who didn't want to get stuck rehashing things with Ben at the bar, left with them. The next day she almost called Kyra to confront her, but called Bruce instead. She thought he might worry a little that she'd run into her ex-boyfriend of six years the night before, but he didn't seem fazed.

"I'm sure Kyra's not the only one who's made a comment," Bruce said. "People are strange about money. You'll probably lose at least one friend after we get married, someone who just won't be able to handle it. I did when I got rich. The way I figure it is that they weren't great friends to begin with."

"Okay, thanks," she said, feeling better.

After the talk with Bruce she stopped worrying about Kyra, and about what her other friends might think about Bruce. She had other things to deal with, mostly the logistics of who was staying at the Blue Barn Inn, which had only twenty-five rooms, and who was staying at the bed-and-breakfast half a mile away, and whether they should offer some sort of shuttle service back and forth so that people wouldn't have to worry about drinking. And she had her own apartment to worry about. She'd given notice, and now it was just a matter of boxing up her possessions, mainly books, and figuring out what to do with her few pieces of furniture, most of which were not coming with her to Bruce's place. And she was worried about Zoe, who still lived in Boxgrove, because she'd just had another massive fight with her boyfriend of seven years, and now she didn't want him at the wedding. Zoe was a rock—well, she was Abigail's rock—but when things went bad with Dan, all bets were off.

With the wedding looming, these were Abigail's biggest worries, and she realized that she was in pretty good shape, considering. The memory of the stranger at the vineyard in California now felt like a fuzzy, unreal dream, something that had happened to her either very long ago or maybe not at all. In some ways, it had even helped clarify for her how much she wanted to marry Bruce. The fact that the evening had been intriguing and romantic made her only crave the solidness, and coziness, of marriage more. Everything was going to be all right.

And then she saw Scottie in the coffee shop.

That whole day she felt like a chasm had opened up in front of her, a big black hole she was powerless to escape. He'd come for her—all the way across the country—and he was going to wreck her life. In a way, it helped that she later got the email; it gave her a chance to answer him, to try to end it before it got any worse. She did feel temporarily better after sending him her response, but that night she was anxious, her mind filling with images from California, a jittery sensation racing across her skin. Just to make it stop, to try to relax her body, she flipped onto her stomach and masturbated, feeling half aroused and half sickened by the thoughts that kept entering her mind. She made herself come, and afterward, exhausted, hollowed out, she at least felt that maybe she'd be able to get some sleep.

But there was still that chasm, black and bottomless, that she couldn't entirely shake out of her mind.

9

Her few married friends had all told her that their weddings had been a blur, that you never got a chance to eat, let alone enjoy, any of the food, and you'd be lucky to get a moment alone with your spouse. Most of that turned out to be true for Abigail on her wedding day, but she still enjoyed herself.

The ceremony, held in the upper loft of the barn, was fairy-tale-like, the entire place lit by white candles. She thought she'd be nervous—thinking back on her few high school experiences on the stage—but she was okay, more emotional than she thought she'd be, cognizant of the enormity of the moment, of what it meant to pledge yourself to one person for the rest of your life. She felt great in her wedding dress. She'd never been a girl who dreamed of wearing the perfect white dress for her wedding, and she'd considered wearing black just to be different, but then she'd found an online site that sold vintage wedding dresses and fallen in love with a butter-toned organza dress from the 1940s. It was simple—a sleeveless bodice and an A-line skirt—but was covered in beads and sequins. It was long enough that it covered her single tattoo, a barren tree that ran from her hip halfway down her left thigh. When she'd seen herself in the dress with her makeup and her hair done (she'd given the hairdresser pictures of Audrey Hepburn from *Roman Holiday*), she'd felt as though she was looking at a stranger, that she was a fictional character, an impostor. She told herself it was a natural feeling, something every bride must feel, but she wasn't sure. The feeling of disassociation had something to do with what had happened in California—Scottie, thank God, had not replied to her email—but it also had something to do with Bruce. Who was this rich, attentive man? And who was she, that she was marrying him? It wasn't just that he was a stranger, it was that she sometimes felt like a stranger to herself as well. Like everything she was now doing to prepare for this wedding was happening automatically. She was going through the steps, almost like clockwork, and not unhappily. It just felt strange. Was she still an arty girl who went to the city to be a writer? Or was she a small-town girl like Zoe? She was neither, it appeared. She was about to be the wife of a very rich man. And that felt as bizarre to her as anything.

Bruce wore a very classic Brunello Cucinelli tux, and Abigail realized that she'd never seen him in any kind of suit before. He looked relaxed and handsome, and the cold that he'd been fighting the past few days had disappeared.

Bruce's father, whom Abigail had met only once, sat with her parents, and they all got along, or seemed to, anyway. Bill Lamb was a retired truck driver, a hardened version of his son who looked uncomfortable in the suit that Bruce had bought for him. But he kept claiming that he was having the best day of his life, and he even danced later in the evening, several times with Abigail's mother, and at one point with all the bridesmaids.

Abigail's favorite part of the wedding was the cocktail reception. The photographer had taken pictures prior to the ceremony, Abigail not feeling superstitious about the groom seeing her dress, so that after they were declared husband and wife, everyone could go straight to the reception, which was set up on a sloping lawn with a distant view of the Hudson River. A few tents had been erected but weren't needed. The skies were clear, and the temperature was somewhere in the sixties. It was perfect. The signature cocktail was a sidecar, served in a coupe. Toasts were made, the oyster bar hummed, and when Abigail's heel sank into the lawn and she nearly fell over, Bruce managed to catch her.

Dinner truly was a blur, but it might have been the two cocktails. Abigail managed to eat half of her sea bass with parsley cream sauce and was amazed that it didn't taste as though it had sat in a warming tray for the last two hours. More toasts were made, including a showstopper by the actor Martin Pilkingham, who embarrassed Abigail by listing off all the Boxgrove actors she'd had a crush on, including Zachary Mason, the actor to whom she'd lost her virginity. Zoe sat next to Abigail through dinner and kept up a good appearance even though she hadn't reconciled yet with Dan. Usually a big eater, Zoe managed just three stalks of asparagus and drank half a bottle of wine, and she was the first on the dance floor after the traditional dances had ended. During the band's second set Zoe slipped and hit the floor, and when Bruce's best man, Darryl Cho, a married computer programmer from California, helped her up, she thanked him by kissing him full on the mouth. The other bridesmaids helped Zoe to her room, then reported back to Abigail that they'd managed to at least get her out of her bridesmaid dress before she passed out on the bed.

Toward the end of the evening Abigail spotted her parents sitting together at a table on the edge of the dance floor. Each had been dancing, and they now looked sweaty and tired. Abigail joined them.

"The original Baskins," Lawrence said. "Together again."

"You guys have fun?" she said.

"God, yes," Amelia said. "Did you see your aunt Mary on the dance floor?"

"How could I miss her?"

"Bruce was very sweet," Lawrence said. "He introduced himself to everyone in our family and acted as though we are all normal."

"And he invited us down to see a show in New York after you two get back from your honeymoon," her mom said.

Abigail, slightly tipsy, suddenly said, "He's going to want to talk with you about the theater. He wants to bring it back."

"What theater?" Amelia said. "Our theater?"

"Yes."

"Oh, God. Please derail him. I don't think I have it in me."

"What about you, Dad?"

"He wants to invest in the theater and bring it back?"

"He does. Very badly."

He took a deep breath. "Two years ago, I would have given my right arm for an investor. But what's done is done."

"Well, look, at least hear him out. He's so excited to talk with you."

After the conversation, when Abigail was returning to the dance floor as the band was breaking into a swing-style version of "Friday I'm in Love," she caught a glimpse of her parents leaning into each other, half smiles on their lips. She had a moment of clarity, not that they were going to get back together, but that they weren't. They were too comfortable with each other post-separation. They were friends, and nothing more.

The last dance of the night was to "Every Breath You Take," the Police song, done in a bossa nova style. She and Bruce danced close to each other, and she could feel his breath against the hollow of her throat as he mouthed along with the lyrics. Not for the first time, she thought how creepy the words of the song actually were.

"What did you think of your wedding day?" Bruce asked Abigail as she rested her head against his shoulder.

She thought she could probably fall asleep before the end of the song.

"Oh, it was okay." She smiled at him and for a moment he looked concerned, then he smiled back, realizing she was joking.

"Yeah, just okay."

"I requested '(Don't Fear) the Reaper,' and the band didn't play it."

"Assholes."

"And I didn't eat one oyster."

"Neither did I," Bruce said.

"But I did get married."

"Ditto for me," he said, and she tilted her head back to meet his eyes. He looked tired, too, but in a good way. Happy-tired.

"I couldn't be happier, Bruce."

"Are you ready for the honeymoon?" he asked.

"Yes, but I've barely thought about it because all I've been thinking about is today."

"And it's not over yet."

"Technically, it is. We're into our second day of marriage already."

After the dance, and after they'd said good night to the few remaining guests, they walked down the flagstone pathway to the carriage house that they were staying in. There was a lone guest standing in a nearby cluster of trees, smoking a cigarette, the smell of it wafting toward them. Abigail, breathing it in, had a sudden vivid sense memory, the smoke bringing her back to that night in California. But it wasn't just the smell of a cigarette that was bringing her back; it was more than that. Whoever was smoking in the trees had to be smoking the same cigarette that Scottie had that night at the vineyard. They'd been Gauloises, those unfiltered French cigarettes that had made Abigail feel as if she'd spun around in place about ten times. She stared toward the man smoking, but he was completely in shadow, only the orange tip of the cigarette showing where he was.

"You okay?" Bruce said.

"Yeah, sorry. Do you know who that is, smoking?" As soon as she said it, panic grabbed at her. What if it was actually Scottie, and what if Bruce made his way over there?

"My friend Mike, probably. Why, you want one?"

"Ha, no." They kept walking. The night had turned cold, and she shivered. She leaned against Bruce as he opened the door to their room, then he lifted her over the threshold, Abigail screaming in genuine shock. The four-poster bed was turned down, and there were fresh flowers throughout the room. Abigail's bags had been brought over, and she got her toiletries and her overnight bag and went into the bathroom. There were flowers in there, too, and several lit candles. The stone floor was heated.

She stared in the mirror for a moment, and told herself that she was paranoid. Scottie hadn't stalked her all the way to the wedding.

He stalked you to New York.

Besides, all cigarettes smelled the same, didn't they? And people were always smoking at weddings, even people who no longer smoked. She'd spotted Kyra smoking earlier, and her uncle Evan, who'd quit years ago. It made no sense that it was Scottie lurking around her wedding. Why would he come? To watch it from afar? No, if he had decided to come, the only reason would be to break up the event somehow, and he hadn't tried to do that. It wasn't him, just some other guest. Maybe even some other guest who liked unfiltered French cigarettes. It was possible.

She washed her face and got out of her dress. She'd brought a sheer nightdress in baby blue that had puffed sleeves and ruffles along the hem and put it on. She felt slightly ridiculous, but it was her wedding night and when else was she going to wear something like this? When she emerged from the bathroom Bruce was already in bed, naked from the waist up. She did a quick spin, the hem of the lingerie floating up, then got under the covers, where she tried not to think of the man in the trees, and Scottie, and the smell of French cigarette smoke.

10

"What do you mean, there's no electricity?"

"There's *some* electricity. For a hair dryer, for example, and if there's an emergency."

"Where exactly are you taking me?" Abigail said, laughing. They were driving north in Bruce's electric Tesla.

"It's all part of the experience. No phones, no television, no computers."

"I'm fine with all that."

"You're just worried about your hair?"

"Pretty much, yes."

"There are plugs in the bathrooms," Bruce said. They had just crossed into Massachusetts. The day had begun in bright sunshine, but now there was a thin haze of clouds building across the sky, and the temperature was dropping. The forecast for the week was for heavy winds and occasional showers. Bruce had claimed that it would make the honeymoon more romantic.

"What about lamps?"

"They have them there."

"Real ones?"

"Most everything is lit by candles at night, and they give you lanterns when you need to walk somewhere.

They look just like old-fashioned oil lanterns but they're actually battery-powered. They're really beautiful. Trust me, a week of living this way, you're never going to want to go back to the real world."

"When were you here before, again? I know you told me, but I forgot."

"A few times. The longest trip was three years ago, right after Chip opened it. I was one of his first guests. He originally envisioned it as a place for people who work in the computer industry, a place to reconnect with nature, take your eyes off the screen. That sort of thing. There are a lot of corporate retreats there, brainstorming sessions, that sort of thing. And now it's actually become popular with honeymooning couples, for some of the same reasons. No distractions. Plus, the food's amazing."

"What do people do there?"

"What do you mean?"

"Are there activities?"

"There are great walks on the island. There's an indoor swimming pool that you have to see to believe. There's a spa, but most of the activities are supposed to be like camp activities but for grown-ups. You don't have to do them, but if you want to, there's archery, and sailing on the pond, and a whole art studio. You can paint pictures and do pottery."

"Really?"

"Yeah. All voluntary, though. Personally, I like the main lodge. You can sit by the fire and read. They bring you drinks. It's pretty sweet. And it's not going to be filled with corporate types, I promise you. Chip told me it's going to be relatively empty. It has a Gothic feel, you'll like it."

Abigail was worried that she'd made him a little defensive about his choice of a honeymoon spot, so she said, "It sounds awesome, Bruce. I can't wait to see it."

They stopped for lunch in southern Maine, eating in the basement tavern of a seaside inn near Kennewick Harbor. Abigail, who'd been starving herself just a little bit in preparation for the wedding, ate a cheeseburger with fries and declared it the best she'd ever had. Bruce had the lobster roll and they shared a bottle of Sancerre.

"I keep having these moments," Abigail said, "when I suddenly realize that I'm married, that *we're* married. It's kind of mind-blowing."

"No regrets?" Bruce said.

"Not yet," she said, and instantly saw something change in his eyes, even in the dim lighting of the tavern. "I'm kidding," she added.

"I know."

"How about you? Any regrets?"

"No. I feel ridiculously lucky, like I don't deserve you. If I feel anything, it's a form of guilt."

"You totally deserve me," she said, then added, "That didn't come out right. *We* deserve *each other*."

"Okay," he said. "No more guilt. Let's start our honeymoon."

There was a small airport about twenty miles north of Portland. Abigail was nervous about taking a plane to the island, but Bruce had assured her that it was totally safe.

"I feel like I read about small planes crashing all the time."

"Mostly because of bad weather, and there's no bad weather today. And it's only about a twenty-minute flight."

They walked into the departure lounge and were greeted by a tall, wide-shouldered man who looked like he was ex-military. He stood behind a desk embossed with the words CASCO AIR, and a logo that showed a plane above a lighthouse. He looked at them both and said, "Heart Pond Island, right?"

"Right."

"Got a good day for it. Is that all your luggage?"

"There are two more bags in the car," Abigail said.

"No worries. I'll send someone to get them. Chip told me that you're his special guests and I was to pull out all the stops, so just take a seat, and I'll let you know when we're ready to go."

They were on the plane in about twenty minutes, a six-seater in which you could see straight ahead through the windshield. It was the smallest plane Abigail had been on, and she thought she was going to hate it, but once they were up at cloud level, with views of the Atlantic Ocean, she began to get excited. *This is my life now*, she thought, *one adventure after another*. She stretched her back, felt a crackle in her neck and a pop in one of her shoulders. The plane lifted slightly, and she experienced a sudden wave of relaxation so intense that it felt like she'd keep on feeling it even if the plane started tumbling toward the ocean. Her fingers were intertwined with Bruce's. He leaned across her and pointed through the oval side window. "See the island?"

It was oblong, with rocky shores everywhere except for one sandy cove. In the center was the pond that gave the island its name. It was shaped very much like a heart, a triangle cut in on one side by a wooded spit of land. As the plane began to lower and circle around, Abigail could make out two clusters of buildings, one on either side of the pond.

"Where do we land?" she asked Bruce, and he pointed out a landing strip that seemed too short along the southern edge of the island. A gust of wind came along, and it felt as though the plane almost skidded on the air. Still, Abigail was calm, telling herself that the pilot had it all under control, and pretty soon the plane was bumping down onto the gravel landing strip, then pulling up toward a medium-sized hangar. The pilot lowered the stairs and all three stepped out into the salt air, cooler here than it had been even at the airport. Abigail pulled a sweater from her bag and pulled it on over her head, as the plane's propellers ticked to a stop.

"This way," the young pilot said, and Bruce took her arm as they began to walk toward the hangar, just as a stocky man with a reddish beard pulled up in a Land Rover and jumped out of the driver's side, bustling toward them.

"Hey, Bruce," he said, and Abigail was surprised to see Bruce and the red-haired man hug. It was the first time she'd seen her husband physically interact with another man.

"You didn't have to come yourself," Bruce said, "but thank you."

"Of course I did. This must be Abigail."

Bruce introduced her to Chip Ramsay, saying that everything she saw on the island was his. "He's the man," he said. Chip wore cargo shorts and a short-sleeved T-shirt despite the cold air on the island. The hair on his arms and legs was as red as the hair on his head. There was what looked like a walkie-talkie strapped to his belt.

With the pilot's help they collected all their luggage and loaded it into Chip's car. "Quick tour of the island?" he asked. "Or straight to your room?"

"How about straight to our room?" Bruce said.

"That sounds good," Abigail added.

Chip drove them along a dirt road through a thick pine forest, then up a short incline and through two stone pillars that marked a gate. Above them hung a faded sign that said CAMP PASSAMAQUODDY. "Welcome to Quoddy," Chip said. They were suddenly through to a clearing. To their left was an enormous lodge made of dark timber and rough stone. Even with the windows closed she could smell woodsmoke in the air.

"Gorgeous," she said.

They kept driving, turning down toward a row of ten miniature versions of the lodge. They looked like they were the original cabins from when this was a camp. "You guys are in River Rock," Chip said. "It's not where you stayed before, Bruce, but I think you'll like this bunk more."

"Do they have bunk beds?" Abigail asked.

Chip let out a single nasal sound that was probably a laugh. "Sorry, we still call all the cabins bunks. Sticking with tradition."

He pulled up right to the front of the bunk. Its low roof was covered in bright green moss, and its wooden front door was edged in flowering vine. Abigail was admiring it when the door swung open suddenly, and she jumped. A tall Asian man stepped out into the dusk light. He was wearing khaki pants and a crisp white shirt, and he took two bounding steps to the Land Rover and opened the door. Chip said, "Meet Paul. He's going to take care of anything you might need during your stay. Stocking your refrigerator, bringing you extra blankets, wake-up times, although I hope you won't require those. He comes with River Rock, so feel like you can call on him anytime you'd like."

Paul showed them inside. Abigail knew it would be fancy, but she wasn't entirely prepared for just how serene the interior was. There was a large stone fireplace in the center of the cabin—the *bunk*, Abigail reminded herself—a fire already going. In front of the fireplace was an overstuffed leather couch along with a beautiful cocktail table constructed from a single dark green stone speckled with yellow. "That's where this bunk gets its name," Paul said, as Abigail touched the stone. "It's a river rock."

"Beautiful," she said.

"Everything in here is handcrafted, including the bed," Chip said.

Abigail walked over to the king-sized bed, its sleigh-style frame made from dark refurbished wood. There were lit lanterns on either side of the bed, and Abigail thought they were real until she remembered that Bruce had told her they were battery-powered, just made to look real. Above the bed was a framed poster from the movie *Midnight Lace* with Doris Day and Rex Harrison. Abigail spun, and looked at Bruce.

"No, it's not a coincidence," he said. "It's a gift."

It had been the first film they'd watched together, the second time she'd spent the night at his apartment in New York. They'd been talking about favorite thrillers—well, Abigail had been the one mostly talking about her favorite thrillers—and Bruce had brought up *Midnight Lace*, a film he'd watched with his mother when he was young. Abigail had heard of it but never seen it, and they'd watched it in the wee hours while still in bed, eating popcorn and drinking champagne. She'd loved the film.

"That's the nicest thing you've given me," she said

now, about the poster, embarrassed that Chip and Paul were in the room with them.

"Nicer than the ring?" Bruce said.

"Yes," Abigail said without hesitating.

"I think she means it," Chip said, then quickly added, "We want to get out of your hair, and I'm sure Bruce explained everything, but there *are* electrical outlets in the bathroom, and you do have a refrigerator, but that's about it for electricity. There are no screens anywhere on the island, and we suggest you put your phone and laptop, if you brought one, somewhere out of sight. There's no wireless and no cell service. You gave our number to somebody in your family?"

He was looking at Abigail, and she said that she had. Her parents, plus Zoe, had the resort's landline, just in case there was some emergency.

"I won't lie to you. Our guests can get a little wiggy in the first twenty-four hours from not having any access to the internet. Trust me, though, it passes. In one day, you won't think about it, and next week, when you leave, you'll wish you could live every day without a phone."

"I'm excited," Abigail said, meaning it. Even though she'd grown up in an era of social media, her parents had not allowed her a smartphone until she was fifteen years old, and she still reminisced about life before Instagram and Snapchat.

"I'll leave you to it, then. Paul, want to show them the provisions?"

Paul led them to the refrigerator, carefully hidden behind a wall that must have been original to the bunk, but the wall somehow slid soundlessly to the side. Inside the refrigerator there were craft beers, several bottles of wine, and an array of cheeses, charcuterie, olives, and designer water. "This is just a start," Paul said. "Anything else you want, just let me know and I can get it for you."

"Oreo cookies," Abigail said, and Paul nodded at her. She realized he had taken her seriously, and she quickly said, "I'm just kidding. You don't have Oreos here, do you?"

"We don't, but like I said, anything you want, and we'll get it."

"No, no. I was just kidding."

There was a set of French doors that led to a back veranda with a view of the pond, its surface now orange beneath the setting sun. "Cocktails at the lodge at six, but some guests like to have their cocktail hour in their bunk instead."

Abigail looked toward Bruce and shrugged.

"We'll have cocktails in the lodge," Bruce told Paul, then looked at Abigail and said, "I want you to see it."

Paul showed them a few other amenities, including a button they could press to summon him, then he slipped quietly out the front door and Bruce and Abigail were alone. She started to laugh. "You didn't say it came with a butler."

"Get used to it, babe," he said.

"I don't know if I can, but this place is beautiful. I just want to live inside this bunk for the entire week."

"You can do whatever you want."

After unpacking their things, Abigail and Bruce took a bath together in the deep freestanding tub surrounded by candles. Bruce told her that the tub was made from sandstone. "You could just be making that up," Abigail said, "but I believe you."

She slipped through the water and into his arms. They kissed, Abigail aware of the sound of the bathwater lightly hitting the edge of the tub. "It's so quiet in here," she said. "I think I forget how much noise we're constantly hearing."

"If it becomes too much for you," Bruce said, "we could add some ambient noise to the place. There's actually a hidden sound system that we can utilize."

"Of course there is. I think you lied about the no-electricity thing. It's just hidden electricity."

"Yes, that's kind of true."

When they got out of the bath together Bruce dried Abigail off with a massive towel, taking his time, studying her naked skin. Though they'd never talked about it, Abigail could tell just how important visual stimulation was to him. The first night they'd had sex he'd asked her to undress in front of him and watched her with such fascination that it bordered on uncomfortable. She'd made some joke, she was sure, at the time, and it was really the only slightly strange aspect of their sex life. She wondered if it had something to do with the fact that men today, women, too, had grown up watching so much pornography. Maybe the sight of an actual naked woman in front of them was akin to finally seeing the Grand Canyon in reality after years of only seeing pictures. It was both familiar and completely new. She didn't mind, exactly, and when they had sex, he would become more physically engaged, less visually so. It was totally common, she realized, and the only part of it that bothered her was wondering if he'd lose interest in her as the years passed, as her body changed.

Abigail left the bathroom first and sat naked on the edge of the bed, assuming that Bruce was going to want to have sex. She felt ambivalent, as she always did up until the moment his hands started to touch her. As she waited for him while he dried off, her eyes instinctually scanned her immediate vicinity for her cell phone before she realized she'd already stowed it away in the drawer where she'd put her underwear. It was going to be strange not having a phone. How did one fill those little gaps in time? Bruce emerged from the bathroom, the towel wrapped around his waist. She watched him walk across the room. He had a trim, athletic body—he never went more than two days without going to the gym—but he wasn't graceful, and when he walked Abigail could always visualize the awkward teen he'd probably been, skinny and perpetually at his computer. It made her love him more, not less.

He dropped his towel on the floor and was pulling up his boxer briefs when Abigail realized he wasn't going to try to initiate anything. She was surprisingly disappointed and said his name to get his attention. He turned, and something in his face—a distraction in his eyes—made her decide not to call him over to the bed.

"Nothing," she said, then got up herself and walked to the bureau she'd claimed when they'd unpacked.

11

The main hall of the lodge felt more like a castle than an old summer camp. The fireplace could easily fit an entire basketball team inside it, and the room's ceiling rose three stories. An enormous chandelier made of brass and candles hung above the center of the hall, and Abigail wondered how it was possibly lit. Did one of the butlers run out here with a huge stepladder when no one was looking?

There were only about a dozen people mingling in the hall, most standing near the fireplace or sitting in overstuffed chairs.

"Bar?" Bruce said, and together they walked across the stone floor, covered here and there by expensive-looking rugs, toward a fully stocked bar made from dark wood carved to look like vines growing up columns. The bartender was middle-aged, with a graying mustache that flared a little on either end. Like Paul, the man charged with taking care of their bunk, the bartender was dressed in khakis and a crisp white shirt.

"Bruce, my man," he said in an indecipherable accent. "Welcome back."

"Hello, Carl. I'd like you to meet Abigail, my wife."

"I heard. I heard. Congratulations. What can I get you? A champagne cocktail?"

"I think we can do better than that," Bruce said. "I don't suppose you remember that Manhattan you made me last time I was here?"

"Of course I do."

"How about two of those?"

Abigail turned and looked at Bruce, a little surprised he'd ordered for her. It was not something he'd ever done, not something that anyone she'd ever dated had done for her. He met her eye and immediately said, "You like Manhattans, don't you?"

"I do. Sorry. I was just surprised."

"That I ordered for you? It's a onetime thing, I promise. You have to try this drink. It's perfection."

"WhistlePig Rye and Punt e Mes," the bartender said.

When she tasted the drink, she had to agree that it was delicious, the best Manhattan she'd had. She was still a little annoyed, though, not because he'd ordered the drink for her, although that was part of it, but because it was increasingly obvious that Bruce had spent a lot of time at this resort, and that he'd brought her to a place that felt like *his* place. She wondered if the honeymoon would have been more special if they'd gone to a place that was new to both of them. It was a little thing, though. She focused on the taste of the drink and the majesty of the lodge.

"Mingle or stay put?" Bruce asked.

93

"How about we stay put for the length of this drink, at least?" she said.

"Good choice."

Two men approached the bar, and Carl asked them what they wanted. The men were young and hip, both dressed in jeans and casual sweaters, both bearded, and Abigail thought that they were probably young wealthy computer entrepreneurs like Bruce. She was surprised he didn't know them. The men ordered something called Peeper on draft, then talked in hushed tones. Like everywhere else on this island, it was quiet in the lodge, almost eerily so.

As though he were reading her thoughts, Bruce said, "There's music here some nights. Chip has bands flown in."

"Like rock bands?" Abigail said, trying to imagine it.

"More like string quartets, but also a lot of experimental bands. Electronic stuff." He named a bunch of artists Abigail hadn't heard of.

Bruce started talking about the dinner, the philosophy behind the food, what to expect. Abigail listened, but also thought about where she was, who she was with, and all that had happened over the past few weeks. Since meeting Bruce she'd had these little moments when she felt as if she'd taken a step away from herself and could see the surreal nature of her new life. It was partly the money, the fact that she'd suddenly gone from struggling to pay her rent to being with someone who was probably a billionaire (she didn't know exactly how much money Bruce had, nor had he asked her to sign any kind of prenuptial agreement), but it was also partly to do with Bruce. In these moments she would be suddenly acutely aware that he was a stranger. It didn't last long, this feeling, and she'd remind herself how much they'd shared since they'd met. Not just experiences, but long conversations. She'd heard all about his childhood as an only child of an unhappy marriage. When he was twelve his mother had left his father for another, more successful man. He'd told Abigail the whole story one night at his apartment, the two of them staying up until dawn, falling asleep just as the light began to enter the apartment. So why did he occasionally feel like a stranger? Why did he feel like a stranger right now, the two of them sipping Manhattans a little more than twenty-four hours after they'd gotten married? She knew the feeling wouldn't last. It never did. Maybe it was just something she'd feel on and off for a few years. The only people in her life who didn't feel like strangers were her parents, of course, and Zoe, who had always told Abigail everything she felt and experienced. Everyone else—her college friends, Ben Perez—all felt slightly mysterious to her, like she never knew precisely what was going on in their minds.

"Another?" Bruce asked, and it took Abigail a moment to realize he was asking her about her drink, empty now.

"Another drink, yes. Another Manhattan, no, if you want me to make it to the dinner table. Glass of wine?"

Carl was putting two martinis onto a tray for a server,

who then carried them toward the fireplace. Abigail wondered if it was really necessary for there to be a server when there was a bartender already in the hall. But maybe the Quoddy Resort was sometimes busier than it was now. She could only count about ten people, not including them, in the lodge.

After they got their drinks, a glass of Malbec for Abigail and an IPA for Bruce, they wandered the lodge, looking at some of the wall hangings and artwork. One whole wall was composed of framed engravings, mostly images from fairy tales. A girl pushed an old woman into an oven. There was a knight fighting a hairy, naked beast in a forest. Several included wolves; the largest engraving showed what looked like a Roman god turning a man into a wolf, his head transformed, his body still a man's, wrapped in a toga. The most recognizable showed Little Red Riding Hood meeting the wolf in the forest.

"'The woods are lovely, dark and deep,'" Abigail said aloud.

Bruce looked confused.

"Sorry, I'm quoting Robert Frost."

They moved to a wall that showcased photographs from the original camp, all black-and-white, groups of grim-faced boys posing in front of their bunks. "I think it was only an active camp from the 1930s to the 1960s. It was pretty run-down when Chip bought it."

"All boys?" she asked.

"This camp, yes. The one on the other side was the

girls' camp. They'd do social events, I'm sure, together. Dances."

"Panty raids."

"Probably."

At the fireplace she and Bruce introduced themselves to a few of the other guests. It was mostly men but there was one other young couple, Alec and Jill, each holding a glass of champagne, a raspberry at the bottom of their tulip glasses. Bruce and Alec quickly started their own conversation, as Jill said to Abigail, "We got married last weekend, then stayed a few nights in Bar Harbor, and now we've been here for three days. It's unbelievable, this place. Wait till you try the food."

"It better be amazing or I'm going to be annoyed. Everyone keeps telling me about it."

"Oh no. I hope I haven't overhyped it." Jill, who was model-gorgeous with natural blond hair but with a sliver of a nose that must have been surgically altered, looked genuinely worried.

Abigail said, "I'm just kidding. I'm easily impressed by food, trust me. If it was pizza night I'd be thrilled."

Jill looked relieved, and Abigail asked her where she was from, not surprised to hear that she was from North Dakota. It wasn't just the wide eyes and the politeness, but some of the flat accent was still audible. It turned out she'd lived for five years in Los Angeles, trying to break into acting—"It's so much harder than you'd think"— and then she'd met Alec, a film producer who'd made several action films that had all done well overseas. She mentioned one film in particular, a mountain-climbing thriller that had just debuted on Netflix, but Abigail hadn't heard of it.

"How are you doing with the no-screens policy?" Abigail asked.

"Oh my God. I was dying for a little while, but I'm better now. I can't tell you how many times a day I think about checking my phone."

"I think I'm actually looking forward to it. Not having a phone."

"Don't get me wrong. It's great. Honestly, I feel like I've lived more in the last few days than in the last couple of years. I've been swimming every day. I painted a picture this morning. Alec and I are . . . so connected. It's been amazing." She spoke rapidly and her voice was pitched unnaturally high, and Abigail wondered if this was how she always spoke, or if she was having less fun on her honeymoon than she claimed.

"How long are you here for?"

"Five more days. I'm thinking of trying sailing even though I'm kind of terrified of deep water. It just seems that if I'm ever going to get over my fear, right now is the time, do you know what I mean?"

"I do," Abigail said. "You've been busy. What's Alec been doing?"

"He's been here before, a few times, so he's just really into relaxing. He likes to hike in the woods, and then he's been reading. They're all books he's thinking about optioning for film, of course, but he claims that it's not really work."

Jill looked over Abigail's shoulder, and Abigail turned her head. Three men had just entered the lodge and were walking slowly toward the bar.

"A lot more men here than women?"

"I know," Jill said. "Most of them are tech people from California. They get sent here for team-building. At first I felt like I was honeymooning at some sort of men's club, but I guess it's all right. Honestly"—she leaned in and whispered—"I was kind of hoping that our honeymoon would involve a sunny beach, but I guess we can do that sort of trip any old time."

"It's nice here," Abigail said. "But it's not tropical."

"No, it's not," Jill said, and finished her champagne, the raspberry rolling down the inside of the glass and bumping against her teeth. She fished it out with a finger and ate it, just as one of the resort's employees—a woman this time, but in the same khaki pants and white shirt—came out and stood next to Bruce. He stopped talking to Alec and turned to her, and she said that their table was waiting.

The dining room was immediately adjacent to the hall, about half the size but still enormous, and with floor-to-ceiling windows. There was still just a little bit of light in the sky, enough so that the pond was visible. She and Bruce were brought to a table for two near one of the windows. The woman who seated them lit their table candle, then presented them each with a single piece of paper with the menu choices. It was a four-course meal, two or three choices per course.

"Good lord," Abigail said. After studying the menu, she looked around the room. Most of the tables were set for two, but there was a long communal table that ran down the center of the room, and several of the men she'd seen at cocktail hour were now being seated there. The atmosphere was incredibly hushed, and she privately decided that it would be better if music was playing in the background, even though she was sure that was against the aesthetics of the resort.

A waiter arrived, same outfit, but he had a large dark beard, and long hair knotted into a top bun. Abigail ordered the lobster tortellini to start, the pomegranate sorbet, then the seared Maine salmon for the main course, and a blood orange crème brûlée for dessert. After Bruce placed his order the waiter asked if they wanted the sommelier to come out to talk about bottles, or if they'd prefer wine pairings by the glass with each course. Bruce looked at Abigail, who shrugged and said that the wine pairings would be fine. After the waiter left, Abigail said, "What's the actual employee-to-guest ratio at this place, do you think?"

"I don't know exactly."

"But it's got to be something like five-to-one, at least, right?"

"From what I've heard, more guests are arriving late tonight. There are times when there's no one here, and then there are times when there are all-company retreats, or an entire wedding."

"So, when no one is here what does the staff do?"

"They're all on yearly salary, and it doesn't change depending on the number of guests. Some months are busy, some months they can take off and go traveling. That's the way Chip described it to me. For all of them it's a two-year commitment."

"It makes me feel bad that the sommelier could just be sitting back there desperately hoping that someone will ask for him and he can actually do something."

"He's pretty busy, I think. He does all the wine pairings."

"I know. I'm just saying."

They were both quiet for a moment. Now that the candle on their table was lit, the window reflected the two of them. After a brief hesitation, Abigail said, "Don't tell me if it makes you uncomfortable, but how much does it cost to come here?"

Bruce's brow creased slightly, and Abigail quickly said, "No, don't tell me. I shouldn't have asked."

"No, no," he said. "It's fine. I just hesitated because there's not an easy answer. I was an original investor in this place, so I'm essentially a part-owner, and I pay yearly dues."

"So you can come anytime?"

"Pretty much, yes."

"So it turns out that you picked our honeymoon place because it was actually cheap."

"Exactly," he said, smiling.

Their first course arrived, Abigail's tortellini and the beef tartare for Bruce. "Just out of curiosity, what does it cost for someone who's not a part-owner?"

"I'm not going to tell you," Bruce said. "It might ruin your dinner."

"You can tell me after dinner."

"Sure," Bruce said, smiling, and she was pretty sure he wasn't going to.

Abigail cut a small piece from her single tortellini, sprinkled with slivers of black truffle, and took a bite. She immediately concluded it was the single best thing she'd ever put in her mouth.

After dinner, a little bit uncomfortably full, but mainly sleepy, Bruce and Abigail got up from their table and walked back into the hall. There were a few men around the bar.

"Nightcap?" Bruce asked.

"Oh God, no," Abigail said. "But you should get one."

"Maybe I'll order a whiskey at the bar and have it sent to our room. You sure you don't want anything? A Baileys?"

"Thank you, no, I'm fine."

She stood in the center of the hall, immediately under the chandelier, which seemed dimmer somehow. Maybe the candles had burned down or maybe they weren't candles after all, just an elaborate illusion. She stared at it, but she didn't have her distance glasses with her and the chandelier was blurry. The periodic sense of unreality that she'd been feeling since meeting Bruce flooded her again, but this time it was accompanied by an empty feeling. It was the combination of extreme luxury and the feeling she couldn't quite shake that Bruce was still somehow a stranger. There was something else as well. It was the emptiness of this resort; it reminded her of a theatrical set after the season was over. It echoed.

She looked toward the bar, where Bruce was waiting to talk with the bartender. Her vision blurred drastically, a sign she was very tired and a little drunk. She heard footsteps, loud against the stone floor, then soft, then loud again, someone walking across one of the scattered rugs. Then she realized the footsteps were coming toward her, and she turned, expecting to see Jill or Alec, or else another employee pushing an after-dinner drink on her.

But it wasn't Jill or Alec, or an employee of the resort. It was Scottie from California, a tentative half smile on his face.

Abigail's legs went weak, and for a second she thought, *I'm going to faint, right here in the middle of this hall.*

Scottie stopped, and then he must have seen the color leaving her face because he immediately moved toward her again, closing in as though to catch her from falling.

Abigail raised a hand, though, and he stopped short of

actually touching her. She regained some of her composure, and said, "What the fuck are you doing here?"

"Shh," he said.

"Don't shh me. What are you doing here? I'm on my honeymoon."

"Look," he said. "I got your email, and I'm sorry if you were telling the truth, but I just didn't believe you. I just need . . . I want an hour of your time."

Abigail turned toward the bar, where Bruce was now talking with the bartender. "Seriously, you need to leave."

"Walk down to the pond tomorrow morning, early, and I'll be there. Please."

Abigail turned from him and walked, on unsteady legs, toward the bar, and came up behind Bruce, placing a hand on the small of his back. "Oh, hi," he said.

"Can you make that two whiskeys, Bruce?" she said, her voice shaky-sounding, at least to her. "I changed my mind."

12

When she could see the faint light of dawn begin to penetrate the drawn curtains of the bunk, Abigail got out of bed, pulled a sweater on over her pajamas, and quietly opened the doors that led to the veranda. She stepped outside into the cold misty morning, and looked down toward Heart Pond, wondering if Scottie, or whoever he really was, was already there.

She'd already decided that she wouldn't meet with him. She was tempted, figuring that maybe if she was forceful enough she could talk him into leaving her alone, leaving the island, never contacting her again. But, down deep, she knew that going to meet him alone would only lead him on. It might even be dangerous. He'd stalked her across the country. He'd probably come to her wedding. And he'd actually followed her on her honeymoon. What else was he capable of?

She hadn't slept at all. Walking with Bruce from the lodge to their bunk, each with their faux-lantern, she could feel herself start to shake, a delayed reaction to the appearance of Scottie in the hall of the lodge.

"Cold out here," she'd managed to say, the lanterns carving out small pockets of light in the blackness of the night. Above them the sky was filled with more stars than she'd ever seen.

"It's not that cold," Bruce said. She kept waiting for him to ask about the man who'd come over and talked with her in the middle of the hall, but maybe he hadn't seen the interaction. They'd only talked for about thirty seconds.

After entering the bunk, Bruce looked at her and said, "You really are cold. You're shaking." He hugged her close to him, and the feel of that hug, the warmth of his body, was almost more than she could bear. When he tried to release her, she gripped harder, pressing her face against his chest.

"I love you so much," she said. "And this place is amazing. Thank you for bringing me here."

He kissed the top of her head, right at the part in her hair, and she shivered. "I have to pee," she said, and went to the bathroom. When the door was closed behind her, she stood in front of the sink, her hands on the marble countertop, and took deep breaths. Her stomach buckled, and she bent over the sink, sure that she was going to be sick, but nothing came up.

He's followed me here.

On my honeymoon.

She wondered for a moment how he'd even known where they were going, but then she remembered the wedding announcement in the *Times*, how it stated that the bride and groom were honeymooning on Heart Pond

Island off the coast of Maine after the wedding. Was that announcement how he'd gotten her name as well? How much more did he know about her? And what did he expect from coming here?

She remembered the smell of cigarette smoke at her wedding. Had he been tracking her ever since that weekend in California? She squeezed her fists together, then unclenched them, pressure building in her chest.

When Abigail had first started high school, she went through a period of extreme anxiety, overwhelmed by the multiple classes, the homework, the test-taking. She'd also been overwhelmed by the rumors that were suddenly flying around in the wake of Boxgrove Theatre's production of *Spring Awakening*. Her parents were under attack, and kids were whispering that they were the town perverts, all courtesy of Kaitlyn Austin, Abigail's nemesis. She'd briefly gone to see a therapist, but all the therapist wanted to talk about was Abigail's earliest memories. Instead, it was her father who sat her down and gave her several very helpful hints on dealing with stress. He had her make lists, then tackle projects one at a time, or, if the projects were too big, break them up into smaller parts. It worked, but she'd still lain awake at night worrying. So he taught her a system of dealing with worry, a way to break it into mental questions and lists. She started to do that now, in the bathroom, concocting a strategy for how to face this immediate problem. She began to relax, but then heard a commotion in the bunk, the sound of voices, and her stomach went cold again.

What if Scottie had come directly to the door to confront Bruce?

Abigail steeled herself and opened the bathroom door. Paul, whom she was internally referring to as a butler, was lowering a tray onto the coffee table in front of the fire. He quickly departed, Bruce thanking him, and Abigail told herself that she'd need to think about the Scottie situation later, after Bruce had fallen asleep.

On the tray was a cut-glass carafe half filled with whiskey, a bucket of ice, and a small plate with four cookies on it that looked almost like Oreos, but they were warm to the touch.

"Homemade Oreos," Bruce said. "The chef made them for you."

"Good lord," Abigail said, but the thought of putting one of them in her mouth made her stomach buckle again, and she really did think it would be a miracle if she got through the rest of the night without being sick.

Bruce was stretching out on the couch, a whiskey already poured. "Have one," he said, and she didn't know if he meant a drink or a cookie.

"Actually, I can't," Abigail said. "I think I overate at dinner and my stomach is a little off. I might just get into bed."

"That's fine," Bruce said. "Mind if I sit here with my drink for a moment?"

"No, please do. Tomorrow night I'm not going to eat all four courses. I just . . . I don't feel great."

She undressed and got into her pajamas, then brushed her teeth at the sink, wondering if her face looked guilty just to her or if Bruce had been able to read the panic in her eyes. She rinsed her mouth, washed her face, and studied herself again. She had always been pale, but right now Abigail thought she had a chalky, unhealthy pallor. She actually pinched her cheeks to bring color to them, like a heroine in a Regency-era novel trying to look prettier.

She went directly from the bathroom to the bed. It had been turned down, but before getting in Abigail loosened the sheets at the foot, knowing it would have been made too tight. She looked up at the poster of *Midnight Lace*—the image of Doris Day's face under a twisting Saul Bass-like graphic—and tried to remember the happiness she'd felt just a few hours earlier when she'd first seen it. But that happiness was gone. She slid under the covers, her pajamas crackling against the flannel sheets, and felt tears well up in her eyes. The gift of the poster really was one of the nicest gifts she'd ever received. Bruce had reminded her, not for the first time, of her father, and how thoughtful he was, how eager to please. The thought of hurting him was almost too much to bear.

She was relieved that Bruce was still by the fire with his drink. It was hard for her to imagine having sex right now. She turned onto her stomach, the position that she usually fell asleep in, and pressed her face into the too-firm pillow, prepared to pretend she was sleeping.

As far as she could see, there were two possible scenarios. In the first, Scottie really did believe that the two of them had fallen in love in California, and he wanted a moment to try to convince Abigail of this. Why he had decided to try this on their honeymoon was another question, but in this scenario, she imagined that Scottie was more or less sane, just acting out of true infatuation. If this was the case, then Abigail thought there was a chance, a slim one, that she could convince him to leave her alone. The other scenario—the more likely one—was that Scottie was unwell, maybe even delusional, and that simply talking to him wasn't going to work. If that was the case, then Abigail knew that the smartest and safest move would be to tell Bruce about Scottie right away, to alert the authorities (where were the nearest authorities, anyway?), and throw herself on Bruce's mercy. There were two ways to do this, Abigail thought. She could tell Bruce the entire truth, that she had slept with this man in California. Tell him she'd been drunk, and that she regretted it the next morning, and beg for his forgiveness. But Abigail knew that if she told Bruce the whole truth, the marriage would be over. He felt so strongly about his mother's infidelity that there'd be no chance he'd forgive her. The other option, of course, was to tell him half the truth. Say that she'd met this guy on the night of her bachelorette party. She'd been drunk, and maybe she'd flirted a little with him. He'd tried to kiss her, and she'd rebuffed him, but maybe not strongly enough. And now he was here, stalking her. Of course, he could tell his side of the story to Bruce, but it would be his word against hers, wouldn't it? He couldn't prove they'd slept together.

Abigail thought this option—she was calling it the half-truth solution—was the best. The problem was that she'd have to do so much lying. In a strange way, she believed that she hadn't lied yet to Bruce. She'd cheated on him, of course, but it wasn't like he had asked her directly if she'd ever been unfaithful to him since they'd met. Well, that wasn't entirely true. He'd asked her during the lunch they'd had at that midtown Mexican restaurant after she'd gotten back from California. She'd assured him, hadn't she? Or had she just made some sort of joke? Either way, if she went with the "half-truth solution" there would be a lot of lying involved. Not only was Abigail a terrible liar, she knew that it would be a fatal way to start a marriage. And would Bruce ever really believe that this man, after simply talking with Abigail at a vineyard, would stalk her all the way across the country?

She listened as Bruce went into the bathroom, brushed his teeth, then emerged. He was moving quietly, and Abigail was hopeful that it meant he wouldn't try to wake her once he was in bed, but after he got in beside her, he gently placed a hand on the small of her back, making circular rubbing motions with his thumb. Abigail shifted, mumbled into her pillow, then said,

"Good night, honey," in what she hoped sounded like a sleep-slurred voice.

"Good night," he said, but moved his hand lower down so that it rested at the rise of her buttocks.

"Sleepy," she said into the pillow, and he took his hand away.

She lay as still as she could, breathing the way she imagined she did when she slept, and after twenty minutes Bruce flipped onto his side and began to snore.

On the veranda in the morning, not having slept at all, she realized she still hadn't decided exactly what her plan was. In case of the "psychotic stalker" scenario she had decided to not go down to the pond and confront Scottie. She did know she would have to speak with him eventually, and she was counting on there being a time when that could happen without Bruce knowing about it. She would make it as clear as she possibly could that she had zero interest in him, and if he didn't believe her, or if it was clear that he wasn't going to go away, then she would go to Bruce and confess. She still hadn't decided whether she'd confess the whole truth, or the half truth, but she'd figure that out later. Either way, the thought of that sickened her, not just for what it would do to their marriage, but for how much it was going to crush him. "When in doubt, tell the truth" was something her mother used to say to her, and she knew that if the time came, she would have to do that. She'd made her decision and now it was out of her hands.

There was a strange wavering cry that came from the pond, followed by another, similar cry. She thought it was probably loons, even though she'd never heard one before. But somewhere in her past—or in a book she'd read—she'd heard that their cries were ghostlike. She watched the sliver of the pond that she could see. Its surface was glassy in the early morning light, and a hazy mist was rapidly dissipating.

The doors behind her opened and Bruce stepped out onto the veranda. "You're up early," he said.

"Temporarily up," she said. "No guarantee I'm not going back to bed. Did you hear the loons?"

"No," he said.

"I think they were loons. Either that or the pond is haunted."

"What do you want to do for breakfast?" he asked.

"Can we have it brought here? Scrambled eggs on toast?"

"Sounds perfect. Oh, is that one?"

The loons had made their cries again.

"Yep," Abigail said, and for a brief moment she almost turned and told him everything, but she just couldn't bring herself to do it. She knew that once the words were out, the rest of their lives would instantly change. She didn't want to lose him, and she didn't want to hurt him.

"I'll order breakfast," Bruce said, and went back into the bunk, closing the doors behind him.

13

After they'd eaten, Abigail asked Bruce if he wanted to go swimming at the pool.

"I was thinking of taking a walk around the island," he said.

"Okay," she said. "Do you want to meet for lunch?"

"Sure," he said. "If we don't see each other back here, then lunch at one-ish in the lodge?"

She agreed, thinking it felt a little strange that they were splitting up, but she was actually glad for the opportunity to be alone. It would give her a chance to find Scottie, or a chance for him to find her, and to talk.

She'd packed both a one-piece and a bikini but put on the dark red one-piece. She didn't know exactly what the indoor pool would look like, but she was hoping for swimming lanes. It would feel good to burn some energy.

She put jeans and a sweater on over her bathing suit, then kissed Bruce goodbye and walked up the path toward the lodge. She felt exposed, the blank eyes of the bunks all watching her. There was a man up ahead, exiting the lodge and making his way down toward the pond, and she thought for one stomach-tightening moment that it was Scottie, but he turned her way and she could see the white of his beard. It wasn't him.

She entered the lodge even though Bruce had explained to her that the pool and spa area was just past the lodge and into the woods a little way. But she had decided that it was worth a shot to see if she could get some information on her stalker. It bothered her that he knew who she was but she had no idea even what his real name was. Once inside the lodge—there was the distinctive smell of something fresh-baked coming from the dining area—she glanced around, looking for anything resembling a front desk. She was about to head in the direction of the dining room when one of the employees—it was the woman, actually, who had seated her and Bruce at their table the night before—fast-walked across the hall toward her.

"Hi, Mrs. Lamb, what can I help you with?" she said.

"I actually have a . . . What's your name?"

"It's Mellie."

"Thanks, Mellie. I was wondering if you could help me out. I saw someone last night that I know, but I can't remember his name."

"Do you know what bunk he's staying in?" Mellie said.

"I don't. Sorry. I can describe him to you."

"Sure."

Abigail thought for a moment, and then said, "He has a brown beard and blue eyes, and last night he was wearing either very dark blue jeans or black jeans, and a roll-neck sweater."

Mellie smiled, then said, "Scott Baumgart."

"Oh," Abigail said, and there must have been a look of surprise on her face.

"Is that not him?" Mellie said.

"No, that sounds right. Scott."

"He got in late last night."

"Thanks, Mellie."

"Not a problem, Mrs. Lamb."

"You can call me Abigail," she said. She hadn't officially taken Bruce's last name yet, although she knew he'd like her to do it. Still, it felt strange to be referred to as a Mrs., let alone a Mrs. Lamb.

"Not a problem, Abigail. Anything else?"

"I was planning on going for a swim."

"Lucky you. You know how to get there?"

"I think so. Back outside, and toward the woods."

"I can show you the secret passageway, if you'd like," Mellie said.

Abigail agreed and followed Mellie behind the bar and into a part of the lodge that felt as though it was for employees only. There were stacks of chairs and boxes of wine, and there was actual fluorescent lighting in tracks along the ceiling. They went down some cement stairs, Mellie walking fast in her khakis and white shirt, and Abigail briefly wondered if it was a good thing or a bad thing for Mellie to be stuck on this island with so many male employees. They were in a dimly lit hallway that suddenly veered to the right, and then they were in an even dimmer tunnel, carved from rock, with a much lower ceiling that curved like an archway.

"Wow," Abigail said.

Mellie turned back, smiling. "This is a secret, so don't tell anyone I brought you down here."

At the end of the tunnel, at least fifty yards, Abigail began to smell chlorine, and the air changed, becoming warmer, more humid. There were double glass doors, and the two women pushed through into another hallway, this one carved from stone as well, but more luxurious, with soft lighting and a higher ceiling.

Mellie pointed to the left and said, "There's a changing room just down a little ways. Everything's in there."

"Thank you, Mellie," Abigail said, and made her way down the hall, then pushed through another glass door marked with a stenciled w. Inside, it felt less like a changing room and more like a spa. The walls were stone and all the furnishings were made from blond wood. She found a closet where she could hang her clothes and took off everything but her bathing suit. She was, not surprisingly, the only one in the changing area, and for a moment she longed to be at a different type of resort, one that was full of women and children. It was too quiet in here, almost creepy, and she kept thinking about her stalker. There was no way that Scott Baumgart was his real name, and she wondered how he'd managed it. Had he paid in cash? Or had he used his real name to register, but then asked the staff to call him something else? She supposed it was possible that he really was a Scott, but what were the chances? *She'd* come up with the fake name of Scottie on the night they'd slept together. Hadn't she? He'd called her Madeleine and she'd countered with Scottie. Because of *Vertigo*. That was the way she remembered it. If his name really was Scott, he'd have mentioned it, right?

She heard a distant sound, like a door closing. Leaving her clothes behind, she went in search of towels, finding a neat stack of them near the exit, along with swimming caps and goggles wrapped in plastic. She grabbed one of each and walked out toward the pool, hoping she wouldn't be alone out there. The quiet of this place was getting to her.

There turned out to be two pools, one a standard lap pool with eight lanes. She was happy to see that one of the lanes was occupied. It was a man, but she knew right away it wasn't Scottie. The man hurtling through his strokes was dark-skinned, and Abigail thought she'd seen him the night before, noticing him because he was one of the few people of color, either guest or employee, here at Quoddy Resort. The only peculiarity of the lap pool was that the far lane extended into a curving tributary that went under an archway built into the stone wall. Abigail skirted the wall to see where it went and there was the second pool, built just for lounging and designed like an underground grotto, vegetation everywhere, rocks plunging up out of the water, even a small waterfall. It was magical, actually, and Abigail felt a stab of anger at Scottie for keeping her from enjoying this moment.

While she was standing there trying to figure out if she should actually do some laps or just lounge around in the grotto, the door across from the women's changing room swung open and a staff member entered. He walked over to Abigail and asked her if she wanted anything. "A smoothie? Or a tropical drink?" Abigail, tempted to order a Bloody Mary, declined, and the employee, who'd introduced himself as Brad, showed her a button she could push if she changed her mind.

After he left, Abigail stepped into the water of the lap pool, donned her cap and the goggles, and began her slow, awkward crawl that kept pulling her to the left. As she swam, she tried to empty her mind of what was happening, but it wasn't working. Even though she'd decided earlier that morning that if she couldn't talk Scottie into leaving her alone she would tell Bruce some version of the truth, she was beginning to wonder if maybe she should lie, after all. Scottie was messing with her life, and maybe she needed to protect herself. She imagined a conversation with Bruce, maybe over lunch.

I didn't bring this up last night because I didn't want to freak you out, she'd say. *But there's a guy here that I met out in California. He was a pest, kept asking me if I was sure I was ready to get married, and maybe I talked with him too long, but he's here now. He must have become obsessed or something. I didn't tell you last night because*

I didn't want to wreck anything, but I think you need to know.

She imagined herself crying. And then she imagined Bruce springing into action, having Scottie removed from the premises. No doubt Scottie would try to tell a different story, but Bruce would believe *her*, wouldn't he? And maybe, in this case, lying would be the best thing to do for everyone involved. Maybe it would be the kindest thing to do for Bruce?

Her arm came down on the rope that separated the lanes—she was drifting left again—and she bobbed to the surface to take some deep breaths. The water was a perfect temperature, reminding her of the feel of Woodhouse Pond, her favorite swimming spot near Boxgrove. The man who'd also been doing laps had disappeared, and Abigail wondered if he'd swum through the connecting tunnel into the grotto. She decided to follow his lead, but after getting in a little more exercise. She even thought that when she got to the grotto she'd press that secret button and get herself a Bloody Mary, maybe even a pitcher. She picked up her pace, exhausting herself, and she felt good for the first time that morning. Even though she had slept with the stranger from California, that didn't give him any kind of right to fly across the country to try to fuck up her marriage. The anger felt good, as though it were filling her, and she almost considered going straight to Bruce and telling him what was going on—the half-truth version—right away. She wanted it over and done with so she could really start her life. Instead, she crossed the lanes of the lap pool, then breaststroked her way through the tunnel and past the greenery and into the grotto. The water was lit from below and the ceiling was bowed, shaped like a planetarium, shimmering with light from the pool.

The man was settled to one side of the gently flowing waterfall, his head back along the pool's stone rim, his long, muscular arms stretched out to either side. He seemed to be breathing hard, but nodded in her direction as she swam into the middle of the pool.

"I'm ordering a drink," Abigail said to him. "What can I get you?"

He smiled and said, "What are you having?" His accent wasn't American. She thought it was probably English even though there was a little bit of a lilt to it, as if he might be from the Caribbean.

"I can't decide between some sort of healthy smoothie and a Bloody Mary, so I thought I might order both."

"I can't let you drink alone. I'll have a Greyhound."

"What's that?" Abigail asked.

"Vodka and grapefruit juice. Get two of them. That way you'll have three drinks."

She got out of the pool and walked, dripping, to the button. About five seconds after she pushed it, Brad entered the pool area; he must have been waiting just outside the door. "Can we get some drinks?" she asked, then gave her order.

The man's name was Porter, and it turned out he was from Bermuda. After the drinks had arrived, she told him how she was on her honeymoon with Bruce, and he told her how he'd come here with a small group of insurance executives. The rest were sailing on the pond this morning.

"Not your thing?" Abigail asked.

"Actually, I grew up sailing, and didn't want to see it done poorly by my colleagues. Besides, I'd been to this pool earlier and there was no way I wasn't coming back before I left."

"Has it been this quiet the whole time you've been here?"

He took a long sip of his Greyhound, some of the salt from the rim clinging to his upper lip.

"When did you get here?" he said. "Last night? There was a big group that left yesterday morning, but, yes, it's quiet. Definitely quiet."

Abigail had finished her Bloody Mary, tasted her own Greyhound, and was now halfway through her smoothie. She was a little tipsy and had to pee. But it felt good to be in the pool, making small talk with this stranger, and not obsessing over what she was going to do about the Scottie situation. She was all set to tell Porter that she had to go to the changing room for a moment but that she'd be right back, when the door quietly opened. She felt cool air move through the grotto room and expected to see the waiter coming to see if they needed more drinks. But it was Scottie, dressed in jeans and a hooded jacket. She could tell it was him by the way he purposefully strode along the edge of the pool to where she and Porter were lounging.

"Hi, Abigail," he said.

"Hey," Porter said, filling in the unnatural pause. Abigail hadn't spoken yet. "You must be Bruce. Nice to meet you."

"I'm not Bruce," Scottie said.

"What's your name again?" Abigail quickly asked Scottie, and he glanced at her with almost a hurt look.

"Scott Baumgart," he said, crouching and shaking Porter's hand.

"Scott and I met on my bachelorette weekend, and then totally by chance he showed up here," Abigail said. "Small world."

"No shit," Porter said, then stretched his hands out, looking at his fingertips. He said, "I'm pruning up. It's time for me to take off."

Abigail didn't know if he was actually wanting to get out of the pool or if he was sensing the weird tension between her and Scottie.

"Nice meeting you, Porter," she said, then turned to Scottie and added, "I'd love to talk with you for a few minutes. Can we meet outside the changing room?" There was no way she wanted to be alone with him in the pool area, she in her bathing suit, he looming over her with all his clothes on.

"Sure," Scottie said, and Abigail followed Porter up the stone steps out of the pool. She walked past Scottie without looking at him and went straight into the changing room.

She took her time showering, then slowly got dressed. There was a pitcher of ice water available—had that been there before?—and she drank two tall glasses. There were actually three exits from the changing room, one that went back out to the pool, the one she'd come in from that led to the tunnel back to the lodge, and another exit, which Abigail assumed led toward the ground-floor entrance. She decided that Scottie would most likely be waiting for her there. Before pushing through the doors, Abigail went through a mental checklist. She tried to remind herself that when she'd met Scottie he'd seemed like a nice person. He was attentive, he told her about his unhappy marriage, how much he loved his dog, how much his own parents loved his wife. He wasn't necessarily a monster. He was a human being. She needed to try to appeal to this side of him first. Tell him that she was sorry he'd come all this way, but she really was in love with Bruce, and she wanted to make the marriage work. Ask him nicely to just leave.

And if that didn't work? Well, then, she was fully prepared to unload on him, tell him he better get the fuck off this island before she alerted the authorities. Tell him that as far as she was concerned nothing had happened between them in California, and that Bruce would believe her. She hoped it wouldn't come to that, but she needed to be prepared.

She pushed through the doors, which brought her to a staircase that led up to a reception area, although, as with all the reception areas here, there was no front desk, just the constant presence of a lingering employee. Like the changing room, the reception area was made of light wood, and one wall was covered with succulents while another had a built-in waterfall, a sheet of perpetually falling water.

Scottie was perched on a white chaise longue under a high window that showed the dark woods outside. Abigail didn't want to talk inside, so she walked straight to the door and out into the cool air.

14

At the back of the building, a path of stones led to a wooden bench that faced a grove of birch trees. Abigail sat down, and Scottie sat next to her.

"You made a new friend," he said.

Abigail was confused for a moment, then realized that he was talking about Porter, the man in the pool.

"I did," she said, already annoyed, and decided that she should probably just skip the treat-him-like-a-nice-guy plan.

"What kind of friend is he?" He unzipped his jacket a little, and she saw that he was wearing a flannel shirt, maybe even the same shirt he'd been wearing in California. Looking at him now, she wondered how she'd ever found him attractive. He was handsome, in that wiry way she liked, but his skin was too orange, as though he went to tanning booths. Also, he was far too intense, the way he sat with his head cocked her way, his hands—he wore three rings—thrumming on his kneecaps like he was waiting to pounce.

"What kind of friend is he?" She repeated his words. "We were having sex in the pool five minutes before you arrived."

He recoiled slightly, and she decided not to completely abandon her plan to win him over. "I'm kidding," she said. "I just met him this morning. But we need to talk about us, about you coming here. It's crazy, you know that, right?"

"I do," he said. "I know it's crazy, but I also know that what happened between us was special. It was the best night of my life, Abigail."

"Before we go any further, I need to know your real name. It's not fair that you know mine."

"It's Scott, or you can keep calling me Scottie if you'd like." He blinked twice, and Abigail wondered if he was lying.

"But that was just your made-up name for that night. I made it up for you," she said.

"I know, but you guessed my real name. I suppose it had something to do with me saying that I was going to call you Madeleine. I didn't realize it at the time, but I think I called you that name because of *Vertigo*, maybe I was subconsciously channeling Scottie from that film. And you picked up on it. That was when I first knew that we were meant to be together."

"I think it was a random accident," Abigail said.

"You don't really believe that, do you? There are no random accidents."

"I actually believe that everything is a random accident. I'm sorry. I really do." He started to interrupt her, but she kept going. "Look, will you do me a favor and hear me out? Let me talk for a while, uninterrupted."

"Okay."

"What happened between us in California was a huge mistake. I drank far too much, and it should never have happened. That doesn't mean that I don't find you attractive, and that, if I was available, I wouldn't be interested in pursuing things with you. But I'm not available. I am in love with my husband, and protecting what we have together is the most important thing in my life right now. I am asking you . . . no, I am begging you, Scottie, to please just drop this. We had a nice night, and that's all there is to it. We are *never* going to be together. Not under any circumstances, and definitely not if you do anything to jeopardize my marriage. Is that clear?"

He had begun gently shaking his head about halfway through her speech and he was still doing it.

"It's clear, but I don't believe you," he finally said.

"What part don't you believe?"

"I don't believe you're in love with your husband. If you really were, then you'd never have slept with me three weeks before your wedding."

"Like I said, I made a mistake, and I have to live with that mistake. It's very possible that I had some reservations three weeks ago, but after we were together those reservations went away. I'm sorry if it hurts to hear that, but it's the truth. I'm not a perfect person. I fucked up, and if Bruce finds out about it, if you think you need to tell him about it, I will fight to the end of my life to win his trust back." She saw what looked like self-doubt sneak into Scottie's eyes, and she kept going. "We're just strangers, you and I," she said. "I'm sorry if you thought otherwise."

"Do you remember when we were in my room at the vineyard?" he said.

Abigail didn't immediately say anything, thinking he was going to continue, but he didn't. "I do," she finally said, "but I was drunk, Scottie. I really was. That whole night is a blur to me."

"The whole night?" He smiled expectantly.

"I don't know what you want me to say," Abigail said.

"It was good sex. It was the best sex."

"Like I said, it—"

"And there was that one moment—I know you remember it—when we were making love, and our hands intertwined, and just for a moment I felt it pass between the two of us. My soul went into yours, and your soul went into mine. I know that you felt it, too."

Abigail shook her head. "I didn't. I'm sorry, but I didn't."

"Maybe you just don't remember it, but it happened, I promise you." He'd leaned in, and Abigail could see tiny beads of perspiration along his hairline, even though it wasn't warm out.

"Even if we had this moment, this intense experience, it doesn't change anything, you realize that," she said.

"It does. It changes everything."

Abigail's hair was still damp from her shower and she was beginning to get cold. She shivered a little, then said, "It doesn't. I've said all I have to say. This is over, Scottie."

"There's only one way I'll consider this over," he said, and shifted a little closer to her along the bench. "You need to prove it to me. I know that we had that moment, and I do believe you that maybe you don't remember it. I get it. But I'm not going to leave here unless you agree to make love with me one more time."

Abigail expelled a breath, then laughed a little, not caring if it pissed him off. "That will never happen."

"Why? You already cheated on your husband. What's one more time? And if you're right and we mean nothing to each other, then I'll know. And I'll leave you alone."

Spreading out her words, Abigail said, "I am on my honeymoon. I will never sleep with you again, and if you don't leave me alone, I will call the police."

"Then Bruce will find out everything."

"I'm asking you to please not do that," Abigail said.

"That's not for you to decide."

"I realize that. That's why I'm asking. Please don't tell him. Not for me, but for him."

"Why not? He should know the truth."

"You say you think we have a connection, then you should honor it. Please, for me. Don't tell him. It would hurt him too much."

"It would hurt *you* too much, you mean," he said.

Abigail realized that what Scott was trying to do was keep her here talking to him, and she was starting to get annoyed. "Look," she said. "Do what you want. If you care for me like you say you do, you'll leave me alone, let me live my life. And if you decide you want to hurt me, then go ahead and tell Bruce what you want to tell him. I'll tell him my story, and we'll see who he believes. Okay?"

"He'll believe me," he said.

"Fine. If that's what you think."

"I'll tell him about the birthmark."

Abigail paused for a moment, confused, then remembered the birthmark under her left breast, shaped like a crescent moon, lightly pink and threaded with red. When she was young it was very visible, up near her top rib, but then when she developed breasts it had become hidden, and she'd pretty much forgotten about it.

Abigail stood, annoyed that her legs were shaky. "Fine, tell him anything you want. It's up to you. I can't stop you."

"I'm two bunks down from you. It's called Pinehaven. I'm here for four more days. Come down some night after your husband has fallen asleep. If you give me one more chance, I'll let you go. I promise. He'll never know."

"Fuck you," Abigail said, "and while we're at it, fuck you for following me to New York and for showing up at my wedding."

She walked away from him down the path before he could say anything back to her. Her heart was racing, and her arms tingled. She checked her watch. It was not quite eleven. She'd have time to go back to the bunk, get changed for lunch. She hoped Bruce wasn't there, that he was still on his walk. She needed more time to think about what had just happened, and what to do next.

When she got back to the bunk it was empty. Out of habit, she grabbed her cell phone and checked to see if there was any service, but there wasn't. If she had service, she'd google "Scott Baumgart" to find out if that was really his name. Maybe he was a lunatic with a police record? Also, if she had service, she could call Zoe, tell her what had happened, and ask her for advice. That was what she really wanted to do, more than anything. She looked up Zoe's phone number on her contact list and wrote it down on the inside cover of the paperback novel she'd brought with her to read. Suddenly, more than anything, she wanted to speak with her best friend, to hear her voice.

She left the bunk and walked swiftly toward the lodge. The day had turned a little warmer, but the sky was still cloudy, a solid bank of gray, a hazy spot where the sun was located. In the hall of the lodge one of the employees was stacking wood by the fireplace, and Abigail asked him where the phone was.

"What phone?" he said.

"You must have a landline, for guests to use?"

"Of course. Is it an emergency?" The man, about her age and with a military buzz cut, looked genuinely concerned.

"No, not a huge emergency. There was something that I needed to tell my friend before I left for here and I totally forgot. I just need to at least leave her a message." Why was she having to explain this?

"Not a problem," he said, and she followed him up a stairwell to a balcony that ran the length of the hall, then through an open door that led to an office space, in which there were five desks, three of which had large desktop computers. There was a printer station, and the walls were covered with large detailed maps that looked to be of the island. Mellie, the woman who had brought Abigail to the pool this morning, sat at one of the computers, her back to them, and when the man gently touched her on the shoulder, she let out a short scream that made Abigail jump as well.

"Jesus." She turned to them, swiveling on the chair. "You scared the shit out of me, Glen. Don't sneak up on me like that." Then she looked at Abigail and said, "I'm sorry. I thought I was alone up here."

"Don't worry about it," Abigail said. "I get scared like that at least once a day."

The woman laughed, and Abigail said, "Mellie, right?" Then she glanced at the computer screen behind her, wondering if what she was looking at had anything to do with her reaction. But the screen was blank, just a box in the middle where a password would go.

"Abigail, what can I help you with?" she asked, recovering.

"I was hoping to use a phone for a quick call."

"Oh sure," she said, glancing at Glen. "I can show you where it is."

"Thanks, Mellie," Glen said, and retreated out of the room, while Abigail was led to one of the desks that didn't have a computer, but which had a phone on it.

"Dial nine to get an outside line," she said, then left Abigail alone.

Abigail opened her paperback—it was her well-worn copy of *We Have Always Lived in the Castle*—and punched in the number. She heard several ominous clicks and then there was a distant ringing.

"Hello?"

"Zoe, hi, it's Ab."

"Everything okay?"

"Yes," Abigail reflexively said, then added, "Well, no, actually. I can't talk long, but I need you to do me a favor, okay?"

"What's wrong?"

Abigail, aware of the presence of Mellie, leaned forward over the phone and lowered her voice. "Remember that guy in California? At the bachelorette party?"

"Uh-huh."

"He's here."

"What?"

"He followed me here. He thinks we're in love."

"He's there on the island? Staying there?"

"*Yes*. And I'm pretty sure he was at the wedding, too, skulking around."

"What?"

"I know. It's nuts."

"Jesus," Zoe said. "Does Bruce know?"

"No. Not yet. I might just tell him . . . I don't know."

"What would he do if you told him?"

"He'd leave me. It would all be over. Our marriage would be over."

"Then don't tell him," Zoe said.

"The guy . . . this guy, whatever his name is, says he's going to tell Bruce about us. I don't know what to do. I'm freaking out."

"Ab, I'm so sorry. I don't know what to tell you."

"Can you do me a favor? Can you look him up? He says his name is Scott Baumgart—probably B-A-U-M-G-A-R-T—although I'm not totally sure he's telling the truth. See if you can find something out about him. He said he was a carpenter but that he did regional theater. That might help. And he said he lived in San Francisco."

"I'm walking right now. Dan's car's in the garage so he took mine and now I have to walk to work."

"You don't have to do it right now, but as soon as you can, okay? There's no internet here, no service at all, but I can call you back on this line."

"What's his name again?"

Abigail told her, and they agreed that Abigail would call back sometime later in the evening to get a full report. After hanging up, Abigail stayed at the desk for a moment, wondering how much Mellie had heard, but when she turned to go, she found that Mellie had disappeared from the room. She was alone, and she stood for a moment, wondering if there was a computer she could get onto. But just as she was considering her options, she heard someone bustling by in the hallway and abandoned the plan. She found her way back to the main hall, where a few more people had gathered and the bar was now open. There was a seat open by the fireplace and Abigail decided to take it, wait for Bruce to show up.

15

"Thought I'd lost you," Bruce said as he settled in across from her ten minutes later. He was wearing a fleece with his company logo on it, and hiking pants, and his cheeks were flushed as though he'd been outside all morning.

"I thought I'd lost *you*," Abigail said. "It's so strange not to have cell phones, otherwise I'd just have texted you."

"How was your morning?"

"I'll tell you all about it, but right now I'm famished."

Lunch turned out to be a buffet. Abigail actually wasn't that hungry, her stomach still in a tight knot from her encounter with Scott earlier that morning, but she managed to have some tomato bisque, which came with slivers of toasted sourdough topped with Gruyère cheese.

"So you had a good morning?" Bruce asked, for the second time, after they'd finished their meals.

"Yes, that pool is beautiful, but no more of this separation, okay? It's our honeymoon and we should do things together."

"Agreed. No more separation."

They walked back to their bunk together, the day darker and the sky beginning to spit rain. It felt like dusk and the inside of the bunk was dark. Bruce began to light a candle by the bed.

"No, don't," Abigail said.

Bruce shook the match out, and Abigail undressed and slid under the covers. She could hear the distant roll of thunder, and the window that looked out toward the pond lit up with a weak flash of lightning. Bruce began to undress as well. Unlike the night before, when the thought of having sex with Bruce made her almost queasy, she was now physically aching for him to touch her. Scott might wreck their lives together, but he couldn't wreck this particular afternoon, Abigail thought.

Bruce slid under the covers quickly. Despite how much he liked to look at her when she was naked, he was modest himself, often turning away when he undressed.

"This is nice," Abigail said, as she slid a thigh across him and their lips met. The light from the window was projecting streaks of rain onto their skin. "Let's stay here all day, okay?"

"Let's," Bruce said, and shifted underneath her. He wasn't hard yet, so she slid down his body and took him in her mouth, his hips rocking slightly, a hand cupping her breast. She pulled herself back up and was surprised when Bruce flipped her onto her back, buried his face in her neck, and entered her too fast. She grimaced, and he slowed down, but only for less than a minute. He positioned a pillow under her, returned his face into the crook of her neck, and thrust frenetically until he was finished.

Later, after the storm had passed, there was a light knock on the door. Bruce was sleeping, but Abigail, despite having slept for a solid hour, was now wide awake.

Even though she assumed the knock was Paul, coming by to find out if they wanted cocktails delivered to their bunk, Abigail instantly thought of Scott, barging in to tell Bruce everything and destroy her life. But she didn't think it would be him, at least not yet. He would still be holding out hope that Abigail would have sex with him one more time. Maybe if she could just keep him believing that it was a possibility she could get through this nightmare of a honeymoon.

Abigail got out of the bed, slid her robe on, and went to the door, cracking it open. Paul stood outside, in rain gear, just as she expected, and Abigail ordered two Manhattans to be delivered.

After dinner that night—Abigail skipped the appetizer and dessert but did eat a pretty tasty saffron risotto topped with a lobster tail that had been poached in butter—she and Bruce went back into the hall, where a jazz trio had been playing all night. There were more guests around—a small party of businessmen had arrived that afternoon—and despite looking for him, Abigail didn't spot Scott. As her eyes scanned the room, she felt as though the men—Jesus, why were all the guests men?—were glancing back in her direction, surreptitiously almost. It was warm in the lodge, but she felt the skin of her arms break out in gooseflesh. She suppressed a shiver. At the bar, Carl, his mustache heavily waxed, poured a beer for Bruce and a Baileys on the rocks for Abigail. The band was playing something familiar, and it took a moment for Abigail to realize that it was a jazz version of "Creep" by Radiohead. More chairs had been added around the fireplace, and they brought their drinks over, Abigail taking the seat with a better view of the hall. She'd been the one to suggest lingering after dinner—she was hoping to sneak away at some point, go upstairs to the office and see if she could call Zoe back. She realized it was unlikely that there was someone still in the office who would let her use the phone, but she wanted to give it a chance. If she knew Zoe, her friend would have done everything possible to figure out who her stalker was, and she was anxious to hear the report.

"Mind if we join you?" It was the couple they'd met the night before, Alec and Jill were their names, Abigail thought, and both she and Bruce nodded and said, "No," as the couple settled in across from them. Alec was wearing fancy-looking distressed jeans and a black T-shirt with leather stitched into the neckline. The T-shirt hugged him at the waist. As had happened the previous night, they instantly broke into conversations along gender lines, Alec and Bruce starting to compare notes on what they'd had for dinner—"That Wagyu beef, I mean, fuck me"— and Abigail asked Jill how her day had been.

"We were going to go sailing on the pond, but, you know, the weather." Jill, who was wearing a white cocktail dress that fell just above her knees, shivered and added, "Honestly, I didn't know it would be so cold here, did you?"

"Have you been to the pool yet?"

"God, yes, it's the best, but . . ."

"But what?"

Jill bit her lower lip, and Abigail noticed that beneath her very artful makeup she looked tired and pale. Jill leaned in while breathing out and Abigail could smell the alcohol on her breath.

"So, thing is," she whispered. "There's this guy, also here on the island, totally by random chance, who I was involved with a while ago, and twice now I've run into him at the pool."

Abigail, stunned by the strange coincidence, managed to ask, "Does Alec know that he's here?"

"God, no. Alec doesn't even know about this guy. At all. And if he found out about him, I think it would totally wreck our honeymoon. So, I'm just letting it wreck *my* honeymoon and trying to keep it to myself."

Abigail was about to tell Jill about her very similar situation, but instead she asked, "Are you sure it's random that he's here? You don't think he . . ."

Jill's jaw tensed, the tendons in her neck popping out, and Abigail had a sudden vision of what she would look like in about fifty years—rail-thin, still blond, and very tightly wound.

"I wondered about that, but, no. It's just an accident, I think. *I hope.* The thing is, he and I, we were engaged two years ago, and then it ended really badly. I didn't tell Alec about any of this because I didn't want him to freak out—he's the jealous type, and this guy—"

"Is he black?" Abigail asked, without really thinking.

Jill's eyes widened, and she swiveled her head. "Why? Is he watching us?"

"No, no," Abigail said. "I think I might have met him this morning, in the pool. Is he from Bermuda?"

"Yeah, that's him. He's in the pool every morning."

"He seemed nice, actually," Abigail said.

"He was nice. He *is* nice. I used to be in Bermuda all the time because I was in the chorus on a cruise ship that went back and forth from New York to Hamilton. Let me tell you, not as much fun as you'd think, and he rescued me from all that, at least I thought he had."

"So, what happened?"

"Ugh. We got engaged and then I got a job in Vancouver for three months and he couldn't get away from work, so we were apart from one another. And, you know, it turned bad."

"Why don't you just tell Alec that he's here? I mean, it's not your fault, and it's not like he thought you'd never had any boyfriends before he came along."

Jill breathed in through her nose, then took a long sip of her white wine, finishing the glass. "Walk with me to the bar," she said, standing up.

Abigail stood, still holding her untouched Baileys. The two men stopped talking and looked inquisitively at them. "We're going to the bar," Abigail said. "What can we get you?"

Alec and Bruce, each with a beer, declined, and Jill put her arm through Abigail's as they walked the twenty feet toward the bar. They stood about three feet back from the line of men waiting for drinks, and Jill said, "Sorry. I was getting paranoid that Alec could hear everything I was saying. I talk too loud when I drink. Am I talking too loud?"

"No, you're whispering. I can barely hear you."

"Good. Here's the thing. I told Alec that I was a virgin when we first met. I know, I know. It's ridiculous, but *he* was a virgin, at least that's what he said, and it was very clear that he wanted me to be as well. I didn't feel good about lying, but I did it, and then we started to get serious, and I couldn't get out of it. And here's the other thing—God, I can't believe I'm telling you all this, but it feels so good. He is *super*-insecure about sex. It did not go well at all on our wedding night, and it's very obvious that he, uh, feels inadequate not just in his performance, but I think he feels inadequate in his size."

"Is he small?" Abigail asked.

"I mean, he's not large, but what do I know? He's fine. But if he found out that (a) I lied about never being with a guy before, and (b) that guy is here right now, and he's the big, handsome black guy . . ."

"I get it. He'd fall apart."

"He'd totally fall apart."

"Ladies." It was the bartender, and Jill ordered another glass of wine. Abigail thought how incredibly strange it was that the two of them were in situations that were so similar. She'd been on the verge of saying something to Jill, telling her that at least her ex-boyfriend who'd shown up wasn't attempting to blackmail her into sex. But she stopped herself. For one, she didn't really want to upstage her new friend, who was clearly having a bad time, and for another, she didn't know if she wanted anyone else on this island to know about what was happening to her.

"I don't mean to be laying all this on you," said Jill, stepping away from the bar toward Abigail. "It's your honeymoon, too, and—"

"No, I'm glad you told me. Look, it's just a bad coincidence. Nothing's going to come of it, so just try to enjoy the rest of your stay."

"That's the other thing," Jill said, taking Abigail by the arm again and leading her a little farther away from the bar. "I'm *not* enjoying this trip. I hate this island. It's creepy. I feel like every move I make I'm being watched by about five staff people. They're everywhere. Honestly, if one more person sneaks out from behind a doorway and asks me what I want I think I'm going to scream."

Abigail laughed. "I know what you're saying."

"I'm right, right? I mean, the food is good and the drinks are good and our cabin is beautiful, but seriously, I'd give it all up right now for some cheesy resort down in Cancún, with actual other fun couples around, and bad food, and a piña colada in a plastic cup. I just need some freakin' sun. Look at my skin—I'm turning into a ghost." Jill held up an arm to actually let Abigail look at it, and Abigail couldn't help but laugh again. She felt a little bad about having judged Jill earlier for her nose job and her skinny body. "And honestly, there's just not enough people here, and there's like *no* other women. Thank God for you. And I love the pool, but it's actually scary in there when it's just me by myself, or me and my ex-boyfriend."

Abigail nodded. "Yeah, the pool is a little scary when you're all alone."

"Right?"

"Tell you what. Let's go together tomorrow morning before lunch. We'll hang out in the grotto pool and order piña coladas and request that they come in plastic cups."

"Oh my God, you are making me so happy right now. Can we really do that?"

"Of course. You and I, and I suppose we should ask the husbands to come along, too, if they want."

"Mine won't. Well, maybe he will if I make him do it, but he says he hates to swim. He's lost a lot of weight recently—actually, he's lost about a hundred and fifty pounds—and so he has some excess skin and I think he's self-conscious about it."

"Oh okay," Abigail said.

"God, I'm a blabbermouth tonight. I've told you all my secrets and now you know pretty much everything about my husband. Please tell me something scandalous about you so I don't feel like a total idiot."

Again, Abigail nearly decided to tell this stranger about her predicament, but something held her back. Instead, she said, "I think I hate this place, too. I actually called my best friend Zoe today just because I wanted to hear her voice."

"How'd you call her?" Jill asked, her eyes widening.

"I used the landline in the office." Abigail tilted her head toward the balcony. "Actually, I told her I'd call her back tonight because we got cut off and there was something we still needed to talk about. I was thinking of sneaking up there now."

"Go. I'll cover for you, tell them you went to the bathroom."

"Okay, maybe I will," Abigail said.

"Go! And we'll get together tomorrow, right?" Jill said.

"Yes, let's do it. Eleven-thirty in the grotto pool? Maybe we can even get lunch. Order something like nachos."

"Sounds like heaven," Jill said.

Abigail finished her Baileys and put the empty glass on the bar, then walked casually toward the stairwell that led to the offices on the second floor. She took the stairs two at a time and was happy to see lights on in the hallway above. When she got to the office door it was closed. She knocked and waited for an answer. When none came, she swung the door open. She felt guilty, like she was doing something illegal, but she'd been allowed up here earlier to make a call, and she figured it would be okay to make another one. If she got caught, or if Bruce found out, she could tell him that Zoe was in crisis, and that she felt like she had to call her back this evening.

She let the door swing closed behind her and stood for a moment, letting her eyes adjust to the dimness of the room. Then she navigated her way to the desk she'd sat at earlier, picked up the phone and dialed Zoe's number.

"Ab?" Zoe picked up right away.

"Hi, it's me."

"I'm so glad you called back."

"Everything okay?"

"Yeah, I've just been doing detective work all day and I want to show off about it."

"You found him?"

"I think I found him, but I can't be sure. His name's not Scott Baumgart. I'm pretty sure it's Eric Newman."

"How'd you find him?"

"Well, first I did a ton of searches for a Scott Baumgart and nothing really came up, nothing that made me think it was him, anyway. And so then I just started doing searches based on everything we know about him. Carpentry. The theater. San Francisco. And I found this one article from about five years ago that was in a local newspaper. It was about this theater north of San Francisco. The Lagunitas Community Theater."

"Yeah, he said he acted in community theater," Abigail said.

"The article was basically about how all the actors at the theater did double duty. Like the lead actress worked in the box office and one of the actors designed all the programs. And there was this one line that said that the actor Eric Newman was an accomplished carpenter and helped build the stage. So I looked up Eric Newman and there wasn't a ton, but he has a website for a freelance carpentry company, and he has a few credits from being in plays, but not for a while. Not for a few years."

"Did you find a picture of him?"

"Just one. It looks like a professional headshot, and it's really pixelated, but he looks like the guy from the bar that night. I mean, I didn't get a good close-up look at him like you did, but I kind of remember what he looked like."

"Brown beard, blue eyes."

"He has a beard in the picture, but it's black-and-white so I can't tell anything about his eyes. He's your type, though."

"Cheekbones and squinty eyes?"

"Yes, definitely," Zoe said.

"I think that's him."

"I do, too. I think we totally nailed him. So, here's the thing I haven't told you yet."

"Okay," Abigail said, and something about Zoe's tone of voice made her stomach flip a little.

"You said he was married, right?"

"Yeah, that's what he told me. That he was married, and that he was unhappy."

"So, I found an article from about two years ago. There was an Eric Newman who was on a honeymoon with his wife down in Baja California, and she drowned. The wife drowned."

"Do you think it's him?" Abigail asked, thinking there were probably many Eric Newmans.

"Here, I'll read it to you. 'Eric Newman, the groom, runs his own carpentry business in San Francisco. He met Madeleine Cartwright when she hired him to put molding up on the ceilings of her recently purchased Victorian.'"

"Jesus," Abigail said. All she'd heard was the name of the bride.

"It's him, don't you think? It has to be."

"Yeah, it has to be," Abigail said, then added, "Zoe?"

"Yeah."

"So, we gave each other fake names at the vineyard. Like, it was a game we were playing, each of us deciding what to call one another, and he decided to call me Madeleine."

"What? That's nuts. Ab, you need to report this guy for following you there. Seriously, right now. It doesn't matter if Bruce finds out. If he truly loves you, he'll forgive you. This guy's probably a total psychopath."

"I think maybe he's just obsessed with me. I don't know. Maybe I reminded him of his wife and he kind of cracked."

"He also could have killed his wife."

"What do you mean? What did the article say?"

"Well, it didn't say anything like that. But I don't know, maybe he drowned her and got away with it."

"Okay. You're freaking me out."

"You *should* be freaked out," Zoe said. "Seriously, you need to tell Bruce about this. You need to get off that island."

"Okay. I'll think about it. I'll deal with it. Zoe, sorry, but I told people I was going to the bathroom and we've been on the phone forever."

"Call me tomorrow when you get a chance. Promise."

"I promise. I'll be safe."

Abigail hung up the phone. She wanted to sit for a moment, digest all the information she'd just been given, but she knew she'd been away too long. She stood, began to wend her way back through the desks toward the door that led to the hallway, when it swung open and one of the staff members came in, flicking on a light. "Oh hello," he said to Abigail.

"Sorry," Abigail said. "I was just using the phone. Mellie showed me where it was earlier."

The staff member—she recognized him as one of the servers in the dining room—shrugged and said, "That's fine."

"Hey," she said. "I was just wondering. I've been talking with a friend who's not doing so well. If I needed to get off this island, how long does that take?"

"You flew here, right? It's about twenty minutes."

"No, I mean, how long does it take to arrange a flight,

get someone to come here from the mainland?"

"Not very long. Casco Air always has a plane available, unless the weather's bad."

"Thanks. Just checking. What's your name?"

"It's Aaron, Mrs. Lamb," he said, and something about the fact that he knew her name made her feel a little on edge. Did all the staff know everything that was happening with the guests? Well, of course they did. There weren't that many guests, and Bruce was a part-owner, after all.

Back downstairs Bruce and Alec were still in their chairs, still talking, and Jill was sitting near them, staring at the back of her hand. For a moment she had thought Jill was looking at a cell phone, but of course she wasn't. As Abigail walked toward the group, Bruce looked up at her and made a face that she immediately read as, *Save me from talking to this guy any longer.*

Abigail went over and touched Bruce's shoulder, told everyone she was exhausted and wanted to call it a night.

16

The next morning Abigail told Bruce about her plans to meet Jill at the pool before lunch.

"You've made a friend," he said.

"Not really. She's just . . . I think she's feeling a little outnumbered here on this island by all the men."

"Yeah, I get that," he said. "How about you?"

"Oh, definitely outnumbered. You're more than welcome to come, though. Remember that we weren't supposed to separate."

"Come where?"

"Swimming. With Jill and me. She's going to invite Alec, too."

"Alec's trying to get me to invest in a movie about a serial killer who's killing one woman in every state in the country. He goes, 'You know how some mountain climbers want to bag the biggest peak in every state? This killer wants to bag a woman in every state and get away with it.'"

"Sounds horrible," Abigail said.

"I agree. It will probably make a fortune."

They were eating breakfast outside on the veranda. It was still cool, but the skies had cleared and everything was bathed in a soft morning light. Abigail had actually slept the night before. She hadn't thought it was possible— her mind buzzing with all the new information she'd gotten—but after going over and over her conversation with Zoe on the phone and with Jill after dinner she'd actually slipped into a deep, dreamless sleep. When she woke up, there had been about two minutes during which she just lay there in the comfort of the bed, her mind blank, before it all came rushing back. She couldn't stop thinking about what Zoe had said about Scott Baumgart, real name Eric Newman, and how his wife had drowned on their honeymoon. It was obvious that what had happened with him was a driving force behind him being here stalking Abigail, but was he some kind of psychopath, or was he simply grieving? And what was the deal with Jill, and an ex-boyfriend of hers showing up during her honeymoon? What were the chances that something so similar would happen to both Jill and Abigail?

Bruce stirred beside her in the bed, and Abigail formed a plan. This morning she would go and see Jill at the pool. If they were alone, she'd tell her what was going on with her and Eric Newman. It would be good to get another opinion. Abigail decided that the best thing to do—no matter how dishonest it was—was to simply tell Bruce this afternoon that she needed to leave the island right away. She hadn't quite figured out what she was going to say to him yet. She considered just telling him that she was having panic attacks, being so cut off from civilization, but was worried that he'd try to get her to confront her fears instead of calling for the plane to get them. Maybe she'd complain of severe stomach pain, try to convince him she had appendicitis. Or she could go with the idea she'd already considered when making the phone call—telling him that Zoe was in crisis. If she could convince him that it was bad enough, then he'd be forced to get her off the island. She hated the idea of doing that—of all the lying—but she now realized that getting off of Heart Pond Island was what needed to happen. It would solve the problem of Eric Newman, at least temporarily.

"I'm going for a walk again. You want to come along?" Bruce said, after finishing his eggs Benedict.

"Sure," Abigail said. "Just so long as we get back here around ten-thirty."

After leaving the bunk, they walked down a well-trodden path to the edge of Heart Pond, then out along a wooden dock. Up close, the pond seemed larger, almost like a lake. Abigail lay down on her stomach on the warmed wooden slats of the dock and peered into the clear water. A fish darted by and Abigail ran her fingers along the surface of the pond, the water surprisingly warm. "We could swim in here," she said.

"Well, you could," Bruce replied. "I'll go sailing."

Abigail turned over and sat up. She'd forgotten her sunglasses and shaded her eyes as she looked around the edges of the pond. There was a boathouse, probably where the sailboats were kept, and next to the boathouse there was a stack of kayaks, plus a few canoes. It was all pretty rustic, and Abigail was surprised. Considering the renovations made on the main camp, she'd imagined that there'd be top-of-the-line boating equipment down at the pond. She kept moving her eyes along the shoreline and spotted another boathouse on the other side of the pond. Above it loomed a lodge, shrouded by dark woods.

"Is that the other camp?" she said.

"That was the girls' camp, yes. We're going to start renovating that in the spring."

"Then you can put all the women there and you won't have to have any at your camp," she said, raising her eyebrows at Bruce.

"That's the idea," he said.

"Can we go over there and look around?"

"We're not supposed to, I think, because it's unsafe."

"You're part-owner here. You should be able to check it out."

"Whatever you say," Bruce said. "But let's walk to the cliff first so I can show you the views."

They walked along the shoreline past the boathouse and picked up another path that took them up along a ridge through spruce trees and birches, then turned away from the pond and emerged from the woods onto an open bluff. They were high enough so that the Atlantic Ocean, sparkling in the morning sun, spread out all around them.

"Wow," Abigail said.

"Yeah, not bad."

They walked across the bluff along a barely visible path. On either side were low shrubs, several with red berries. A large bird hovered above them in the sky, and Bruce pointed it out, said it was an eagle that was nesting over near the pond. When they got to the edge of the bluff, they met up with a wider dirt path that skirted the cliff edge, dark gray outcroppings that sloped down to a rocky shoreline. "Can we get down there?" Abigail said.

"It's about a half-mile walk but there's a path."

They walked along the cliff edge, the breeze off the ocean suddenly gusting. They reached a copse of twisted trees, then picked their way down a steep path that deposited them in a cove. Large rocks, slick with seaweed, spread out into the ocean. The beach itself was covered with medium-sized rocks, black, gray, and green. Here and there were deposits of seaweed or the remains of a gull. Bruce picked up several small stones, then found a strategic location where he could skip them out along the water. "It's slack tide," he said.

"What does that mean?"

"It's gone all the way out, and there's this brief period before the tide starts to come in again. It's called a slack tide."

Despite growing up in New England, and then living in New York City, Abigail had spent hardly any time by the ocean. Her parents had always been too busy, especially in the summer season, and the few big trips they'd gone on as a family had always been to New York to see plays.

And summers in western Massachusetts meant trips to swimming holes and nearby lakes. She loved the water, but rarely got to the ocean's shore. Despite that, there was something nostalgic about being here now. The tidal smell, and the distant sounds of gulls, made Abigail feel young again. As Bruce searched for perfect stones to skip, she began to pile stones on the shore, using the smoothest ones she could find, starting with a circular base and working upward. She was still thinking about her predicament, still thinking about telling Bruce that they needed to leave the island, but as she built her pile those thoughts began to disappear. She was wholly focused on her task, suddenly filled with purpose. Looking for good building blocks for her pile, she'd found a beautiful, perfectly round white stone with a single band of pinkish red around its middle and slid it into her front pocket to save it for the top.

"You're building a cairn," Bruce said. He was suddenly next to her, and she realized that she'd stopped hearing the sound of skipping stones for a minute or so.

"A what?" she said.

"It's a cairn, a pile of stones like the one you're making."

"Where I come from, we call it a pile of stones," Abigail said.

"Well, it's a good-looking pile of stones."

Abigail had just reached the top; any more and it was bound to collapse. She touched the white stone through her jeans and was about to pull it out and put it on top when she decided to keep it instead. She liked the way it felt in her pocket. "Find a pretty stone for the top," she said to Bruce, feeling a little bad that she'd been snippy about the whole "cairn" thing.

"Okay," he said, and searched around the rocky beach, coming up with a speckled green stone that was almost perfectly round. Abigail carefully placed it on the top of her pile and stepped back, satisfied.

"When do you want to have kids?" Bruce suddenly said, and she turned to him, not able to keep the surprise off her face.

"Not this very moment," she said, "if that's what you're thinking."

"No." He laughed. "Sorry. I guess I just thought of kids because here we are playing on the beach."

They'd discussed children before, but only in the vaguest terms, each saying that they did envision themselves one day having a family. "Let's discuss it after our honeymoon, okay?" Abigail said, smiling widely so that it didn't sound harsh.

"Sure," Bruce said.

The sun had climbed in the sky and they both stretched out along the rocks. They were protected from the ocean breeze and Abigail removed her fleece and put it under her head as a pillow. The sun felt nice on the skin of her arms, and she lifted her shirt a little to expose her stomach. Bruce reached out a hand toward her, and she took it, intertwining their fingers. *This is the moment,* she told herself. *This is the moment I should tell him about what's happening. Just tell him everything, and it will be out of my hands.* But she couldn't bring herself to do it. It was like standing on the edge of a high diving board and being unable to jump.

The sun dipped behind a single ragged cloud, and her skin instantly turned cold, then warm again when the cloud moved swiftly away. She was beginning to drift off. Under her eyelids multicolored dots swam and she chased them, moving her eyes, but the dots kept skirting just outside of her vision. Then she was lightly dreaming, walking along the second-floor balcony that hung in the lodge. The hall was filled with people, hundreds of them, and they were all silent, just staring up toward Abigail on the balcony. And even though they were looking right at her she wondered if they could see her, and if they did, would they come for her? Two people were speaking, two men, their voices coming from somewhere in the crowd, but then she was on the beach again, cold, because another cloud, bigger this time, had blocked the sun. She sat up, groggy.

Bruce was no longer next to her. He was standing about ten yards away, his hands on his hips, talking to someone whom Abigail couldn't see because they were blocked by Bruce. Still, she knew it had to be Eric Newman, Scottie, whatever his name was, and that he'd followed them here. She didn't move, and a snatch of conversation reached her—Bruce's voice exclaiming enthusiastically about something. The sun came out again and she put her hand above her eyes. Bruce bent to pick up a stone and she saw that it really was Eric Newman, wearing a white fisherman sweater and staring directly at Abigail through a pair of wire-rimmed sunglasses.

Bruce must have caught Eric looking Abigail's way, because he turned around and said, "You're awake."

"A little bit," she replied, and thought of lying back down on the rocks, hoping Eric would just go away. But it was too late for that. She stood up, her body stiff—how long had she been out?—pulled her fleece back on and walked toward the two men. Bruce was smiling, so it was obviously not a confrontation, at least not yet.

"Abigail, this is Scott. Scott, this is Abigail."

The lenses of Eric's sunglasses were not completely opaque, and she could see the intensity of his stare. "We met, didn't we?" she said to Eric, not reaching out with her hand. "First night I was here. In the lodge. You said I looked familiar."

"Oh yeah," he said. "That's right."

"I thought you said your name was Eric Newman, or am I confused?" She said it without thinking, but he stammered a little in his reply and Abigail felt a brief moment of triumph that she'd put him off balance.

"Uh, well, it's Eric Scott Newman. I like to be called Scott."

"Uh-huh," Abigail said.

"Bruce just told me that you're on your honeymoon,"

160

he said, and there was a click in his voice as if his mouth was dry. "Congratulations."

"Thanks," Abigail said. "Are you married?"

She caught Bruce turning his head toward her out of the corner of her eye, maybe hearing something in the tone of her voice. Maybe she was going too far, taunting her stalker, but it felt good. Her own words were filling her, and despite the presence of two tall men, she felt tall herself.

"I was," Eric said. "But it didn't work out."

"Oh, I'm sorry. So, you're here alone, or are you with a group?"

"No, just here by myself. Heard some good things about this place. Wanted to get out into nature. It's beautiful, don't you think?"

"It's goddamn life-changing." That was Bruce, jumping back into the conversation. "Not just *here*." He gestured with his hand toward the view. "But at Quoddy. Getting away from screens, from your phone, from everything."

"Yeah, I love it. Makes me a little sad to be here alone, to tell you the truth." He flicked his eyes toward Abigail.

"Look, man," Bruce said. "I get you. If you want to join us for dinner, tonight or any—"

"No, no way." Eric held up his hands, Abigail noticing all the chunky rings again. Had he been wearing all of those in California? "You guys are on your honeymoon. I wouldn't dare."

"Well, if you change your mind."

"Yeah," Abigail said. "If you change your mind, join us."

"I won't, but thanks. And I should let you both be alone here now as well. I was just passing through, really, and now I'm starting to think about brunch."

Hearing the word "brunch" made Abigail check the time on her Fitbit. It was ten-thirty already—how long had she been sleeping?—and she realized that she had to hurry if she didn't want to be late to her swimming pool date with Jill.

"Take it easy, you two," Eric said, and spun and left, heading toward the steep path that led back up to the bluff.

"You were asking him a lot of personal questions," Bruce said when Eric was out of earshot.

"He gives me the creeps, that guy. He came up to me the first night we were here, while you were getting drinks at the bar. He said he was sure he knew me from somewhere, and he asked me if I'd been to Piety Hills Vineyard."

"So he must have seen you there, on your bachelorette weekend."

"Yeah, but I don't remember him. It's creepy, don't you think?"

"Doesn't sound that creepy to me, but we can avoid him. It definitely didn't sound like he was interested in having dinner with us."

"Thank God for that," Abigail said, then reminded Bruce that she was supposed to go swimming with Jill this morning, and they began the walk back to the resort. They didn't talk again about Eric Newman on the walk, but Abigail was acutely aware that she had just actively lied to Bruce for the first time, that she'd laid the foundation for further lies, if it came to that.

She didn't get to the grotto pool until eleven thirty-five. There was no one there, and Abigail was relieved that she hadn't kept Jill waiting.

She slid into the warm water of the pool, pushed herself from the side, and skimmed along the surface. After she had swum back and forth a few times a staff member mysteriously appeared, the same man who'd been there the day before, and Abigail asked him if there'd been a woman here earlier. He told her no, and Abigail ordered a Greyhound.

At noon Abigail gave up on Jill. She drank the dregs of her drink and stepped out of the pool, leaving a trail of water as she walked to the changing room.

17

At dinner that night Abigail kept looking toward the door to the dining room, hoping to see Jill and Alec.

"Who are you watching for?" Bruce said, slicing into his rabbit.

"Oh, sorry," Abigail said. "Jill. I haven't seen her all day."

"You going to let her have it for standing you up?" Bruce smiled.

"No, I'm just worried, I guess."

"What are you worried about? She's on her honeymoon, too. She's probably just spending the day inside with Alec."

"Yeah, you're right." Abigail's main course was a vegetable tart, now all gone, and she was nervously scraping up the remnants with her fork.

"And don't forget. They'll bring you your dinner to your room if you want. That's probably what they did."

"Right," Abigail said. "That's probably what they did."

Abigail saw Eric Newman in the dining room, eating by himself at one of the corner tables. He'd brought a book with him, and there was something pathetic about the way he was sitting alone at the table, the book propped open in front of him, but with his eyes nervously scanning the room. After their encounter on the beach Abigail felt a little better about the possibility that he would simply stop bothering her. He clearly hadn't been prepared for being called by his real name, or for being questioned about his wife. Maybe he really was just a pathetic delusional man who believed that he'd found his soul mate. Maybe, by challenging him the way she had, Abigail had destroyed some of his illusions about her.

"I'm tired tonight," Abigail said as they ate their dessert. She didn't want to linger in the hall after dinner, even though she was still hoping to see Jill and find out what had caused her to miss their swimming date.

"Me, too. Straight to the bunk after this?"

"That would be nice."

The air was cool as they made their way down the sloping lawn toward their bunk, holding their fake lanterns. When they were near their door something rattled in a nearby shrub and Abigail jumped.

"What's that?" she said.

"Probably a raccoon, or maybe a fox," Bruce said. He approached the shrub and they both heard something slink away.

"It's strange to think there are animals on this island," Abigail said as she entered the bunk.

"Why?"

"Because they'd be stuck here. I mean, how'd they even get here in the first place? Birds I understand, because they can fly away, but where did the foxes come from?"

"They came from other foxes. Do you need me to explain it to you?"

Inside the bunk the fire had been lit. Abigail went to the hidden refrigerator and pulled out a wine-sized bottle that turned out to be a beer called King Titus. "Wanna split this?" she asked.

"Sure," Bruce said, and they drank the dark beer together on the couch near the fire, playing a game of backgammon. It was the closest to normal Abigail had felt since before Eric Newman had approached her in the lodge two nights earlier. After playing four games, and each winning twice, they agreed to go to bed, even though it felt early.

Bruce fell asleep first, curled up in the fetal position, breathing deeply. Abigail lay naked under the covers, still awake, thinking about everything that had happened over the past few days. The fire was dying, but it still cast soft flutters of light across the walls and ceiling, and the occasional crackle broke up the oppressive silence of the bunk. She closed her eyes but found she wasn't tired. She had a trick when she wasn't sleepy. She didn't count sheep, but she did count all the productions she could remember from Boxgrove Theatre's history. It almost always worked. The first play she usually thought of was *Deathtrap*, then she went through the rest of that entire season: *The Merchant of Venice*, *Blithe Spirit*, *Conviction*, an early play by Eve Ensler, and there was one more that Abigail couldn't remember. She knew it wasn't another

Shakespeare—they only ever did one Shakespeare over the summer—then she remembered that they'd actually done *Into the Woods*, a rare, and unsuccessful, foray into musical theater, or at least that's what her parents had concluded.

Abigail went back over several other seasons, then began to tire, and just as she was on the edge of slipping into sleep, she heard what sounded like a branch scraping against the window. It stopped, and she wondered if she'd been dreaming it, but just as she was about to fall asleep again, it started up.

She slid out of the bed, pulled on her nightgown, which had been bunched up on the floor, then pulled her robe from the back of the chair. The fire had died out entirely and the bunk was cold and dark. She went to the window that faced the open lawn in front of the lodge and peered out. She didn't immediately see anything and wondered if it really had been a branch moving in the wind, when she noticed a figure crouched in one of the low shrubs that ringed the bunk. She caught a glimpse of blond hair and pale skin, and realized it was Jill, hunkered down, squatting. There was a three-quarter moon in the sky and Abigail could see the fear in her face, the wide eyes and set jaw. Abigail waved to her before realizing that she wouldn't be able to see through the window, then went to the front door and opened it as quietly as she could. It was windy outside, and her robe flapped open as she stepped onto the threshold. She pulled the door closed behind her.

"Jill?" she whispered, and stepped toward the shrub she'd seen her hiding in. "Jill, it's Abigail."

Jill stood up and took a step backward. She was wearing a long satiny nightgown that was either white or yellow. Down her right side, under her arm, there was a dark stain on her nightgown that looked black in the moonlight. "Are you hurt?" Abigail asked, and Jill took another step backward, looking confused. She held up her arm, the inside of which was also coated in what was clearly blood.

"Who are you?" Jill said.

"It's Abigail, Jill, what's wrong?" She moved rapidly toward her, and Jill turned and began to run across the lawn toward the line of trees that bordered the end of the bunks.

Abigail froze for a moment, wrapping her robe around her, shocked by what had just happened. The moon was bright, and Jill was moving fast, her white nightgown whipping around her. Abigail didn't know if she should dart back into the bunk and wake Bruce, but if she did that Jill would be long gone. Abigail began to chase her across the lawn, the grass damp under her bare feet.

As she ran, the moon must have moved behind a cloud, because it darkened. Even so, she could see that Jill had reached the line of trees. She disappeared into the woods.

Abigail slowed down, breathing rapidly, staring into the darkness. "Jill," she shouted. She stepped right up to the edge of the woods, staring into them, letting them come into focus. There was nothing to see, though, and nothing to hear, except for the wind whipping through the tops of the trees. Inside the woods was total darkness. Even so, Abigail, shaking now from the cold, took a few steps farther. She could feel the fallen pine needles sticking to the soles of her feet, and she could smell damp soil and rotting vegetation. "Jill," she shouted again, but she knew that she was gone.

Suddenly scared, Abigail turned and raced back across the lawn toward her bunk. A few lights were on at the main lodge and they jangled in her vision as she ran. She considered going straight there, but decided she needed Bruce with her.

She pushed through her door and into the bunk, going directly to the bed and shaking Bruce by the shoulder. He woke, as he always did, sluggishly, looking at Abigail as though he didn't know who she was or what she wanted.

"Bruce, wake up," she said, still shaking his shoulder.

"What? What's wrong?"

"It's Jill. I just saw Jill outside. She was bleeding and I chased her into the woods."

Bruce, sitting up now, rubbing at an eye with the heel of his hand, said, "Say that again."

She told him exactly what had happened as they got dressed.

"Let's hit the button, call Paul," Bruce said.

"It could take too long, Bruce. Let's just go straight up to the lodge and let whoever's up there now know about it. There needs to be a search party. They need to alert the police, is what they need to do."

"Okay, relax. They'll take care of it."

When they got to the main hall of the lodge, there was light coming from the balcony level, but Abigail just shouted into the dark cavernous space, "Anyone here?"

The chandelier, the one that looked as though it were made of real candles, suddenly lit up, and she heard racing steps on the stairwell, and then Paul, their own personal staff member, was coming across the hall to meet them. He moved quickly but his face was placid.

"There's an emergency," Abigail said.

"What can I do?" Paul replied, and Abigail told him quickly that she'd been awoken by a tapping on her window, and then she'd seen Jill with blood on her. She'd chased her into the woods. "You need to call the police," Abigail said, and Paul nodded.

"Take a seat, both of you, by the fire. I'm going to go wake up Chip, but I'll be right back. In the meantime, can I get either of you a warm drink?"

Abigail, being led to a seat, said, "You need to send out a search party. She was only wearing a nightgown, and it's cold."

"I'll be right back, okay?"

"Jesus, should we just go look for her ourselves?" Abigail said to Bruce, as Paul raced back up the stairwell.

"Relax for a moment, okay?" Bruce said. "He's going to get Chip, and he'll take care of it. I promise."

"But they need to call the police. Something was really wrong with her."

"They will, but it's only been about five minutes. Besides, maybe she just drank too much or something. Maybe it's a personal matter."

"She was bleeding, Bruce," Abigail said. "All down her side."

There were footsteps again. Paul was leading Chip Ramsay to them. She hadn't seen him since they'd landed on the island three days earlier. The large red beard was unmistakable, combined with the carefully buzzed hair. He was wearing a green silk robe and had slippers on his feet.

"Tell me what you told Paul," he said to Abigail as a greeting, perching on the edge of a free chair.

She took a deep breath and quickly recounted her story, ending by saying again that someone needed to go to Jill's bunk and talk with Alec, the husband. Or they just simply needed to call the police. Bruce was quiet, watching Abigail while she spoke.

"Okay," Chip said. "I do need to ask you a couple of questions first. Are you absolutely positive that the woman you saw was Jill Greenly?"

"I'm sorry, I didn't know her last name, but it was Jill from the other honeymooning couple. Married to Alec."

"That was their name. Alec and Jill Greenly. And you're sure it was her?"

"Yes," Abigail said, loudly.

Chip slowly nodded, frowning a little.

"I don't understand," Abigail said. "Do you not believe me?"

"So, the thing is," Chip said, "Alec and Jill Greenly are no longer here with us."

"What do you mean?" Bruce asked.

"They left this afternoon. Mrs. Greenly wasn't feeling well, so a plane took them both back to the mainland."

Abigail found she was shaking her head. "No, no," she said. "They didn't, or at least Jill didn't, because I saw her tonight."

Bruce reached over and took Abigail's hand, and without thinking she snatched it away from him.

"I took them to the plane myself," Chip said. "I watched it take off, and I got confirmation when they were safe on the mainland. Is there any way that you might have seen someone else, or that, possibly, you were dreaming?"

"I wasn't dreaming," Abigail said at the same time that Bruce said, "She's not making this up, Chip."

"I know. I know. I'm not suggesting. I'm just looking for a logical solution, that's all, and one possibility is that you had a very vivid dream."

Abigail said, "I was not dreaming. I was outside and chased Jill across the lawn and she went into the woods. I came back and woke Bruce up. Bruce, you felt me. I was cold."

"I didn't notice, Abigail, sorry," Bruce said. "But let's be logical. Abigail says she wasn't dreaming, so she wasn't dreaming. What if Jill came back to the island somehow?

Maybe she forgot something, or maybe—"

"I know everyone who comes onto this island," Chip interrupted. He rubbed at the edge of his nose with a finger.

"Then there's only one conclusion," Bruce said, then turned to Abigail. "You saw someone else, who looked like Jill. How many women are on this island, Chip? We'll have to check."

"Okay, I'll do it. There aren't many. It shouldn't take too long."

"It was Jill," Abigail said, but she said it quietly. In her mind she was going back over exactly what had happened, trying to figure out if she could have possibly been wrong.

Bruce stood, then crouched in front of her and said, "We'll find out what happened, I promise. We'll figure it out." He stood and turned to Chip, who had just stood up himself.

Abigail stood, too, hit with a wave of exhaustion tinged with nausea. "Can I call Jill?" she said, the words coming out just as the thought occurred to her.

"What do you mean?" Chip said.

"You must have her number, or the number of her husband. I want to call her, hear her voice, make sure she's all right."

"Sure, I can look into that. In the morning, okay? It's three a.m. now. Try to get a few hours of sleep, both of you, and we'll square this all away in the clear light of dawn."

Abigail clenched her jaw, but she was tired—how much total sleep had she had since the wedding?—and a little bit of doubt had crept into her mind. Once, as a child, she had woken up and told her parents that a large black bird had been crouched on her chest and had fled out the window after she pushed it away. It had been so vivid that she believed for years it had really happened. But what had just happened to her was even more vivid, far more real than the bird.

"I don't know," she finally said out loud.

"As soon as it's light," Chip said, "I'll send everyone I can into the woods to look for this woman. I promise."

"That sounds good," Bruce said.

"Okay," Abigail said.

Bruce was quiet as they walked back down to their bunk. The moon was still bright enough so they could see clearly without needing lanterns, and Abigail was thinking about how the cold ground felt against her bare feet, how it had felt the same way earlier when she'd chased Jill. "Chip will take care of it," Bruce said, as he held the door for her. Abigail entered without saying anything.

18

With dawn light edging the windows, Abigail was about to get out of bed, even though she'd barely slept. But she closed her eyes for just a few moments, and the next thing she knew she was pulling herself up from a complicated dream, and Bruce was not beside her. It was almost ten o'clock.

She dressed quickly, running over the events of the previous night, then splashed some water on her face, swished her mouth with mouthwash, and left the bunk. It was a perfect autumn day, the air crisp and the sky a hard ultramarine blue. On her way to the lodge she glanced toward the pond, a single sailboat creasing its surface. Anger flared up in her. Why was someone sailing when Jill, or some other woman, might still be in the woods, bleeding and scared?

Even before she pushed through the doors into the lodge, she could smell cooked bacon and freshly baked bread. Over by the unmanned bar Bruce and Chip Ramsay were talking to a third man, someone she hadn't seen before. He was tall, with stooped shoulders and white hair that was thinning at the front. She began walking toward them and Bruce noticed her, instantly breaking away from the group and coming across to intercept her.

"I thought I'd let you sleep," he said.

"What's going on?" she asked.

"The good news is that Jill is fine."

"They found her?"

"No, Abigail. They called her. This morning. Chip did. He talked with both her and Alec, and they were already back in California."

Abigail felt a dropping sensation move coldly through her torso, despite the good news. "When?" she said, realizing as soon as she spoke that she sounded angry.

"It's good news, Abigail," Bruce said. "I know you're sure you saw her, but you didn't. I just think . . . I think you must have had a really vivid dream that felt one hundred percent real to you, but it wasn't."

"No," she said. "If it wasn't Jill, then it was someone who looked just like her. It wasn't a dream. I know what dreams are, and that wasn't one. It was real. Who's Chip talking to?"

Bruce took Abigail's arm, said, "Here, come with me. Talk with him. He's the island detective."

"He's a police detective?"

"He's a private detective," Bruce said, and the man must have heard, because he turned toward them both, quickly reaching out his hand toward Abigail.

"I'm Bob Kaplan," he said. "Chip here told me you had an interesting night." He smiled at her, revealing very straight but very yellow teeth.

"I don't know if it was interesting," Abigail said. "It was pretty awful."

"I know you've told Chip and Bruce all about it, but I'd love to hear what you saw."

Abigail turned to Chip. "You talked with Jill?" she asked.

"I did. About twenty minutes ago. Alec, too."

"I want to talk with her as well."

Something crossed Chip's eyes. They were odd to begin with, flat almost, and too far apart. "I just did," he said. "And they'd just gotten to California. They were exhausted and needed to sleep."

"It's not that I don't—"

"I'll try them again a little later, when you're around. I understand that it'll help if you hear Jill's voice."

"Okay, thanks," Abigail said, wondering if she should be more forceful, but something in Chip's eyes was stopping her.

"How many women are on this island?" she asked, the words coming out at the same time as the thought.

"There are actually not too many at this particular moment," Chip said, his voice scratchy. He cleared it. "There's Mellie, who works here. I think you've met her."

"I did. It wasn't her."

"I've spoken with her and she wasn't out last night."

"What about guests?" Abigail asked.

"Actually," Chip said, "now that Jill has left the island, you're our only female guest. Tomorrow there's a whole group of female executives coming from Atlanta, but right now it's just you." He said it almost apologetically, as though he'd been working hard to ensure gender equity and he'd been failing.

"I just . . . I know it wasn't a dream," Abigail said, and all three men frowned sympathetically at her. She felt a surge of anger, but more than anything she wanted to get away, grab some coffee, and try to wake up a little.

"We *did* search the woods," the detective said, pulling at the long lobe of his ear. "Of course, there are a lot of woods around here, but we didn't spot anything out of the ordinary. We can . . . I can organize another search later."

"Never mind," Abigail said. She just wanted the conversation to end. "Obviously, I had the world's most realistic dream. Either that or I'm going crazy. Bruce, did you eat breakfast?"

"No, not yet," he said. "I'll go with you to get something."

All she really wanted was coffee, but Bruce made her drink a large glass of fresh-squeezed orange juice, and then she picked at a blueberry muffin.

"I want to leave this island," she said after Bruce had finished a second plate of eggs.

She completely expected him to immediately dismiss her, so she was surprised when he said, "I agree. We should leave. Maybe coming here wasn't such a great idea."

He looked crushed as he said the words, and Abigail said, "No, it's not this place. It's nice here. It's just, I don't think I can enjoy myself after what happened last night. I can't just stay here and pretend I didn't see anything, or pretend I really believe it was all a dream."

"I totally get it. When do you want to leave?"

"Can we leave this afternoon?" she said.

He nodded. "Yes, I'll arrange it."

"You understand, don't you?" Abigail said.

"I do. I get it."

After walking back to the bunk, they both began to pack in silence, when Bruce said, "Oh, I forgot to talk with Chip, tell him to book the plane."

"We could call Paul," Abigail said, and she was moving toward the call button.

"No, let me run up and talk with Chip. Also, I was thinking about what we could do before the plane comes. Take a walk, maybe. Or go for a swim. It might feel good, get some of the tension out."

"I want to look around the woods, Bruce," Abigail said, her back to him. "I'm going out this morning. I need to see if there's any sign of her, of the woman I saw." She turned, expecting Bruce to look disapproving, but he was nodding.

"I get it," he said.

"I'm going right after I finish packing."

"I'll come with you," Bruce said.

"If you want to help you can look separately, because it doesn't make any sense for you to come with me. We should spread out."

179

"I don't want you in the woods by yourself."

"I won't get lost. It's an island."

"Look. Just wait for me and we'll search together, okay?"

She made a noncommittal sound, and he said, "We'll go together."

After Bruce left, Abigail quickly finished packing her things, then changed into her walking shoes. She had already decided to search the woods herself—she'd seen a bleeding woman enter them the previous night, and she needed to at least go look for her. Bruce might be upset, but she didn't care. It was increasingly clear he thought she'd dreamt the whole thing. They all thought she'd dreamt it. The thought almost enraged her, but she told herself to calm down. Maybe it was possible that she'd had a dream. Maybe it had been triggered by the stress of having Eric Newman on the island. Her subconscious had projected all those anxieties onto the image of Jill, bleeding and running away. Abigail moved her head rapidly back and forth and shook out her limbs, just to get blood moving through them. Either way, whether there was something terrible happening on this island or she really was losing her mind, she needed to look in the woods.

The day had warmed up even more and two staff members were carrying archery targets out onto the lawn. She walked along the row of bunks, her eyes raking over the bunks' names, looking for the one that Eric Newman was staying in. What name had he given her? Pinehaven, she thought. She spotted it, the second-to-last along the row, and walked rapidly past, not looking toward its windows, hoping that he wasn't inside, looking out.

Somehow, the threat from Eric Newman had lessened in her mind. It was partly due to the Jill incident from the night before, and partly due to the way he had acted down at the cove with her and Bruce. She was now convinced he was just a sad, obsessive creep, more bark than bite. But what if he had seen her walk past his bunk? What if he followed her into the woods? Well, let him. It was far less terrifying than what she'd seen the night before. Besides, if he followed her it would give her someone to yell at, maybe even punch. Somehow, she'd stopped being particularly frightened of her stalker.

After finding the place where she was pretty sure Jill, or whoever she was, had entered the woods, Abigail saw that there was actually a path, poorly marked, that led into the scrubby woodland. She took a few steps in, then pulled her cell phone out of her pocket. She'd brought it with her because the compass still worked, even without service. And the flashlight would work, too, if she needed it. She was pointed east, and figured she'd walk straight ahead for a while, then turn back, going directly west. That way she wouldn't get too lost and wouldn't spend time searching the same area again and again. She began to walk, keeping an eye out for any signs of footprints or drops of blood. In the woods, the ground was almost a luminescent green at times, its mossy surface broken by complex patterns of emerging tree roots. Once she'd gone about a hundred yards she began to occasionally call out, "Hello," but her voice sounded strange and lonely, so she stopped.

Something moved high up in the trees and Abigail looked up to see a large bird, maybe the eagle she'd seen earlier with Bruce, wheeling away against the blue of the sky. She was suddenly exhausted, and overtly aware that what she was doing was not only futile but maybe dangerous. Even if she'd been imagining things, she was still alone in the woods. And it had grown congested the farther she'd walked, the ground thick with bushes she couldn't identify, some with clusters of dark, poisonous-looking berries, some with sharp leaves.

She went a little bit farther, spotting a break in the trees marked by a pool of light, and went to it, stood in the sun, letting it warm her skin. The ground was blanketed in the strange green moss, and she sat for a moment, leaned her back against the crook of a tree. It was time to turn back, she told herself, find Bruce, make sure he had booked the flight, and get off this god-forsaken island. Once she was back on the mainland, with service on her phone, she could call Jill Greenly herself and make sure she was all right. And she would be, wouldn't she? Back in California like Chip Ramsay said she was. And if Eric Newman ever got in touch with her again, she would immediately notify the police. She'd even tell Bruce about it, not about the affair, but about the way he claimed they'd had one. She was now willing to lie, she realized. Maybe it had something to do with the fact that Bruce clearly didn't really believe what she'd told him about seeing Jill. If Bruce didn't believe her when she was telling the truth, then maybe it would be okay to tell him one major lie, just the once. It was a rationalization, she realized, but she was okay with it.

She shut her eyes and listened. There was the faint sound of trees moving in what little wind there was, the clicking of limbs and the creaking of trunks. She could hear gulls in the distance. And that was it. She felt like a child again. The height of the trees, and their constant slow-motion movement—as though the woods were underwater—made her feel small and insignificant. Something was happening, and it was beyond her comprehension. And no matter how quietly she sat on the cool ground, the woods would never let her in on their secret.

It was time to go back.

She stood, wiping the dry pine needles from the back of her jeans, and saw a figure moving quietly through the woods toward her, about fifty feet away. Eric Newman, his head swiveling from side to side, clearly looking for her.

She froze, her body going still like a deer sensing danger, and just when she was wondering if she could outrun him back to the lodge, he spotted her, and stopped walking.

"Don't run," he yelled, putting his hands above his head, as though she were pointing a gun at him.

"What do you want?" she said, her voice loud but shaky.

"Just to talk. Sorry. I saw you pass my window and watched you enter the woods. I followed you in, but I won't come any closer. I'm not trying to frighten you."

"Too late for that," Abigail said.

"I'm sorry. Really, I just want to talk."

"What do you want to talk about?" Abigail said.

"I saw her, too. The woman in the nightgown last night."

19

Abigail took a breath. "How do you know about that?"

"Everyone here knows. That private detective interviewed me this morning. He didn't mention you, but I saw you follow her last night. Across the lawn. I haven't been sleeping and I was looking out the window. I know it's strange."

"Did you tell them that? Did you tell them you saw someone?"

"Of course. They asked me if it was someone I recognized, but it wasn't."

"You hadn't met Jill Greenly?"

"She was a guest here?"

"Yes. That's who I saw last night, but they told me she left the island yesterday afternoon, that it couldn't have been her I'd seen."

"They told you she'd left?"

"Yes."

"How did they tell you she did that?" Eric said.

"What do you mean?"

"Did they say she flew?"

"Yes. That's what they said."

"She didn't," Eric said.

"How do you know?"

He took a step forward, and Abigail said, "Stay there. We're close enough."

"Okay," he said, stopping. "Unless she left by boat, she didn't leave the island, because no plane came to this island in the afternoon. After I saw you and your husband by the cove, I walked over toward the landing strip. There's a spot where you can sit, and if you look really hard you can see a lighthouse on one of the islands in Casco Bay. I sat there till it was almost dinnertime. There were no planes. I'd have seen them."

"Maybe you—"

"I'm telling you, there weren't any. There's something wrong with this place. I felt it the moment I got here."

"The moment you stalked me here."

"I'm sorry . . . sorry for everything I've put you through. There's no excuse for it now, I realize, but that's the real reason I followed you here today. I wanted to tell you that I won't bother you anymore."

"What changed your mind?"

"When I saw you and Bruce yesterday, as you know, on that beach. I felt your anger, and I realized . . . I guess I realized that I was wrong about us. I really did think that we were meant to be together, the two of us. I think I went a little insane."

"You think?" Abigail said.

Eric smiled, then looked down at the ground. His hands were now in the pockets of his jeans. "I went a lot insane. The thing is, you look like her. You look like . . ."

He hesitated, and Abigail said, "I look like your wife."

"Not her coloring. She had bright red hair, and her skin was very pale, but your eyes are the same, and the way you talk is the same."

"Well, we're not the same," Abigail said.

"I know. I'm sorry I came here. I'm sorry that I didn't give up when I got your email, but I thought that if you saw me again . . ." He shrugged.

"You followed me to New York, didn't you? A few days before I got married."

"I did. I just wanted a chance to see you, to let you see me. I thought you might be having second thoughts about the wedding."

"Let's get out of the woods, okay?" Abigail said, and began to walk back the way she had come.

"Can I come with you?" Eric asked.

"Just walk over there," Abigail said. "I still don't know if I trust you."

"What are you doing out here? Are you looking for that woman?"

"I guess. I'm looking for any evidence that what I saw last night really happened," Abigail said.

"Well, now you have me. I saw her, too."

"But you didn't recognize her?"

"I didn't see her face, and even if I had, I didn't know her." He was walking parallel to Abigail, his hands still in his pockets.

187

"Why did you say that you think there's something wrong with this place?" Abigail asked.

"Because there is. I may be insane, but I know that much. First of all, this resort is not a viable business. It can't be. There are far more staff members than there are guests. And everyone seems to know each other—all the guests, I mean. I just think it's some kind of front for something else altogether."

"And all the guests are men."

"Yes, I noticed that, too. Something's off."

"I know what you're saying," Abigail said. "But if it's financed by billionaires, I guess they don't care if they lose money. And I guess most billionaires are men."

"Your husband is one of the financiers, I guess."

"I actually don't know too much about it, but yes. I think it was created as a place for tech people to go that doesn't have screens. A place to get back in touch with nature, and even though it's open to other people, it's not really a regular business."

"That makes sense," Eric said. "But I still think there's something else creepy going on. What if it really was Jill Greenly we saw, and they're lying about her?"

"I've been thinking about that," Abigail said. "If it really was Jill, then maybe she was attacked by her husband, and maybe he followed her into the woods and killed her and the resort is covering it up because they don't want a scandal. Or maybe because her husband paid them off. I just don't know. All I know is that I need to get off this island."

Abigail was aware that she hadn't mentioned Porter, Jill's old boyfriend, who was, coincidentally, on the island as well.

"When are you leaving?" Eric said.

Abigail turned to look at him and realized that he'd slid a little way toward her so that they were only about ten feet apart. She didn't say anything, but she began to walk a little faster.

"Bruce is making arrangements now. We're leaving this afternoon."

Eric nodded. "That makes sense."

They walked in silence for a moment. Abigail could now see the open lawn through the trees, and she heard a noise, a whoosh followed by what sounded like an ax hitting wood. She realized almost immediately that it was someone shooting arrows at the targets she'd seen being set up.

"How long will you stay?" Abigail asked Eric as they stepped from the woods back out onto the lawn.

"Two more days, I guess. Do you want me to let you know if I find out anything more?"

"Sure," she said, not knowing if it was the right thing to say, if he would read it as an invitation to continue their relationship. But she didn't really care. If he found out something, she'd want to know. And all the fear and anger she'd felt toward him earlier seemed to have disappeared.

She heard another whoosh, followed by the *thock* of an arrow hitting the target. There were two men holding bows, and two staff members watching them. She was suddenly annoyed by the whole existence of this resort, the idea of adults coming to a place to pretend they were at some kind of summer camp, but a summer camp with gourmet food and constant alcohol.

"Is that your husband?" Eric said. Abigail looked up the hill and could make out Bruce coming down, recognizable by his awkward, long-limbed gait.

"Yep," Abigail said. They were alongside Eric's bunk now and he was heading toward the door.

"Again, I'm sorry for all I put you through," he said. "I hope you get home safe."

"What do you mean?" Abigail said to Bruce.

"They're booked, but they can come early tomorrow morning." They were back in their bunk together. Bruce was changing his shirt. He'd already let her have it for going out into the woods by herself, and now he was letting her know that the plane couldn't come that day.

"I don't understand," Abigail said. "It's such a short flight. I mean, there must be some way to get off this island today."

"I'm sorry. Chip felt terrible, too, but apparently one of their planes is out of commission, and they're backed up."

"Jesus," Abigail said.

"Don't have a fit, Abigail. They're coming early tomorrow morning. You'll just have to rough it here one more night." He smiled sarcastically at her, and Abigail felt an urge to rush at him, shove him in the chest. It wasn't that the plane couldn't come, it was the way he was so nonchalant about it. "Why don't we go swimming, or, hey, I'll even go back into the woods with you if you want," he said.

"Look," Abigail said. "Listen to me for a moment."

Bruce, who had been rummaging through his suitcase, turned and looked at Abigail, his lips pressed together and his brow furrowed.

"This place is freaking me out. It's not just seeing Jill last night—and, yes, I am pretty fucking sure that the woman I saw was Jill—it's everything else. First of all, there's no way that this place is a viable business. There're about twenty guests, all men, all your friends, and every time I turn around there's some new staff person coming out of the woodwork. I mean, tell me what this place is all about."

Bruce said, "I already told you. Chip wanted to start a place for people in the tech world—a getaway—a place to unwind. And women come here all the time, just maybe not right now at this moment. And, yes, they're mostly rich women. That's the purpose of this place. People in demanding positions who need to shed some of their worries and anxiety."

"It's not working. Not for me."

Bruce reached out a hand. "Hey, honey. Honey, relax."

"That's not helping, either."

"So, tell me what will help, okay? I'll do whatever it takes."

"I want to leave here. There can't be just one plane service. I mean, if there was a medical emergency then you'd get someone here, right?"

"Well, if there was a medical emergency then the Coast Guard or someone would come, but that's not the case. It's less than twenty-four hours. That's nothing."

"I don't want to spend another night here."

"It's just one night," Bruce said. "I'll be here with you. You don't even have to leave this bunk if you don't want to. We can have our dinner here, then go to sleep, and in the morning the plane will come and get us. I don't know what the big deal is."

"The big deal is that I saw a terrified woman—the *only* other woman on this island, by the way—who was bleeding and ran away from me, and now you're telling me that I have to spend another night here. It just doesn't make sense. All I've been told since I've gotten here is that anything I want they can get for me. Now I want to leave, and suddenly it's a whole day's wait."

Bruce didn't immediately say anything. He was breathing through his nose and bouncing almost imperceptibly on his toes.

"What?" Abigail said.

"I think you're being a spoiled bitch." He said it in a low voice, but she heard every word, and immediately tensed. It wasn't just the words but the hushed tone. He sounded very different. "Excuse me?" she said.

"You heard me." He was looking at her, but his eyes were resting just a little bit off to the side, not quite making eye contact. Words raced through Abigail's head, but she was still shocked at seeing this side of her new husband. Part of her was scared as well.

"Fine," she said at last, her voice a little shaky. "You do what you want to do, but I'm going to leave today. There's got to be another flight service."

"Be my guest," he said, now definitely not looking at her.

"What's going on with you?" she said, taking a step forward, even though she didn't want to.

"I could ask you the same question. I bring you to this amazing place, and you don't appreciate it. It's all about *you*, all the time, isn't it?"

"I did appreciate it," Abigail said, spacing the words. "But because of what I saw last night I would like to leave. If you don't understand that, I don't know what else to say."

"Fine," Bruce said, and walked toward the kitchen.

20

Abigail left the bunk and began walking up toward the lodge. The men were still at their archery, and every time she heard the sound of an arrow hitting its target her body tensed. As she climbed the stone steps that led to the entrance to the lodge, the doors swung open and Chip Ramsay was exiting. "Abigail," he said. Then, after really looking at her, he added, "Everything all right?"

"Bruce said there's no way to get off the island today," she said, stopping in front of the doors.

"I'm so sorry about that. He told me how much you wanted to leave, and I get it, but I've been talking with Sean all morning at Casco Air and there's just no way. They're down two planes, and they're totally booked. Bruce told you they'd be here first thing tomorrow morning, right?"

"He did. The thing is that I would really like to leave today. There must be another plane service."

"There isn't really, not for this area."

"But what would you do if there was an emergency? If someone needed medical help?"

"Do you need medical help?" Chip asked, genuine concern in his eyes.

"No, I'm just wondering."

"We'd notify emergency services, of course, and I suspect they'd send a helicopter. It's actually never happened before, knock on wood." Chip reached back and knocked on the door to the lodge.

"All right, thanks," Abigail said. "I do want to make a call. Is there someone upstairs in the office?"

"Aaron's up there, last I checked. If he isn't, then just come and find me. I'm sorry about this, Mrs. Lamb. Really, if there was anything we could do to help, we'd do it."

"When did the plane come yesterday to pick up Alec and Jill Greenly?"

He thought for a moment. "About three o'clock."

She pushed through the doors into the lodge. It was clearly lunchtime, the bar now open, and Abigail spotted Porter, holding a draft beer. He had one elbow on the bar, leaning at a rakish angle, and Abigail thought, *He's pleased with himself.* He spotted her and lifted his head in greeting, a half smile on his lips. Her instinct was to walk away, but she went toward him, said hello.

"I didn't see you at the pool this morning," he said.

"No," she said.

"You okay?" he asked, putting his beer down on the bar as though he wanted to free his hands. She wondered if she looked like she was about to faint.

"I'm okay," she said. "Just not feeling well, and I was hoping to get off this island today and I just found out that the plane can't come until tomorrow."

"Oh, that's too bad," he said in his slight accent.

"Can I ask you something?" she said.

"Of course."

"Did you know Jill Greenly, the other woman who was here with her husband?"

"Ah," he said, and raised his eyebrows a little. "How did you know that?"

"She told me. You two had been engaged?"

"A long time ago," he said. He picked up his beer again and took a long sip.

"You must have been surprised to see her here."

"Yeah, I was shocked. I don't know if I was as shocked as she was, but it was a big surprise to her. An unpleasant surprise, probably for both of us."

"Because of your past relationship."

"It did not end well."

"Yeah, she told me."

"She told you what?" Porter asked, a catch in his voice.

"Oh, not much, really. I barely knew her."

"Lucky you," he said. "Sorry, I don't mean to sound bitter, but . . ."

"But you are bitter."

"Yes, I guess. I'd have been better off never having met her," he said, and Abigail thought he was holding back. For some reason, she heard Bruce's voice in her head, saying the words "spoiled bitch" with so much hatred in his voice.

"Well, you don't have to worry about her anymore. She's gone."

"What do you mean, she's gone?" he asked.

"I mean she's left. This island."

"Has she?" He looked surprised, and it was clear that Porter, at least, hadn't heard the whole story about what Abigail had seen the previous night. Either that or he was pretending he hadn't heard.

"She left yesterday afternoon with her husband. By plane."

He looked confused for a moment, but all he said was, "Oh, I didn't know that," his eyes searching the room as though he were looking for someone. Abigail looked up at his jawline, noticed a small muscle twitching. Clearly, even the idea of Jill Greenly made him anxious.

"I'll let you go, Porter," she said, and he looked back down at her, scratched at his collarbone with his free hand. It drew Abigail's eyes to his open shirt; he was wearing some sort of necklace made from braided leather. Whatever was hanging from it was hidden by his shirt.

He finished his beer in one long swallow and said, "You going in to get some lunch?"

"I'll be there soon," she said, and went toward the stairwell instead. She wasn't sure exactly what she'd been hoping to get from talking with Porter, but just the fact that he seemed evasive, nervous almost, confirmed for her that he might have had something to do with what happened to Jill Greenly. Maybe he'd been the one who attacked her last night.

The office door was open, but no one was inside. The

room was filled with the barely noticeable hum of electricity and the flicker of bad lighting. She heard footsteps behind her and turned to face the same staff member she'd met when she'd come to this office previously.

"Hi, Mrs. Lamb," he said. He was carrying papers in one hand and an arrow in the other. Abigail's eyes must have rested on the arrow, because he held it up and showed her the end. "Apparently when an arrow is missing its feathers it doesn't fly right."

"It's fletching," Abigail said automatically.

"What's that?" he said.

"Sorry. It's the name for the feathers on an arrow." The word had jumped into her head because of Ben Perez, her ex-boyfriend, who'd once written a poem with the word in it. They'd had a disagreement, Abigail claiming that no one would know what the word meant. It was so strange to suddenly think of Ben here on Heart Pond Island, where she felt about as far away from New York City and her old life as possible.

"Fletching," he said. "I'll remember that. I'm Aaron, by the way, if you don't remember."

"Hi, Aaron."

"You here to make another call?"

"I am." Abigail's plan was to call Zoe, get her to jump onto her computer and research ways to get off this island. Maybe she'd find another charter service that would agree to fly to Heart Pond Island. If anyone could figure it out, Zoe could.

"Come on through," Aaron said, and led Abigail to the same desk she'd used before. He bent over the phone, cradled the handset between his shoulder and his head, and pushed a bunch of buttons on the phone. She stared at his cleanly shaved neck. He had closely buzzed hair on the back of his head and the sides, but a long blond lock at the top that he had to push back now that he was bent over.

"Here you go," he said, pulling the chair out for Abigail. "I hope you don't have a problem getting through. Phones have been tricky this morning."

"What do you mean?" Abigail said.

"They've just been in and out a little bit. No big deal. If you have trouble getting through, just keep trying."

"Okay," Abigail said, but she felt angry just hearing about the possibility. Even if Zoe couldn't help her get off the island, she desperately wanted to talk to her, just to hear her voice.

"It sometimes happens," Aaron said, smiling.

Abigail dialed Zoe's number from memory, was thrilled to hear a ringtone, but after about five rings she was cut off and a busy signal interrupted the call. "Fuck," she said to herself. She tried it again and the same thing happened. Then she dialed her own cell phone number. This time it was just a busy signal, not even a ringtone. She turned back to look for Aaron, but he was no longer in the office. It was all she could do not to pick up the phone and throw it across the room. Of course it didn't work. Of course they weren't going to let her make a phone call. And then some of her rage was replaced by a surge of fear. She looked around the office again, scanning the ceiling for cameras. Were they watching her? She picked up the handset again and dialed 9 to get an outside line, then punched in 911. It began to ring and she almost hung up. What was she going to say if this actually worked? *Hello, I'm being held against my will at Heart Pond Island. I think I'm in danger.* It sounded ludicrous, but she *was* being held here. It was being done by smiling men in khaki pants, but what difference did that make? She wanted to leave, and they weren't letting her.

Spoiled bitch.

The ringing stopped and went to another busy signal. She hung up the phone quietly and stood as tall as she could to look over all the open cubicles. There must be other phones here, and maybe they worked. She spotted one toward the back of the office. A black office phone next to what looked like a fax machine. She walked over to it, picked up the handset with a shaky hand, and dialed Zoe's number again. The same thing happened, ringing followed by a busy signal. She hung up. Her heart was starting to race, and her breathing felt shallow, as if she wasn't able to get enough air into her lungs. She told herself to calm down, that there was still a chance that all the strange things that had happened in the past few days were nothing more than coincidence.

A woman came into the office, humming to herself.

It was Mellie, the only female staff member that Abigail had actually laid eyes on since arriving here.

"Hello," Abigail said from across the room.

Mellie squinted toward her, then said, "Hi, Mrs. Lamb. Making a call?"

"Trying to," Abigail said.

"Yeah, I heard that the phones were glitching again. Sorry about that."

"How long does it usually last?" Abigail said, walking across the office.

Mellie shrugged, said, "Not more than a day, usually. That's the problem with wanting to have a resort that's entirely cut off from the rest of the world. You wind up being cut off from the rest of the world."

Abigail pressed her lips together and nodded. Mellie pushed a strand of her red hair behind an ear with one of her fingers. She had pale skin covered in freckles. Her eyebrows were so thin as to be almost nonexistent, and she had a deep groove from the top of her lip to the base of her nose. "Mellie," Abigail said, when they were a few feet apart. "Did you hear about what happened last night?"

"Er, you mean what happened to you?"

"Yeah."

"They woke us up early this morning and had us search the island. They said you saw a woman who appeared injured . . . is that right? . . . outside your bunk."

"I saw Jill Greenly outside my bunk. She was bleeding all down her side, and then she ran into the woods."

"I didn't know it was Mrs. Greenly," Mellie said, her thin nostrils flaring a little.

"Yes, it was definitely her, but then Chip Ramsay told me that she'd left the island yesterday. So I guess I was confused."

"You're not confused," Mellie said, lowering her voice. Then she looked toward the door and added, "I shouldn't be saying this, but she's still on the island."

"What?" Abigail said.

"Shhh. I'd lose my job if they knew what I was telling you. She's here, and she's not in danger. No, listen to me. The plane will come tomorrow. You just need to keep your head down until then and you're going to be okay."

"I don't know what . . . Mellie, tell me what's happening here."

Mellie turned back and looked at the door again. Abigail glanced over her shoulder and saw Aaron come back into the office, his head down, reading something printed on a piece of paper. Mellie leaned in close and whispered, "Don't trust your husband."

21

Abigail walked back down the stairway, then turned away from the lodge's hall toward the tunnel Mellie had shown her earlier that led to the pool.

She needed a place to sit for a moment.

There was no one else around as she walked down the dingy hallway, and she was grateful. She didn't know what she would do if Chip or even Bruce suddenly appeared. She'd probably scream.

She took the turn that brought her into the tunnel, darker than she remembered. She was scared, but she also didn't want to go back through the lodge, risk running into someone she'd have to talk to. Her instinct was to run, but part of her knew that if she allowed herself to panic, she'd never stop. So she walked through the tunnel as calmly as possible, finally pushing through the double glass doors into the warm, chlorine-tinged air. She thought of going into the women's changing room— she'd have it to herself—but she actually wanted to be outside instead, not closed in by walls. She walked past the entrance to the changing room and kept going. There was an unmarked door at the end of the hall, and she pulled it open, relieved to find that it led to the outside world. The cold air felt so good that she just stood for a moment with her back against the door and breathed in and out, even closing her eyes for a moment.

The slight breeze on the air carried voices that sounded as though they were coming from the front of the building. She couldn't make out the words, just the deep jokey inflections of men talking, and Abigail cut around toward the back of the building, passing the bench and finding that the path continued past a cluster of what looked like spruce trees. She peered behind her to make sure no one could see that she was entering the woods, then kept walking along the path, now paved with flat rocks. She came to a wooden sign nailed into the side of a tree. Carved into the sign were the words SILVANUS WOODS, and there was an etching of a man's face, ringed with ornate leaves, designed as though they were growing from his skin. The sign itself looked old—it was speckled in places with dark green lichen—but the nails that held it to the tree looked new. The name Silvanus rang a faint bell in her head—she'd taken Latin in high school and remembered enough to wonder if Silvanus was some sort of Roman god.

She took a few steps past the sign, enough to see that there was a clearing up ahead. She felt trapped, not really wanting to see what was there—her mind conjuring the image of Jill, blood spilling down her side—and not wanting to turn back. She moved tentatively ahead, said, "Hello?" in what she hoped was a normal voice. If there was someone in the woods, she definitely did not want to be surprised by them.

No one answered, and she stepped into the circular clearing. At the middle was a firepit ringed with blackened stones, and a little farther out a circle of benches, crudely fashioned from logs. Abigail found a place to sit that gave her a view of the path back toward the resort, so that she could see if anyone was coming. Despite the sign with the strange face on it, she felt temporarily safe here. It probably was a feature of the original boys' camp, a place to gather at night, light a fire, and roast marshmallows. An innocent place, unlike whatever had happened here over the past few days.

Now that she was sitting, she thought back over the words Mellie had said. That Jill was still on the island and that she was okay. That she should just keep her head down until the plane arrived tomorrow. That she shouldn't trust Bruce. Abigail tried to build a narrative that fit everything that had happened here so far. Her best guess was that Jill and her new husband had had a fight that resulted in Jill getting badly hurt. Chip Ramsay decided he didn't want the publicity, and they somehow subdued Jill, then lied to Abigail about her whereabouts. But why was it important to keep Abigail on this island one extra day if they were going to let her leave? She just couldn't quite figure it out. And how did Bruce fit into it? Maybe because it was now clear that Bruce was not simply a guest here but a part-owner of this place and a close friend of Chip's. If the Quoddy Resort had decided to cover something up, then Bruce would have been part of that decision. And what about Eric Newman being here? Maybe that was just a coincidence. And then was it just a coincidence that Jill's ex-fiancé was here as well? If so, it was a huge coincidence. But what other possibility was there?

When she'd been younger, she and her father had played a game he called "What Movie Are We In?" They'd be sitting out in the backyard watching a flock of sparrows assemble on a tree, and he'd say, "What movie are we in?" and she'd say, "*The Birds*." Once, they'd spotted two men sitting in a car across the street from their house, and he'd asked the question, and she'd said, "*Home Alone*," even though he'd been thinking of *The Friends of Eddie Coyle*. Sitting in the woods now, she asked herself, "What movie am I in?", hearing her father's voice in her head. Definitely a thriller, she thought, maybe one of those cheesy 1980s infidelity thrillers. *Fatal Attraction*, or maybe that movie with Mark Wahlberg where he was stalking Reese Witherspoon. But did she really think she was in that kind of movie? She did earlier, but now everything had changed. Eric Newman scared her, but not as much as what she'd seen the night before, or the similarities between her situation and Jill's. No. It felt like she was in some kind of horror movie, and that things were going to get gruesome. Nothing was really adding up, and now here she was sitting in a clearing in the woods with a creepy sign. So what movie was she in? Not a classic slasher flick like *Friday the 13th*, but something weirder. And then she thought of *The Wicker Man*, not the terrible Nicolas Cage remake, although she had a soft spot for that film, but the 1970s original with Christopher Lee. Like in that film, she was on an island, and strange things kept happening, and she didn't trust anyone, not even her husband. She wondered if she was going to end up being burned alive.

The trees around her swayed in unison as a breeze cut through. The air smelled like pine and salt, and in the distance she could smell the fruity aroma of smoke coming from a chimney. And there was something else, the smell of tidal rot, of decay. She stared up at the sky through the trees. High above, birds drifted, and for a moment she closed her eyes and imagined that she could fly. It had been a recurring dream her whole life, the sensation of flying, of being plucked up by a breeze and riding an air current. She'd had the dream frequently when she'd been younger, leading Zoe to believe that Abigail had been a bird in her previous life. ("And I was a cat," Zoe would always say. "We would not have gotten along.") Right now Abigail was thinking about what she would give to be able to push off from the ground and float upward and away from this island of horrors. As it was, she would have to wait for a plane to arrive, something entirely out of her control.

She formed a plan. She would go back to the bunk,

not say anything to Bruce about her encounter with Mellie, and tell him she wanted to arrange for meals to be brought to the bunk. Then she'd just hunker down there and hope.

Please, God.

The plane would come tomorrow morning and she would be on it.

And once she was back on the mainland, she'd have some semblance of control again, and she could figure out what to do about the Bruce situation. It was a situation now, wasn't it? The words he'd said to her—*spoiled bitch*—and the way he'd said them, with what sounded like genuine hatred in his voice, had not left Abigail's head all morning. And he certainly had something to do with the cover-up of whatever had happened to Jill. The more she thought about him, the more she realized that she'd made a huge mistake getting married to a man she didn't know all that well. He was a stranger, after all, and she'd been blinded because he seemed kind, and old-fashioned, and generous.

And rich, Abigail, don't forget that.

Yes, and rich. There would be a time for Abigail to try to understand just how much that had played into her decision, but now wasn't the time.

And maybe there is a good explanation? Maybe Bruce isn't part of it?

Spoiled bitch.

Abigail stood. As much as she wouldn't have minded

staying longer in the woods, alone, she had made a plan and it was time to enact it.

The bunk was empty. It was what Abigail had been hoping for. She knew that she'd eventually have to face Bruce, but she didn't mind putting it off.

She went to the refrigerator and pulled out a container of fruit salad, plus the plate of cheese and meats that had been sitting there since they'd arrived. Then she grabbed a raspberry lime seltzer, taking a long swig directly from the bottle. She ate all the cheese that was on the plate, then picked the fruit she liked from the salad and ate that, too. After changing into pajama bottoms and a T-shirt, she crawled into bed, putting the seltzer bottle next to her. When Bruce came home, she'd just tell him she wasn't feeling well and that she wanted to stay in the bunk until the plane was on its way.

She couldn't sleep, so she propped herself on two pillows and watched as an oblong of light coming from the west-facing window worked its way across the duvet cover. She got out of bed, cracked the door, and peered around its edge so that she could see up to the lodge, wanting to make sure that Bruce wasn't coming down the slope toward the bunk. She didn't see anyone, so she shut the door and went to the closet that Bruce was using. He'd hung his clothes, but she couldn't immediately see where he'd put his empty travel bag. She looked on the shelf at the top of the closet, but it wasn't there, and then she found it on the floor of the closet, pushed toward the back. The closet was much larger than she'd thought possible; it was deep, and there was an alcove on the side with extra shelves. Abigail knelt, unzipped the leather bag, and ran her hands along the inside. His cell phone was there, and she pulled it out, turning it on. He'd changed his backdrop picture to one of the photographs from the wedding, a candid shot, both of them laughing on the dance floor. It felt like a moment that had happened in a different lifetime. She checked to see if the phone was locked, and it was. She'd watched him punch in his four-digit passcode a few times, but she couldn't remember it now. Besides, what was the point of unlocking his phone when there was no service on the island?

She put the phone back in the bag and felt around for anything else in the zipped-up side pockets. There was one paperback book, something academic called *Hierarchy in the Forest*. Abigail thumbed through the pages. There was an inscription inside the front cover:

> *To Bruce,*
> > *Good stuff here—*
>
> > > *Your brother, Chip*

Abigail assumed that was Chip Ramsay. After all, how many Chips did Bruce know? Not that it meant much to her. The subtitle was *The Evolution of Egalitarian Behavior*. She put the book back.

There were more items in the other interior pocket. An engraved lighter, an unopened package of Altoids, and an ornate silver ring of a man's face constructed of leaves, just like the face she'd seen on the sign in the woods. She stared at it, mesmerized and disturbed. The words "green man" popped into her head. She could picture a sign hanging in front of a bar somewhere, or maybe it was a pub sign from the trip she'd taken with Ben to England after they'd graduated from college. She couldn't quite put it all together, except that she now knew for sure that whatever was happening here at Quoddy Resort was tied in with her husband. It couldn't be a coincidence that he owned a ring—a ring he kept hidden from her—that had the same image on it as the sign leading to that clearing in the woods.

She returned the ring to its pocket in the travel bag and slid the bag back into the closet, careful to make sure it looked like it hadn't been disturbed. Whatever the ring meant, Abigail didn't want to spend the next eighteen hours alone in the bunk with Bruce. She didn't know where else she could go, but she didn't want to be here. She changed back into jeans and a sweater, looked through the window to see if she could spot him on the lawn, but it was empty. Even the archery targets had been taken down. A sudden horrible feeling passed through Abigail, more like an image, actually. That all of them—everyone here at the resort—were up at the lodge meeting to discuss what to do about Abigail. That's why it was so quiet outside, even on this beautiful day.

Her against them.

A part of her wanted to pack up as much food and water as she could carry and run into the woods, wait there. But wait there for what? For the plane? For some sort of rescue operation?

Movement caught her eye and Abigail spotted Eric, who'd probably just emerged from his own bunk, cutting across the lawn. Without thinking, she darted outside and went to him. As strange as it was, he was possibly a friend, maybe the only friend she had here.

"Eric," she half shouted as she closed in on him.

He stopped and turned. "Hey," he said.

"Can we talk?"

"Sure. I was just heading up to get some lunch. Do you want to join me?"

"Can we go to your bunk, actually? I know that sounds . . . It's not what it sounds like."

"Okay. Sure."

Together they walked back to his bunk. Eric was quiet, and she wondered what he was thinking. She hoped he wasn't thinking that she'd changed her mind about their relationship, but that was the least of her worries right now. They reached the door, and he held it open for her. Inside, it was laid out differently than her and Bruce's bunk, but with the same luxury feel. The walls were stained a darker brown, and there was a moose head mounted on the wall above the bed.

"Can I get you anything?" Eric asked, as Abigail sat on the dark green sofa near the unlit fireplace.

"No, I'm fine."

"What's going on?" He perched on the edge of a leather club chair facing her. He wore jeans and a faded Ween T-shirt, and there was something about his outfit, so casual, almost collegiate, that reassured Abigail. She had a brief, alarming flash of the two of them together in California, her sliding his jeans down his narrow hips.

"Remember when we were talking in the woods this morning?" she began.

"Uh-huh."

"And you said that you thought there was something strange about this island, something off."

"Yeah."

"Because there was no way it was a real business, right? That's what you said."

Eric nodded.

"Was there anything else? Anything else that you think is strange about this place? Or was it just that?"

He hesitated, and Abigail could tell that he was thinking, trying to decide what to say to her exactly.

"What is it?" she said.

"Sorry, I'm thinking. Why are you asking me these questions? What happened?"

"Well, for one, they're not letting me off this island."

"What do you mean?"

"I told Bruce I wanted to leave today, and he said that he'd arrange a plane to get us, but now he's saying it won't come until tomorrow morning."

"Uh-huh," Eric said, and she tried to read his expression.

"So I asked to use the phones that are here, the landlines in the lodge. I just thought that maybe I could make my own arrangements with another airline, or at the very least I could talk with my friend and she could look into it."

"And what happened?"

"The phones are out. They're not working."

"It's suspicious," he said.

"Are you just saying that, or do you agree with me? I need to know. I think I'm going insane here."

He pressed the heels of his hands against his knees and raised his shoulders, then after a moment said, "I'm going to tell you something I'm not supposed to tell you. It might have something to do with what's happening here and it might not, but either way I think you need to hear it."

"What is it?"

He stood nervously. "Ah, Jesus. So what I'm about to tell you will make you hate me, and that's the last thing I want, but it's the right thing to do."

"Seriously, what is it?"

"Okay. Just please let me tell the whole story before you judge. Okay?"

"Sure. Okay. Whatever."

"So when we met at the vineyard in California, it wasn't an accident. I was paid to meet you."

22

The sun must have gone behind a cloud, because the interior of the bunk dimmed for a moment, then returned to normal.

"What?" Abigail said.

"I was paid. To meet you." Eric's whole body was tense, but he was looking directly at her.

"Who . . . who paid you?" Abigail asked.

"I don't know exactly. I mean, I *know*. It was through my agent in San Francisco. I have an acting agent, even though he obviously doesn't get me work that often. But he told me that someone had seen my headshot and wanted to know if I was available for a job that wasn't exactly an acting job. It was good money, a *lot* of money, so I agreed to at least hear about it. I didn't talk directly with whoever was hiring me—it all went through my agent."

"And it had to do with me?"

"Yes," he said. "I was told who you were, and where you would be on the weekend we met. They would book a room for me at the same hotel, and my job was to try and get to know you, and to try . . ."

"And to try to sleep with me," Abigail said, her voice trembling.

Eric took a breath through his nostrils, his lips pursed. "Yes. Basically, that was it. I mean, I wasn't told I *had* to sleep with you or anything. I was just told that my job was to meet you, try and get to know you, and . . . seduce you. Then I was supposed to report back exactly what had happened. That was emphasized by the client, apparently. They wanted to know *exactly* what transpired."

"Jesus," Abigail said, and she couldn't think of anything else to say for a moment. Her mind was spinning, and her stomach hurt.

"I know," Eric said.

"It must have been . . . Do you think it was Bruce?" Abigail said. "I mean, of course it was Bruce. He was testing me. Jesus."

"I really don't know," Eric said. "That was part of the deal, my not knowing. I never met the client. I only reported back to my agent."

"And you weren't told why you were doing this?" Abigail said, feeling a flush of anger. "You didn't think to ask why you were being tasked with trying to fuck a complete stranger."

"I did think to ask. I *did* ask, actually," Eric said. "I just wasn't told, and, obviously, I feel incredibly guilty that I took the job. There's no excuse, but I needed the money. I know that's not good enough. I know that's not really a reason. And if I'm completely honest, I was intrigued."

"Yeah, I can imagine."

"No, hear me out. They showed me a picture of you, so I'd be able to recognize you, obviously."

"What was the picture from? Where'd they get it?"

"They showed me your Facebook page."

"Uh-huh," Abigail said.

"And even just looking at it, I felt something . . . I was attracted to you. Look, I know it's creepy, but I did."

"Did they *just* show you this picture? Did they tell you things about me? I mean, what else did they know?"

"They told me you'd like my acting background because your parents ran a theater. They said you liked old movies. They said you were funny. That's about it."

"Did they tell you my favorite poet was Poe?"

He paused, and Abigail could tell he was thinking about lying. "Yes," he said. "They did."

Abigail squeezed both her hands into fists and clenched her jaw. She let out a partial scream.

"I know, I know, I know," Eric said. "I know how you must feel."

"You don't," she said. "Trust me on that."

"Okay, I don't."

Abigail took a breath, told herself that she could feel rage later. Right now she needed to hear the full story. "So you memorized an Edgar Allan Poe poem in case I brought it up?"

"Yes. I mean, I knew that poem already, if that means anything. But I brushed up. I know it sounds terrible. It *is* terrible."

"And they never said why you were being asked to do this?"

"I asked, but my agent didn't say. When I was told that it was a bachelorette party, then, obviously, I guessed."

"You guessed that you'd been hired by my fiancé to see if I'd cheat on him?"

"Yes, it crossed my mind."

"And you did it anyway."

Eric, already perched on the edge of the upholstered chair, moved forward another half inch. "Listen," he said. "You don't have to remind me that what I did was despicable. I know that what I did was despicable. I knew it when I took the job, and while I was doing it, and afterwards. I'm trying to help you out now because I agree with you, something fucked up is happening here, and I think it probably has something to do with me, with what happened that night. But I'm on your side now."

"And is that why you came here? Because you were worried something bad might happen?"

"It occurred to me, of course. I mean, if what I was doing was helping your groom run a fidelity test, then you failed, obviously."

"Obviously," Abigail said.

"So I was surprised when I saw that the wedding was still happening. So, yes, part of my actions were because I was worried about you, but, really, the truth is, the other truth is, I really did fall for you that night. Or maybe it's just transference or obsession, I don't know. You do remind me of my wife who died, but that's not all of it. And maybe it had something to do with the guilt I had about what I was doing to you. I couldn't get you out of my mind. It was torture, and so I decided to come to New York to look for you, find a way to convince you that you needed to be with me."

"What about the wedding?" Abigail said.

"What about it?"

"You were there, weren't you? I think I saw you at the end of the night."

He let a breath out. "Okay, yeah. I wasn't going to approach you or anything. It's just . . . I don't know what I thought. I thought something might happen, because at this point it wasn't just about you and me, it was also about the man you married. As you said, he gave you a test."

"And I didn't pass," she said.

Eric smiled tightly. "No," he said.

"Did it occur to you that if Bruce was behind the whole thing, he might know who you were?" she asked.

"That's why I used a fake name. I came up with Scott Baumgart because of Scottie, of course, and Baumgart was my mother's maiden name. I was still paranoid that your husband would know who I was. It was partly why I talked with him on the beach. I needed to know if he recognized me, and I don't think he did. Then you went and used my real name."

"That's why you were freaked out. I could tell."

"Yes, I was shocked you knew my real name, but I also realized that if Bruce hired me, he might know it as well. I don't know if it matters now."

"Why do you say that?"

"You're clearly being punished, or you're about to be punished for what happened in California. That's why I'm telling you about this, because I think it has to do with what's going on here."

"What does it have to do with Jill Greenly and what happened to her?"

"I don't know. She's on her honeymoon, right? Maybe she failed some sort of test like you did."

Abigail nodded. "We talked some, Jill and I. There was an old boyfriend of hers here, and she was freaked out about it. It was strange because it was similar to my situation. I mean, what are the chances that there are two honeymooning brides at a resort—the only two honeymooning brides—and each of them has someone they've slept with show up unexpectedly?"

"But I actually *am* here unexpectedly," Eric said. "So maybe it's a coincidence."

"I keep playing that game with myself. The coincidence game. Trying to figure out if there's some kind of conspiracy going on or if I'm just putting all these things together."

"What things?"

She told him about the clearing in the woods, about the sign with the etching of the man's face made from leaves, and how she found a ring in Bruce's travel bag with the same face.

"He's a part-owner here, right?"

"That's what I figured, too. But why did he hide the ring from me?"

"Maybe he wasn't hiding it. Maybe he just doesn't wear it."

"See, now you're doing it. Making up excuses for all these things that don't make sense. Maybe the phone really is out. Maybe I really did dream I saw Jill Greenly outside my bunk—"

"That part we know is true. I saw her, too."

"So what do you think is the most logical explanation? What's your best guess?"

"If we assume that I was hired by your husband to test you, then he knows that you cheated on him. And if it was important enough for him to even set up the test in the first place, then he must have brought you here for a reason. He's going to punish you in some way."

"So what do you think I should do?"

Eric thought for a moment, rubbing a finger along the patch of hair under his lower lip.

"Tell your husband you know what he did, and that you're leaving him. And then move in here with me and we'll wait for the plane together."

"I'm not . . . I don't have feelings for you. If anything . . . I feel like I was raped by you."

Eric looked down at the floor. "I know. You should

222

hate me, but I'm telling you that you can also trust me. And it's also possible that I may be able to protect you for the rest of the time on this island. You can move in with me. It'll be the two of us, at least, against all of them. Not great odds, but better odds than you had before."

Abigail thought of Mellie's words earlier, how she'd told her to just hold on, that the plane would come. What would happen if she actually left Bruce in the middle of their honeymoon and moved into a bunk with another man?

"I don't know," she said.

"Then I have another suggestion," Eric said. "Go to Bruce and just tell him everything, ask him to tell you everything as well. Put it all out there and see what happens. It will be hard, but maybe there is some sort of logical explanation for everything that's been going on. Maybe he'll be reasonable."

Abigail, still thinking, nodded, not in agreement but because she wanted more time to think. The truth was, she wanted to stay here, in this bunk with this man, and wait for the plane to come. This, despite the fact that waves of horror were beginning to wash over her. She really did feel as though she'd been raped. Taken against her will, even though it had felt like willingness at the time. But even though Eric had been the instrument of that rape, Bruce was the architect.

"You okay, Abigail?" Eric said after a while.

"No, not really," she said, just as there was a knock on the door that made her jump.

Eric stood, said, "Wait there," to Abigail in a low voice, then opened the door. From where Abigail sat she could only see the shadow of the person standing in the door-frame, but she could hear the voice. It was Bruce saying, "I'm looking for my wife."

Eric, not hesitating, said, "Well, she's not here."

Bruce said, "Then you won't mind if I take a look around your bunk."

"Yeah, I do mind."

Abigail watched Eric begin to shut the door, then he was leaning hard against it. Bruce yelled, "Abigail, I know you're in there."

"Fuck off," Eric said, and leaned harder into the door, gaining a few inches. He turned toward Abigail, his skin red with exertion, his face questioning, then he lowered his shoulder and got the door to slam. He held it shut as Bruce hollered from the outside, repeatedly kicking at the door. Some of what he yelled was muffled, but Abigail caught words, including "liar" and "bitch."

She got out of her chair and went up close to Eric, whispered, "I'm going out the back."

"No, stay here," he whispered back.

"He's not going to give up. You need to show him the empty bunk."

"Come back, then. Later."

Bruce must have rammed into the door from the out-side, because Eric bucked back a little, then smiled.

"I'm going," Abigail said. "I'll come back."

"Promise."

"I don't know."

She opened the back door quietly and stepped outside. There was no back deck on this bunk, just a narrow oblong of landscaping and then the woods. As she approached the tree line, she heard Bruce again, his voice hoarse from yelling, shout, "Abigail, you fucking whore. I'm your goddamned husband."

23

For a while she walked blindly through the woods, just wanting to put distance between herself and Bruce. Tears filled her eyes, and she kept wiping them away, willing herself not to buckle over and sob, even though that was exactly what she felt like doing.

She had married some kind of psychopath, someone so paranoid and vindictive that he had hired a man to test her fidelity on her bachelorette weekend.

You failed that test, though, didn't you?

She ignored that particular voice in her head for now. Anger welled up in her. He'd wanted her to fail. He'd hired a handsome man, someone perfectly constructed to appeal to her, and that man had peeled her away from the herd, gotten her drunk, and seduced her. No, it was worse than that. It really was a kind of rape. She was sickened that she'd fallen for it, but even more upset that Bruce had set it up. And that Eric had agreed to it. Worst of all, she was still on this island.

You are still on this island because you failed the test.

But why did he even marry me? Abigail thought. If what had happened in California was a test to find out if she was faithful, she'd failed. Why hadn't he dumped her then? That was the part she was having a hard time understanding. There were only two possible answers. Either he'd forgiven her and decided to overlook the infidelity, or she was here to be punished. And if Bruce was so jealous that he set up some kind of fidelity test, then he was definitely not going to forgive her for cheating. So that left only one option. She was here to be humiliated and punished. *And* if she was here to be punished, then he must know that as soon as they got back from their honeymoon they'd have to go through a divorce, or more likely an annulment. It would be messy, whatever it was, so why had Bruce gone through with the marriage? There was a small voice in her head . . .

He's going to kill you.

She stopped and put her hands on her knees and filled her lungs with air. A single sob came out of her, one that hurt her ribs.

No, she told herself. *I know Bruce well enough to know he isn't a killer.*

But did she? She obviously didn't know him well enough to think he'd ever pull a stunt like he had in California.

You failed the test, and he's going to kill you.

No, Abigail thought. *There has to be some other possibility.* Maybe, just maybe, it wasn't Bruce who set up the test in California. Maybe one of his colleagues did it, someone he worked with who was worried that Abigail was a fortune-hunter. Or maybe Eric Newman was making it up and this was all part of his plan to win Abigail away from Bruce. She didn't think so, though it felt like the truth.

She was walking again, the woods thinning out a little, and she spotted a path, recognized it as the one that led down to the pond. She followed it, trying to slow down her thoughts, trying to concentrate on the fresh air and the colors of the trees around her. If she calmed herself, then maybe she'd be able to think more clearly. The path brought her to the pond, empty except for a single canoe on the west side, its single occupant fishing, casting into an area of the pond shaded by trees. The canoe was too far away for Abigail to see who was in it, but she did know one thing. It was a man. It had to be. What she would give for it to be a woman, some guest she hadn't met yet, maybe one of the women from Atlanta Chip said were scheduled for a visit.

Yeah, right, a bunch of women are coming to the island today.

She walked down to the edge of the pond, then took the shore path to the right, her eyes on the boathouse on the other side of the pond, and the lodge above it. Maybe it was only to have a destination, but she suddenly decided that she wanted to see the other camp. She knew it hadn't been occupied for years and that it hadn't yet been renovated, but she allowed herself a glimmer of hope that maybe it had an old functioning landline, or a CB radio, or anything that might help her communicate with the outside world. She picked up her pace, occasionally jogging, as she worked her way along the narrow gravel path that skirted the shore. She reached the boathouse, built near a tilting pier that jutted out twenty yards into the pond, and peered inside. The wood was rotten and speckled with dark moss. There were no boats inside, just a pile of old life jackets that looked as though they'd been chewed apart and turned into some animal's nest.

Retreating back to the path, she walked up a short incline toward the lodge. Like its neighbor across the pond, it was fronted by a large swath of lawn, this one now choked with weeds. There was a cluster of bunks adjacent to the lodge. They all looked decrepit—half were smothered by vines—but the lodge, maybe because it was primarily built of stone, looked sturdy and habitable. Abigail waded across the lawn. As she neared the lodge, she noticed that some of its windows were boarded up and that the handles on the front doors were entwined with chains and secured by a combination lock. She walked up to the doors anyway, tugged at them, and was able to peer through an inch-wide crack. It was dark inside but not impenetrable, and what she saw at first confused her. She was looking at trees, and she wondered if the back of the lodge had somehow collapsed. But there was enough light for her to see the stone floor of the hall and part of the back wall. She looked longer, and it was clear that the trees were props, their bases crossed pieces of plywood. There were enough of these fake trees to compose a fake forest. And in the dark interior of the lodge, it looked like a forest at night. There was one other object that Abigail could just make out. At first she thought it was some sort of jungle gym, but then she realized it was a cage, constructed of metal bars sculpted to look like twisting branches. She thought of the ring she'd found in Bruce's bag, the "green man" ring. Its band had been made to look like intertwined branches, just like the bars of the cage. She didn't know what she was looking at, but it terrified her just the same. Breathing in the air from the lodge, she could detect a faint piney smell and realized the trees were real, just cut down and displayed inside like Christmas trees. There was something theatrical about it, and that thought triggered a realization that came and went, a fleeting certainty that everything here on this island, every person, every tree, was part of a play, and she was the one unwilling participant.

She turned and took in the view. There was the pond, its heart shape no longer evident. The sky was now creased with a few darkening clouds, and a gust of wind rippled the yellowing grass of the sloping lawn. She envisioned them coming for her, men emerging at separate points from the woods, all converging. She walked quickly toward the nearest bunk and found its door open. She stepped inside, the air stale and acrid. Something fluttered in the rafters and Abigail looked up to see the blur of a bird leaving through a hole in the roof. The floor was warped from rain and pocked with bird shit. There were no furnishings left except for the frames of about ten iron cots. She thought about all the girls who'd slept here when the camp had been active, tried to conjure them in her mind, their faces and their voices, but she couldn't do it any more than she could imagine the boys who used to inhabit her own luxury bunk on the other side of the island.

The air inside the bunk tickled her throat and she stepped back outside, shutting the door behind her just as she saw Bruce coming toward her across the lawn.

She considered running, but there was no point. Instead, she forced herself to smile at him and wave. *Pretend that you were never in Eric's bunk*, she told herself. *Pretend you didn't hear his words.*

Fucking whore.

Spoiled bitch.

"I knew you'd be here," he said, when he was close enough to speak. He stopped and put his hands on his hips, as though the hike had exhausted him.

"I went exploring," Abigail said. "I was curious about this place."

"You don't have to pretend with me anymore," Bruce said. "I know you were in that man's bunk. Scott or Eric or whatever his real name is. It doesn't matter. We can talk about that later. I know all about him."

"What do you know?"

"Come back with me and I'll tell you," he said.

231

"You can tell me now."

"Okay. Whatever you want. I looked him up when it became clear that the two of you have some sort of relationship. I did some research."

"How did you look him up from here?" Abigail said.

"Chip did it, actually. Did you know your friend gave a false name when he registered for his stay, not something that's easy to do? His real name is Eric Newman. He's a murderer, or do you know that already?"

"What do you mean?"

"He wasn't convicted because they couldn't prove it, but it was pretty clear that the investigating officers believed he was guilty."

"I still don't know what you're talking about."

"He killed his wife on their honeymoon. They were at a resort and guests there reported that they'd been fighting. Apparently, he thought his wife was flirting with a male waiter. She drowned when they were snorkeling in shallow water. There were no witnesses, so there was no way to get a conviction. All the autopsy could prove was that she died from drowning."

"So maybe she did," Abigail said, not knowing how else to respond.

"I thought you'd probably defend him."

"I don't know why you're so convinced that he and I—"

"Because I know you secretly met the morning you went swimming, and because I know that you were in his bunk today."

Abigail was tired all of a sudden, sick of Bruce's accus-ations. She said, "So, if he's a murderer, then what you're saying, Bruce, is that you set me up with a murderer. You hired a murderer to try to fuck me in California."

Bruce looked genuinely surprised, his brow lowering, his mouth opening then closing. After a moment he said, "I don't know what you're talking about."

"You hired that man to try to seduce me at that vine-yard you sent me to. You set me up. Look, it's over. Our marriage is over. Whatever's happening here is . . . I don't know what this is, but maybe we can be honest with each other. I'm fucking scared, Bruce. Whatever you wanted, I don't think it was this. At least I hope not."

"He was with you at the vineyard?" Bruce said.

"Yes," she shouted, and Bruce flinched. "You sent him there."

Bruce was shaking his head. "No, no, no, no," he said, almost to himself. Then he looked up and said, "You actually slept with him? With that guy? In California?"

"None of that matters now. Our marriage is over."

"Yes, it is."

"Thanks to you."

He came for her, moving with sudden speed, his fist cocked back, his jaw clenched. Abigail was frozen, her body tightening in readiness for the blow. But it didn't come. Bruce had stopped himself a foot away from her. "Don't you dare blame me for you being a whore."

"Jesus."

"Tell me you didn't sleep with him."

"I'll tell you everything if you tell me the truth. Did you send him there—*did you pay him*—to seduce me? To get me drunk and fuck me?"

Bruce was shaking his head again.

"Why are you shaking your head? You either did or you didn't."

"My mother ruined my father's life," Bruce said quietly. "Do you understand that?"

Abigail decided it was time to leave, and walked purposefully past Bruce, expecting him to grab her. Even so, it shocked her when he did, his hand suddenly around her upper arm, his fingers digging in. "You knew how important fidelity is to me," he said. "I know you knew that."

"Let go of me, Bruce," Abigail said, trying to keep her voice steady.

He did, and she took a step away, wanting to rub her arm but not doing it. A dark, swollen cloud had dimmed the day suddenly, and a patter of rain swept in, then swept out again. "Maybe I did," she said, "but you set it up. You set me up."

She started back along the path toward the pond, expecting him to follow her. Instead, he shouted, "Don't worry. You're about to get what you want. That's why I came to find you."

Abigail stopped and turned. "What do you mean?" she said.

"I came to tell you that the plane is on the way. We're leaving this afternoon."

"Really?" Abigail said. Even hearing those words had made her heart start to race with the possibility they might be true.

"Any minute now, apparently," Bruce said, looking up at the sky. "We've got to go get ready."

She finalized her packing as fast as possible, feeling that any hesitation might mean the plane wouldn't come.

Bruce waited quietly on the couch, fiddling with the zipper of his own suitcase. The walk back from the girls' camp felt like it had taken forever. Bruce had been quiet, walking a step or two behind her.

She had wanted to ask him more questions, to get him to admit to setting up the situation at the vineyard, but she didn't want to upset him any further. The plane was coming. And getting on that plane was the most important thing right now.

After doing one last scan of the bunk, she heard the sound of the Land Rover coming down the row of bunks. "Chip's here," Bruce said.

She sat in the back with Bruce up front. Chip had grinned at her as he stowed their bags in the back of the vehicle, but he seemed agitated and jumpy. Periodic bursts of rain peppered the vehicle.

They drove out through the wooden gates of the resort and along the dirt road to the airfield. The rain had picked up, wind whipping it in several directions. It was later in the day than Abigail thought, dusk approaching. She worried that if they didn't get to the airfield in time the plane wouldn't be able to fly back in the nighttime. Did small planes fly at night? What about the wind and the rain? Would they fly in bad weather? She thought they probably did, but she was worried anyway. She'd be worried until she was far away from here.

There was no plane at the airfield when they got there, and Chip got out of the Land Rover to go into the hangar and check on its status.

The two of them alone in the car, Bruce turned around and faced Abigail. "You happy now? You're getting what you wanted." His voice had the same hushed tone she'd heard earlier when he'd called her a "spoiled bitch."

"I'm not happy, actually, Bruce, but I am relieved to be leaving here."

Chip came out of the hangar looking concerned, and a feeling of despair coursed through Abigail. The plane wasn't coming. It was too windy, or too rainy, he'd say. They were playing with her, and the plane would never come.

But then Chip was swinging open the passenger door next to Abigail and saying, "Your winged chariot is well on its way. In fact, I think I hear it."

Abigail got out of the car and looked up toward the sky. She could hear something, too, a low thrum, and then she could see the plane, cresting the tree line, growing larger, coming to take her away from here.

24

It was the same pilot who'd flown them to Heart Pond Island just four days earlier. She'd barely noticed him during that flight, but now she looked at him the way she'd look at someone selling ice-cold water in a desert. It was all she could do to stop herself from hugging him.

"This it?" he said, coming down the short steps from the plane to the landing strip and glancing from Bruce to her and back. He was young, with shoulder-length blond hair, and he wore a puka-shell necklace tight against his muscular neck.

Chip said, "This is it. Thanks for coming out here on short notice."

"No problem. Let me just use your commode and then I'll be ready to roll." He hurried off toward the hangar, just as the walkie-talkie on Chip's hip squawked. He plucked it off his belt, turned his back on Bruce and Abigail, and had a brief conversation that was obscured by a gust of wind, the second big gust that Abigail had felt since they'd walked out onto the landing strip. Abigail looked toward the horizon, where clouds were building.

"We got one more passenger coming," Chip said to them, reattaching his walkie-talkie to his hip. "My guests are dropping like flies." He smiled at them, Abigail noticing his weird flat eyes again, then turned toward Bruce. They shook hands, then embraced. "Take care, my brother," Chip said, and Bruce patted him twice, hard, on the back.

Abigail stood and watched their goodbye, hoping Chip wouldn't try to hug her, too. He didn't, but he did extend a hand her way and she took it, surprised by the softness and warmth of his palm. Like uncooked dough, she thought.

"Who's coming?" she asked, even though she already knew that it had to be Eric Newman. He was following them, or maybe he was simply taking the opportunity of the plane's arrival to escape this island as well.

"Scott Baumgart," Chip said.

"She knows his real name," Bruce said. "I told her all about him."

"I'm sorry if he came here and bothered you, Abigail," Chip said. "That sort of thing doesn't happen at Quoddy. At least it shouldn't. And I hope you won't mind flying back to the mainland with him. It's a short flight, as you know."

"It's fine," Abigail said, although she wasn't sure if it was. Still, it was far preferable to *not* getting on the plane.

Bruce looked at her, an expression on his face that she couldn't read. "I can tell him not to come," he said after a moment.

"It doesn't matter."

238

The pilot was hustling back from the hangar just as a jeep pulled up alongside Chip's Land Rover. Abigail watched as Eric got out of the passenger side, slung a backpack over his shoulder, and made his way toward them. Even at a distance his face looked grim and determined. Abigail wasn't happy to see him, worried that somehow his presence was going to stop her from getting on the plane, from getting off the island. He strode up just as the pilot arrived, and just as the jeep was making a U-turn and heading back to the lodge. "There's one more for you," Chip said to the pilot.

"No problemo," the pilot said, while at the same time Eric said, "It's actually just going to be Abigail and me," his voice unnaturally loud. Then Eric turned to Bruce, pointing an index finger at him, and said, "You're staying here."

"We can all go," Abigail said quickly. "It's fine."

Bruce laughed and said to Eric, "Uh, I can decide if I'm going or not."

"You're not going," Eric said. He turned to Abigail. "He was going to throw you out of the plane."

Bruce said, "What the fuck?"

Then Chip took a step toward Eric and said, "Whoa, whoa, what's going on here?"

"It's what they did to Jill Greenly," Eric said directly to Abigail, now lowering his voice as though it were the two of them having a private conversation. "They told her she could leave and then they threw her out of the plane."

The pilot laughed nervously. "Are you talking about the couple I took back yesterday afternoon? No one threw anyone out of my plane, trust me."

Eric looked directly at Abigail. "I talked to the woman who works at the lodge, right after you and I talked. Mellie. She told me that's what happened to Jill, that she was thrown out of the plane as a punishment."

"Mellie told me they're still on the island," Abigail said. Her stomach was starting to hurt so bad it felt almost like a cramp.

"Stop. Everyone stop," Chip said. "No one is throwing anyone out of a plane. I don't know what Mellie told you, but anything she says you should take with an enormous grain of salt. Let's just say that she is less than trustworthy."

"She told me that Alec and Jill are still here on the island," Abigail said again, hoping to establish just one fact that they could all agree on.

"I hired Mellie as a personal favor for someone, but she is a bit of a fantasist, to put it mildly." Chip turned to Abigail and said, "Alec and Jill Greenly are *not* on this island." Then he turned to Eric and said, "And Jill Greenly was *not* thrown out of an airplane. No one has been thrown out of an airplane. I promise that I will have a conversation with her and find out what exactly is going on."

"I don't care whether you have a conversation with her or not," Eric said. "I just know that I'm getting on this plane with Abigail, just the two of us." He turned and looked at her and said, "I don't care what you do when we land. I don't care if you don't talk to me again, but I need to see that you get safely off this island."

Bruce smiled at Eric, creasing his forehead, and said, "There is no way I'm allowing you to leave with my wife. It's not going to happen. So either shut the fuck up and we can all take this plane back together, or, if you say another word, then *I'm* not letting *you* on this plane. I think Chip will back me up on that."

"You hired me to sleep with your fiancée. You piece of shit."

"You murdered your wife," Bruce said. Then he turned to Chip and said, "Chip, can you call Bob and have him come and deal with this guy before I have to do it myself?"

"Why don't we let Abigail decide?" Eric said, then turned to Abigail and added, "Whatever you want, I'll do. If you want me to back off, I will."

All the men turned intently to Abigail. For a moment she felt dizzy and wondered if she was going to faint, but then it passed, and she just felt exhausted, and sad, her throat aching like she was about to cry. The rain had plastered her hair to her head, and she felt cold.

"I want to go alone," she said. "Just me. I want off the island." Once the words were out, she realized how badly she really wanted that. To be alone on the plane leaving this evil place, Bruce and Eric left behind. "That's what I really want," she said aloud. "I want to be alone, and I want to get away from here."

She looked at the pilot, who seemed to be enjoying the drama. He shrugged as if to say he'd be happy to take her alone. She nodded toward him. "You ready?" she said.

First the pilot laughed, and then Chip joined in. Abigail, confused, looked around. It was only Eric now who wasn't laughing, but it looked like he wanted to, his lips pressed together so tightly that they were the pale color of his skin, and then suddenly he laughed as well, an expulsion that came with a spray of spit. The terror that Abigail had been feeling all day ratcheted up a notch, even though she was also confused, wondering if she'd missed a joke somehow.

"Sorry," Bruce said, now laughing so hard he barely got out the single word. Abigail thought he was addressing her, but he was looking at Eric instead, who'd stopped laughing even though a huge smile still creased his face.

A small voice inside Abigail was speaking, telling them that she was still here, but the voice wouldn't come out. She was aware that her legs had begun to shake, and that there was a loosening in the lower part of her abdomen. Why were they all laughing?

"Look at her, poor thing," Eric said. "She has no idea what's going on." He turned back to Bruce. "She found your ring, you know. And she recognized it. She's already been to the sacred place."

"I think she's going to faint." That was Chip, and Abigail felt all the men's eyes on her at once. Another strong gust of wind blew in, everyone's hair and clothes rustling, even though no one was moving. It all seemed strangely vivid, almost like slow motion, the faces sharply etched so that every detail seemed equal to every other detail. Bruce's dark eyebrows, plucked in the middle. Eric's pale blue eyes. Chip's white skin, pelted with red hair. Specks of rain and mist in the air. And the pilot's soft giggle, erupting in little spurts even though you could tell he wanted to stop. They all swam in front of her, and the small voice inside her head told her that her best chance was to turn and run.

It was about fifty yards to the line of trees at the edge of the landing strip. Her legs felt heavy, but she moved them as fast as she could, the men's laughter still audible, even over the sound of her own frantic running.

She was almost to the woods when something large hit her back and she was dragged down onto the ground, her chin bouncing as she skidded painfully to a stop.

"Got her," came a yell about a foot from her ear, and then she was flipped forcibly onto her back. It was the pilot, and Abigail reached up, got a handful of hair plus part of the necklace, and pulled as hard as she could, his head jerking down, puka shells scattering, and a hank of hair coming loose in her hand. He gritted his teeth and grunted.

"Bitch," he said, and punched her in the chin. The world went briefly dark and unfocused and she squeezed her eyes shut. When she opened them again all of the men—Eric, Chip, Bruce, and the pilot—stood above her looking down. Bruce was grinning, his teeth clenched and his lips wide apart, and Chip was breathing hard, his beard now gleaming with sweat. Eric seemed blank, almost distracted. The pilot had both her arms pinioned to the hard, wet earth. She could feel the cold and damp seeping through her clothes.

"She wet herself," Bruce said, the words almost casual, like a stray observation, and it took Abigail a moment to realize he was talking about her, and that her jeans were soaked in her own urine.

There was a tapping sound and she swiveled her head. Chip was holding a large syringe, flicking at it with a finger. "Wait," she said, but the pilot held her tighter as Chip crouched, then pushed the needle deep into her neck.

25

For some time, she was nothing.

And then she was in darkness. She knew that even before she opened her eyes.

Someone coughed, and she lifted her head. A tide of nausea rose through her, and she put her head back down. And closed her eyes.

And then she was nothing again.

Coughing.

Not her own but someone else's. The sound of it wet and strangled.

This time when she lifted her head the world swam but her stomach felt okay. Wherever she was, it was complete darkness, the kind of black that has no form at all. There was the smell of damp in the air, and something else, a flowery smell she couldn't identify. She sat up, discovering that one of her wrists was handcuffed to the metal frame of the bed she was on. Her other hand was free, and with that hand she reached up and touched her face. She could feel a tender sticky scab on her chin where she'd been punched by the pilot. Her mouth was dry and tasted sour.

"Hello?" she said into the room, her voice sounding cracked and slurred in her own head.

"Hello," came a voice back, from maybe about ten feet away. A woman's voice, anxious, a little hopeful.

"Who's there?" Abigail asked.

"It's Jill Greenly." The words were whispered. "Is that Abigail?"

"Yes, it's Abigail. Oh my God, what's happening? How long have you been in here?"

"I don't know. What day is today?" And then Abigail could hear stifled crying.

"It's Wednesday, I think. Wednesday night or it might already be Thursday. It was Wednesday afternoon when they gave me a shot of something."

"Who gave you a shot?"

Abigail thought back to the events that had happened after the plane had come for them. Eric had arrived, telling her that he wanted to take her off the island himself. Eric and Bruce arguing, and then suddenly they weren't. They were laughing, all of them, and it was like she was in some movie, that moment when it's clear that everyone is evil, that the pod people are everywhere and there's nothing you can do about it.

"It was Chip," she said to Jill in the dark. "Chip who owns this place gave me the shot that knocked me out. But they're all in on it. My husband, and Eric, and everyone. They're all part of it."

"What do you mean?" Jill said. "Who's Chip?"

"He runs this place, but he's in on it."

"In on what?"

"All of it. All of them. I think we're here to be punished or something. We're the only women here."

Jill was quiet for a moment, and Abigail said, "You still there?"

"I'm here. That's what they told me, actually. They told me I was being punished for my sins."

"Who told you?" Abigail said.

"Alec told me the night I tried to run."

"I saw you that night. Outside of my bunk."

Jill started crying again. Abigail waited, even though she wanted to tell her to stop crying so they could talk to each other. She didn't know how much time they had.

"That was you?" Jill said at last.

"Yes, you ran away from me."

"I didn't know what . . . I didn't know what was happening."

"Why were you bleeding?"

"Alec . . . and Porter . . ."

"Porter was the man you used to be engaged to, right? The man who showed up here, and you were upset about."

"I don't know if I should talk about this," Jill said. "They're probably listening."

"So what? We need to know each other's stories. It can only help us."

"I don't know," came Jill's voice, quiet. Abigail thought she could hear her crying a little.

"Talk," she said. "Tell me everything that happened. Who cares if they're listening?"

"Okay," Jill said, after a period that felt close to a minute. "Okay."

"Take your time," Abigail said.

Jill started right away. She coughed, then said, "I didn't tell you the whole story when we talked that night. I said that Porter was a nice guy, basically, but he isn't. I mean, he was at first, but the more I got to know him, the more controlling he got, the more jealous. He told me that he didn't want me to work anymore as an actress, and that after we got married he would forbid me from working. He said it would make him look bad, like he wasn't able to provide enough money for the two of us, which was crazy because Porter's incredibly rich. I said that it had nothing to do with money, that I really did love acting, and wanted to keep doing it. It just got worse and worse between us. We fought all the time, but I kept flying back to L.A. for acting auditions. Then I got a job in Vancouver, a web series that was only paying minimum daily rates, but I told Porter I wanted to do it and that we should break up. He agreed to let me take the job, but he wouldn't agree to the breakup.

"I should have insisted, I know, but I just wanted to get away from him at that point, and the job in Vancouver was for three months. Anyway, in Vancouver I met this guy. He was a bartender, really good-looking, and I knew that at this point Porter and I were finished, so we got together, me and the bartender, just for one night. It turned out—and I know this sounds completely crazy—but it turned out that the guy, the bartender, had been hired by Porter to seduce me, that it was a kind of trap, or a test, and that he was reporting back to Porter."

"Uh-huh," Abigail said, wanting to hear the whole story, to keep Jill talking. Not wanting to compare notes yet.

"It was a nightmare, the whole thing. Porter flew out to Vancouver. Honestly, I thought he was going to kill me. This guy had told him everything, every detail of what we did, everything I said."

"Who was he? This guy? Do you know his name?"

"He gave me a name. I don't know if it was real or not. I never saw him again."

"What did he look like?" Abigail asked, wondering if it was Eric Newman, but thinking that that didn't make sense, that if it had been, then Jill would have noticed him on the island.

"He was beautiful. Hispanic. He looked like this guy from *Quantico*, that TV show. Aarón Díaz, you know him? The thing is, Porter knew this was my type, 'cause I'd told him once. He'd kept asking me, again and again, what actor I'd sleep with if I could, and I kept telling me no one, which was what I knew he wanted to hear, but he insisted, so I said Aarón Díaz just to shut him up. So I think he found this guy, maybe he was some kind of actor, who looked just like him, and set this trap for me. And the very next day this guy I'd slept with disappeared and Porter was in Vancouver and he kept me in my rental apartment for twenty-four hours, just yelling at me. I thought I was going to die—what I really thought was that Porter was going to murder me—but then he just left, and I didn't see him or hear from him again until I got here, to this stupid island, and he was here, too."

"And you thought he was stalking you?"

"*Of course I did.*"

"You told me, that night we talked about it, that it was random chance."

"That's what he told me. I didn't believe him, but I hoped. I also did have an issue with Alec, that I'd lied to him about all sorts of things, including my past relationships, but now I think . . . I know it's crazy . . . but I think Alec is part of it, too."

"They're all part of it, Jill," Abigail said. "That's why we're here. We're here to be punished."

"Oh God," Jill said. Then: "Why? Why are they doing this?"

"What happened the night you were bleeding?" Abigail asked.

"That whole day was a nightmare. I was supposed to meet you and go swimming, remember?"

"Yeah."

"I was getting ready to go, and Alec told me that I couldn't. It was so out of character for him, the way he said it, and I was like, What do you mean? He said he was making my decisions for me from now on, and that he'd decided that I wasn't going to leave the bunk that day. That I was going to spend all day there, naked, with him. He had this look on his face. It was slightly deranged, and I remember . . . I remember thinking that I'd made a terrible, terrible mistake marrying this man, and then I rationalized it, I guess. I told myself that what he was doing was kind of sexy. We were on our honeymoon and he was taking control, telling me he wanted me all day long, naked, just to himself. So I did it. We ordered all our meals to be delivered, and we had constant sex, and I kept telling myself how it would sound on paper, in a romance novel. It would sound great. *Halfway through their honeymoon they spent the day inside, completely naked, only with each other.* But it didn't feel like that. It felt like he was keeping me there, like if suddenly I decided that I'd had enough and wanted to go outside for fresh air he wouldn't let me, or that if I didn't want to have sex again, he would force me to."

She was quiet for a moment and Abigail didn't say anything.

Jill took a long breath. It sounded loud in the small damp room. "I took a nap, right after dinner, I guess it was. I was exhausted. Utterly exhausted, and now that I think back on it, I know I was drugged. When I woke up, hours later, it wasn't just Alec in the room. At first I thought he was talking to himself, or else talking on the phone even though the phones don't work here, but then

I heard another voice and I opened my eyes and Porter was in the room, and they were both standing over the bed looking at me. I was so confused and out of it, and I don't remember everything they said, but Alec kept saying something like, 'This is what you want, isn't it? Both of us together.' And he was kind of giggling. It was insane and I started to scream and Porter held me down, and that was when Alec bit me hard, under my arm. It was so painful that it woke me up a little and I was able to get Porter off of me, although I think he kind of let me go because he was laughing, too. And that's when I ran outside. I don't remember much of what happened. I was bleeding, and I was cold, and I think I was starting to hallucinate. All I know is that I felt the way I'd felt in college one time when someone had given me a pot brownie and it had gone bad. I kept hearing phantom sounds in the woods and I had no sense of time, and then I was wondering if I'd dreamt it all. After a while I knocked on some windows of the other bunks, just hoping that someone would come and help me."

"That's when I saw you," Abigail said.

"That was really you?"

"Yes, I saw you that night. You were bleeding and you asked me who I was and then you ran away. You don't remember that?"

"I do. Maybe. I didn't know it was you. You . . . you looked . . . in my memory, you were standing there and your face was not human. I could tell you were a woman by your voice, but your face was something else. I remember a muzzle and yellow eyes. And then the next thing I remember is being in the woods all night long, thinking that there were wolves everywhere. And then it was dawn, and they came and found me. They gave me some kind of shot, and then I woke up here. I've been here ever since."

She was crying again, great ratcheting sobs this time, and Abigail wished she could go to her. Instead, she occasionally made shushing sounds from across the room, not knowing if they were comforting. Jill eventually said, "Why are they doing this?"

"It's punishment. And because they can."

"But why are we here? What are they doing next?"

Abigail thought she knew what was coming. She'd been thinking it since she woke up in the blackness of this dungeon. She didn't know if she wanted to say the words out loud, but then she decided it could only help. They needed to be on the same page.

"I think they're going to kill us, Jill," she said. "It will probably be some sort of ritual, or a game, the way they've been playing a game ever since we both got here. But they *are* going to try to kill us. They can't let us off this island."

"What if we promise not to tell?" Jill said, and Abigail recognized that she was already bargaining with them. They weren't even here, although they could be listening, and she was bargaining.

"Maybe," Abigail said, and even saying that word out loud gave her a flicker of hope. "Maybe it's all just a vicious game."

"Besides, it'll be our word against theirs. They'll make it so no one will believe us." Abigail could hear the rising optimism in Jill's voice.

"Maybe," Abigail said again, "but we can't count on it. These are rich, powerful men and they can't have us accusing them of what's happened here. There's a good chance they are planning on killing us. We should try to find a way to get off this island, if we can."

Jill was crying again, quietly this time.

"But they can't kill us and get away with it," she said.

"They'll find a way. They're rich men, and they can arrange it. There'll be some kind of accident. Maybe an airplane crash or we drown. And there'll be no witnesses who say otherwise. That's why we need to survive. We need to tell this story."

"Okay," Jill said.

"If there's an opportunity to run, with me or without me, take it. Try to get away and hide somewhere on the island. Hide as long as possible and maybe you can outlast them."

"But only if they're really going to try and kill us, right?"

"Right," Abigail said. "We don't know what's going to happen."

Abigail listened to Jill breathe for a moment. Loud, damp breaths.

"Tell me your story," Jill said. "Why are they after you, too?"

Abigail began to tell her, not really wanting to, but knowing that it was better if they kept talking. Hearing each other's voice made it less scary. She told Jill about the one-night stand in California and how it had been a setup. She was still talking when she heard the hollow clip-clop of steps outside in the hallway, then the door was opening, light penetrating the darkness.

26

It took a moment for her eyes to adjust to the sudden light, but Abigail could see Chip filling the doorway. He wore a light brown collared shirt with a green vest over it, his red hair seeming to glow. Jill began to scream. Abigail turned toward her, instinctually reaching out before being yanked back by the handcuffs. Jill, now that Abigail could see her, was still dressed in the bloodied nightgown she'd been wearing when Abigail had last seen her. Her hair was dirty and matted on one side with pine needles. Chip said nothing, but went toward Jill, and Abigail heard a cracking that sounded a little like a slap. Jill stopped screaming, her body stiffening.

Abigail was now screaming, too, as another man entered the room—the pilot with the lengthy blond hair, holding what looked like an electric razor in his hand. She batted at him with her free hand when he got close, but he easily dodged her. Abigail saw that his lips were wet. He struck her in the chest and she heard a loud crack, her body surging with pain. All her muscles froze, and strange lights flashed in her vision. She thought she was dead and in that brief moment was struck by the ridiculousness of her death.

Then a hood was shoved over her head, everything dark again.

"You'll feel a little prick," came a voice, distant, mocking, and there was a sharp sensation in her shoulder muscle, almost as though she were being pinched. There was almost relief as the world went dark again.

Cold air moved around her, carrying voices with it. She lifted her head, and there was the semblance of light, yellow flickers cutting through the blackness. Her face itched, her skin was hot, and she began reflexively to shake her head. She felt a tug and the cloth hood that had been put over her head was pulled away. Squeezing her eyes shut, she found herself taking in deep lungfuls of air.

When she finally opened her eyes, the world in front of her tilted precariously and she shut them again. Her stomach roiled, and she thought she was going to be sick, so she leaned forward, pressing her head to her knees. It felt as though she was on a wooden chair, and it didn't seem as though she was tied up.

"Wakey, wakey," came a voice. She sat up, opened her eyes again, and kept them open. The scene in front of her slid into blurry place. It was nighttime. She was in the woods, and a cold wind was moving steadily through the trees. The right side of her body was warmer than the left, and she turned to find a fire in a pit, its flames almost as high as the men who stood around it. She squinted to bring them into focus, and one of them laughed, the sound familiar. Bruce, in a turtleneck sweater and jeans, the skin of his face yellow in the firelight. Oddly, disturbingly, he was holding a glass in his hand, what looked like a whiskey, as though he were at a party.

"Yep, she's awake," Bruce said.

Abigail wanted to say something, but when she went to move her lips they barely responded. She ran her tongue over her teeth and lips. Her teeth felt large and strange, and her lips were like rubber.

You drugged me, she said to the men, although the words were only in her head. She closed her eyes again.

She woke to laughter, and lifted her heavy head.

A man danced in front of her, his knees bent at almost right angles, hopping from foot to foot. She couldn't tell who he was because he was wearing a mask that obscured the top half of his face. Green leaves fanned out from the mask. Behind him was a cluster of men, rocking back and forth, some chuckling, and maybe it was the wind, or the drugs surging through her system, but their laughter seemed to come from somewhere else, from high up in the trees.

The world tilted. She squeezed her eyes shut, and blackness washed over her.

Seconds later—or was it hours?—she shivered awake, opening her eyes. For a moment she watched the men without them knowing she was watching. No one was dancing, and no one was wearing a mask; they were around the fire, their voices still dispersed by the wind. They weren't looking at her but at another figure, on the other side of the fire, also on a chair. The scene came into focus, and Abigail knew where they were. It was the clearing in the woods behind the swimming pool, the place she'd been to earlier that was called Silvanus Woods. How many men were there? She tried to count and got to five before the figures blurred again. One of them was bending toward the woman in the chair—Jill, of course—and Abigail watched a man pull a hood from her. She was slumped, and Abigail thought—with a rush of terror—that she was dead, but then she tried to stand, and the man pushed her back down by her shoulders, laughing. The man was Alec, her husband, dressed in a puffy ski jacket and with what looked like a cigar clenched between his teeth.

All the men were looking at Jill, and Abigail scanned them again. Besides Alec and Bruce, there was Chip, a bottle of beer in his hand, Eric Newman, also with a beer and smoking a cigarette, and Porter, wearing only a polo shirt and jeans, his dark skin gleaming in the firelight. She also recognized the pilot with his blond hair, who had given her the shot, and one other man with a large gray mustache, its tips waxed. The bartender named Carl.

She moved her legs a fraction to find out if she was bound in any way to the chair. Not that she thought she could run, not with whatever drug was in her, making her heavy and confused, but she still wanted to know. She moved her legs about six inches and felt pretty sure that the only thing holding her down on the chair was the drugs in her system.

She breathed deeply in through her nose, filling her lungs. The world still spun a little, but the nausea was gone and her head was a little clearer.

"Put on the mask, put on the mask," came a voice, not one she immediately recognized. More laughter, some of it seeming to come from behind her. She willed herself not to look around, lowering her chin slowly back to her chest, deciding to pretend that she was still passed out. *I'll just sit like this for as long as I can*, she thought. *The longer I delay what is happening, the more clear-headed I'll be. I'll fake it. It's not like I'm even sleepy anymore.*

A hand was tapping at her cheek, softly at first, then harder. She shook herself awake and swung out with a fist, striking a thigh. She heard loud laughter, then Eric's chiseled face swam into her vision, his breath sharp with the smell of French cigarettes, his eyes looking into hers.

"She's up," he said, and straightened so that she was now looking at the crotch of his jeans, a wide leather belt, a half-tucked-in flannel shirt.

Abigail took deep breaths through her nostrils again. It made her feel better. She rotated her head on her neck, pain radiating down her shoulders and back, and the world stayed level. *I feel better*, she thought, but lowered her head back down anyway, not wanting anyone to know that she was more conscious than they thought she was.

"No, no," he said, his voice oddly gentle as he tapped his fingers against her cheek again. "Stay awake for us."

"Where am I?" she said, trying to make her voice sound slurred, although it was coming out that way pretty much on its own.

"It's all just a dream," Bruce said, stepping forward to stand next to Eric. She watched him turn back to the men huddled around the fire, gauging their reaction to what he'd just said. They were all grinning, and Bruce turned back to her, a smile of satisfaction now on his face.

"It's like a terrible dream," she said, making her voice sound small, wondering if there was still a chance that she could gain some sympathy from her husband, or maybe even from Eric. But Eric was smiling and Bruce laughed, the same merciless sound she'd heard coming from him earlier by the plane. A barking laugh, like rocks being clapped together.

"Yeah, we all know about terrible dreams," came a new voice, and Abigail refocused her eyes on the speaker. It was Chip with his reedy voice, and all the other men, including Bruce, now looked at him. "How does it feel?" he said, pointing his finger at her.

He seemed to be waiting for an actual answer and Abigail shook her head slowly, suddenly panicking, as if she'd been asked a question in class that she didn't know the answer to.

"How does it feel?" he asked again, his voice louder. He took a step toward her. The fire was behind him, his shaggy beard and sloping shoulders outlined in flickering orange light. Next to him was the blond pilot, now holding the mask he'd been wearing earlier down by his side, tapping it rhythmically against his thigh as though it were a tambourine.

"How does what feel?" Abigail said, and the words came out loud and clear, although her voice sounded strange in her own head.

"How does it feel to be a modern American woman, to live an entirely privileged life, to be able to do everything you want to do, everything you feel like doing, and get away with it?"

Abigail said nothing.

"How does it feel to finally have to own up to your actions? Both of you."

Chip looked over at Jill and so did Abigail. They'd been moved closer to each other, although they were still about ten yards apart.

"Alec, please," Jill said, her voice almost a wail.

"Jill Greenly," Chip boomed. "You are charged with infidelity and wantonness. How do you plead?"

Abigail watched Jill, her head swiveling, her eyes wide. She looked like a panicked cat searching a room for its exits.

"How do you plead?" Chip said again, stepping in her direction, now pointing at her, his arm held high, almost above his head.

It's a trial, Abigail thought. *We're on fucking trial.* She felt a laugh rising in her that she knew was partly hysteria. She tried to suppress it, but it came out anyway. The eyes of all the men shifted toward her.

"We'll get to you, Abigail Lamb," Chip said.

She laughed some more, and Bruce said, "Keep your mouth shut."

She kept laughing, her shoulders hitching up and down almost spasmodically. Finally, with tears streaking her face, she said, "You bunch of fucking cowards."

Bruce bent and took a wild swing at Abigail's head with a closed fist. She leaned back and the punch missed, and because Bruce was bent over awkwardly, the punch spun him and he twisted to the ground, landing hard on his side. Eric helped him up, then held him back.

Abigail felt the laughter rising inside her again, but suppressed it, thinking that Bruce might just kill her on the spot if she laughed again.

"I trusted you," Bruce said, still being held by Eric.

"You set me up," she said. "People who trust each other don't do that."

"You fucked another man on a weekend to celebrate our wedding. On a weekend that I paid for." In the light from the fire she could see spit spraying from his lips as he spoke.

"Fine," Abigail said quickly, sensing that Chip was going to interrupt, that this was not the script he had in mind. "I'm a bad person. I'm guilty. But you didn't need to marry me. You didn't need to torture me and do all this."

"If I hadn't married you, then you'd have married some other man and made his life miserable."

"What does that have to do with you?" Abigail said.

"So you plead guilty, Abigail Lamb," Chip said, jumping in before Bruce could answer. It was clear that in some ways Chip was in charge. Even though he had no personal connection with either Abigail or Jill, he was running the show.

"Sure, Chip Ramsay," Abigail said back, copying his tone of voice. "I'm guilty as charged."

Chip reached out and gently tapped the shoulder of the pilot, who pulled his mask back over his head, then came around behind Abigail and placed his hands on her left shoulder. Eric came around to stand behind Abigail on her other side.

"And you, Jill Greenly, do you plead guilty, also, to infidelity and wantonness?"

Abigail looked over at Jill, who was quietly crying. She watched Jill slowly lift her head and nod, and then Carl was behind her, also wearing a mask that covered the top half of his face, leaving his mustache visible. The masks looked homemade, probably constructed with papier-mâché, then painted green; she had a sudden surreal vision of these men crafting them. Or had they simply found them in the camp's old theater department, some leftover from a production of A *Midsummer Night's*

Dream? Abigail turned back to Bruce, no longer being held back by Eric, and she tried to read his expression. He was excited, his eyes gleaming and his body rocking back and forth like a little boy who needs to pee. But there was also fear in his face, his jaw clenched, his neck rigid.

Jesus, are they really going to kill us?

A flush of cold desperation surged through her body. "Bruce," she said. "Make this stop."

His expression changed, his brow lowering, and for a moment she thought he might put an end to what was happening. Maybe it really was just a performance, designed to scare them, a form of theater as punishment. Then Chip raised his arms again and pronounced, "We sentence you both as whores, and assert our privileges as men to decree punishment in the form of death for both of you."

Jill raised her head and yelled, "Alec!" over and over, her voice growing louder and more hysterical. Carl, from behind her, grabbed at her mouth and covered it. Porter charged in and helped to hold Jill. At the same time, the pilot and Eric grabbed hold of Abigail's shoulders and arms and held her in place.

"Bruce, Alec," Chip said, and both men turned to him. "Are you each prepared to deliver the punishment?"

27

"We are," Bruce said, but Alec only nodded. His face was flushed, and Abigail realized that she hadn't heard him say a word since they'd been out here.

Chip reached into the front pockets of his vest and pulled a short knife from each. Abigail tried to wrench herself free from Eric and the pilot, but they held on to her tighter, pulling her up off the chair, each gripping an arm. Bruce took one of the knives from Chip and Alec took the other. Abigail struggled, flailing her legs, but the men were too strong. She could feel Eric's hot breath on her neck, and the pilot was digging his fingers into the soft flesh of her upper arm.

Looking toward Jill, Abigail saw that she was being held upright by Carl and Porter now as well. But she wasn't struggling. She looked like she was already dead, slumped between them like a rag doll.

Bruce was coming toward her and all Abigail could see was the knife in his hand. *I'm about to die*, she thought, and terror flooded her body again. She was cold, and felt all alone, more alone than she'd ever felt before in her life. She looked up from the knife to Bruce's face, which was still rigid, his teeth bared. She heard Jill groan, but didn't turn. Bruce pressed the tip of the knife against her chest, then pushed.

She felt pressure, but not much else. *It doesn't hurt*, she thought. *There's that, at least.*

Bruce pulled the knife out, and it made a strange, mechanical click. She still felt nothing. Just dizziness and the cold, terrible awareness that she was dying. He pushed the knife in again, laughing, and turned back to look at Chip, now standing alone, a look of triumph on his red face. Abigail looked down at her chest, and there was no blood. She still felt nothing, and then she looked at the knife, its blade bloodless as well.

Bruce was following her eyes, and he put his finger on top of the blade, pushed down, and the blade retracted into its sheath. It was a fake knife, something used in theaters. There'd been several of them at Boxgrove in the props department.

"Just kidding," Bruce said, and took a step backward.

Abigail felt her body go limp, collapsing so that she was only being held up by the pilot. Eric had let go of her and stepped away.

There was no real relief, just a wave of helplessness, coupled with rage. Bruce turned his back to her, did a half bow as Chip applauded.

"Fuck you," Abigail said, and it took everything from her to say those words, but the men didn't respond. The pilot let go of her and she sat back down in the chair. Her body felt as though it had been wrung out. All of her muscles burned. She looked over at Jill, now sitting back in her chair, too. Carl had taken off his mask and he'd just fist-bumped with Alec and then with Porter. Alec, still holding the knife, was swaying in place, his face hard to read. Carl and Porter walked back to Chip as Alec continued to stand over Jill.

"You really thought I was going to kill you?" Bruce said, and his voice was too loud, as though adrenaline was still flowing through his body.

Abigail said nothing. Her throat ached, and she could feel a sob rising through her, but she didn't let it come out. The men, regrouped now, were comparing notes, laughing. She watched them, wondering what was going to happen next. Would she be expected to get on a plane with Bruce, leave the island? What would stop her from telling this story to the police, or to a reporter? Although at the moment she didn't care about all that; she just wanted to get away, to go home, to forget everything that had happened.

"Alec?" It was Porter's voice. He was stretched to his full height, looking through the fire to where Alec still stood with Jill. The other men had begun to look, and Abigail turned her head, knowing, from the tone of Porter's voice, that she was about to see something she didn't want to see.

Alec held a jagged rock in his hand and was slowly battering Jill with it. Or maybe he wasn't doing it slowly, but it looked that way, his arm raising and lowering while the world froze around him. Everyone was silent; there was just the sound of the rock thunking into the side of Jill's head, as he propped it with his other hand. Then he untangled his hand from her hair and brought the rock down in a long sweeping motion, hitting her on the jaw and knocking her off the chair and onto the ground. He dropped to a knee and hit her three more times with the rock, bringing it down harder each time. No one moved, but even if someone had, it would have been too late. The final strike had produced a sickening crack, and one of Jill's legs was spasming.

Porter came around the fire and grabbed Alec from behind, lifting him up and away from Jill. All the men followed, forming a semicircle around Jill's body. Her leg had stopped twitching, but Abigail got a clear look at her destroyed head in the light from the fire.

"Jesus," Chip said, his voice with a hint of actual fear in it. Bruce was staring down, a hand over his mouth. The pilot pushed his mask off his head and it fell to the ground beside Jill.

Abigail stood up on weak legs. She thought everyone would look at her, but they didn't.

A voice in her head said:

Run.

You're a witness, and you need to run.

Chip grabbed Alec's face and held it. "What the fuck, Alec? What did you do?"

Run.

Abigail took two steps away from the chair. The men were only looking at one another.

They have to kill you now, she thought. *Whatever chance you thought you had that they'd let you off this island is now gone. You're a witness to a murder.*

Run.

But instead of running, she simply walked, putting one foot in front of the other, down the path that led out of the woods. She turned a corner, the path now dark because the fire was obscured by trees, then began to run, tripping on a root but managing to stay upright, her toe zinging with pain. The building that housed the pool and spa loomed suddenly in her vision on her right, its structure visible in the moonlight. She slowed a little; she hadn't thought this far ahead, did not know immediately in what direction she should go. What exactly was she doing? Should she try to find someone—a staff member—and tell them what had happened? No, she told herself. Even if some of the staff didn't know what went on in the woods late at night, that didn't mean they would suddenly take her side. Very rich men owned this place and did what they wanted on it. She needed to get off the island. It was her only chance.

She stopped completely for a moment. For right now she needed to hide, to get somewhere where they wouldn't find her. And then she could figure out what to do next.

Should she run into the deep woods down near where the bunks ended? Or toward the pond and around it to where the old girls' camp was? Or should she double back around the lodge, try to hide in the building with the swimming pool, or in the lodge itself?

She ran across the front of the lodge, wondering if it was empty, if everyone on the island who hadn't been to the ceremony was asleep in their beds. She was still wearing her Fitbit and checked the time. It was just past one in the morning. She thought she heard a voice behind her but didn't dare look back, and when she got to the lodge's farthermost side she cut right, deciding that doubling back was the best option. It would keep her away from the open lawn where they could see her, and maybe the move was unexpected enough that she'd get away with it.

She was also already winded, her lungs burning and her limbs weak. At the back of the main lodge she stopped for a moment, listening to the night and not hearing anything. Deciding to take the risk, she moved quietly up the back wooden steps and tried the rear door of the lodge. It swung open and she stepped inside into the dark.

28

She stood as still as possible at the side of the lodge's great hall. It was dark, except for a light from the balcony level that cast down, painting the wooden floor with a few yellow bars. Abigail thought that it was a light kept on all the time. At least during the nighttime hours. The lodge was silent, no voices, no sound of movement. She told herself that if someone entered through the front doors, she could slip quietly back through the hallway she'd come in and make her way down through the tunnel that led to the swimming pool. From there she could exit back out into the night and enter the woods.

But for right now she thought that she was alone in the lodge, and that she might be alone here for a little while. *They'll be looking for me outside*, she thought. *Scouring the woods*. Maybe this was all part of the plan—to kill one woman and let the other escape so that they could hunt her. But Abigail didn't think so. She'd watched Alec murder Jill, and she'd watched the reaction of the other men. It was not supposed to have happened. They'd find a way to cover it up, of course, but that meant Abigail was a witness. They would need to find her.

The panic began to rise from her stomach up to her

throat, and she told herself to breathe, told herself that she was still alive.

Not only that, but she had done something smart, hadn't she, by turning around and hiding in the lodge? She'd fooled them, temporarily.

She wondered what to do next. The thought of running exhausted her. Whatever drugs they'd given her were still in her system, weighing her down, making her thoughts fuzzy. Also, as she kept reminding herself, there was nowhere to run to. She was on an island, and she didn't trust anyone on it. Not the other guests, nor the detective, nor the staff members. Maybe she trusted Mellie, who'd at least tried to warn her, but that didn't mean Mellie could do anything to help. So maybe the best move was to hunker down and hide, use time to her advantage. If they couldn't find her they'd panic. Maybe they'd make a mistake. Still, she knew that if she wanted to do that—to go to ground, so to speak—she needed food.

Without thinking too hard about it, she walked through the dining room, then pushed through the swinging double doors into the kitchen. It was dark except for under-lighting below the cabinets, just enough so that she could make out the gleaming configuration of high-end kitchen equipment. On the back wall she saw two large refrigeration units and moved in that direction.

Inside the first one she spotted a hunk of cheese wrapped in cellophane, plus a bag of apples. She added the cheese to the apple bag and took it with her, grabbing the largest butcher knife she could find on her way back through. She had food and a weapon and realized that she also needed water. Deciding she didn't want to stay inside the lodge any longer than she had to, she went to one of the massive stainless-steel sinks, turned on the faucet, and drank directly from it, filling herself with as much water as she could.

She walked back the way she had come, going through the hall, then along the adjacent hallway, pausing as she realized that the office, with the phones and computers, was right above her. Was it worth checking? Clearly they had done something to make her think that the phone system was down earlier, but maybe it would be up now. Maybe she'd be able to make a call. Steeling herself, she took the stairs, every creak almost stopping her heart, but on the second-floor balcony she found that the door to the office was locked. She turned to go back the way she had come, then froze as she watched a door down the hall swing open, a wedge of light spreading across the floor. The person who emerged was dressed in a long white robe and turned in the opposite direction from Abigail, sliding the door shut behind them, then swinging the adjacent door open and disappearing again. The light wasn't great, but Abigail felt pretty sure the figure had long hair, which didn't mean much, but whoever it was also had very narrow shoulders. If it was a woman, then it had to be Mellie. The more she thought about it, the more she was convinced it was Mellie. It made sense that as an employee she would sleep in the lodge, and the room next to hers was most likely a bathroom.

Abigail couldn't decide what to do, and then suddenly she heard the muffled sound of a toilet being flushed, and the person was back in the hallway. Moving as quietly as possible, she ran forward, quickly seeing that it really was Mellie, who was now watching Abigail approach.

"Shh," Abigail said, holding a finger in front of her lips as she got to Mellie, who looked confused and half-asleep.

"Ab—" Mellie started.

"They killed Jill," Abigail whispered, interrupting. "Her husband just beat her to death with a rock. I saw the whole thing."

Mellie was pale in the dim light, her eyes wide. "I can't help you," she said, stammering a little. "You need to get away from here."

"I can't. That's what I'm telling you. I was a witness to a murder."

"I'm sorry," Mellie said, taking a step backward. "No one here can help you."

"Listen to what I'm telling you. I've been drugged and beat up. It was some sort of elaborate joke, but then Alec Greenly really did kill his wife. I saw the whole thing."

Mellie was shaking her head, her eyes darting, as though the two women were being watched. "I believe you," she said, her voice now a whisper as well. "Everyone who works here knows the things they do. But listen to me: no one here will help you."

"I'm not asking about someone else, I'm asking about you."

Mellie was shaking her head again, and her chin had begun to quiver. "There's nothing . . ."

She stopped speaking because the front door of the lodge had swung inward, and the beam of a flashlight was slicing across the great hall. Mellie gripped Abigail's arm and pulled her into a narrow bedroom, dark except for the moonlight coming through a large screened window. "Go out the window onto the roof. It's only about a five-foot drop to the ground." She was raising the screen, carefully, so as not to make any noise.

"Can't I hide here?" Abigail whispered.

"I can't. No. Please leave. I won't tell them you were here, but that's all I can do."

Abigail thought she heard footsteps on the stairs that led up to the second level, and she swung a leg through the window, sliding out onto a slightly angled metal roof. She carefully worked her way down to the edge and saw that Mellie was right, it was only a short drop. She gripped the edge of the gutter and lowered herself down as she heard the screen sliding back into place. It was quiet outside, lighter than it had been in the lodge. The moon, not covered by clouds, allowed her to see fifty yards toward the tennis courts, surrounded by woods, and to her left was the road that led away from the camp and toward the airfield. She skirted the building, moving to her left, until she got to its edge, then ran low and fast across the road and into the woods on the other side.

The ground here began to slope down toward the pond, but instead of heading in that direction she picked her way through the trees toward the back side of the row of bunks. She heard a shout behind her, probably the man who had nearly discovered her in the lodge, but she didn't think he'd have any idea which direction she'd gone. As she moved through the woods, she saw the beam of another flashlight sweep across the surface of the pond. She kept going until she reached the back of the first bunk, wondering if all of them were unlocked, imagined that they were. Her plan was to get inside one of them, so long as they were empty, and to hide either underneath a bed or in a closet. Eat her food, try to get some sleep. If she could survive through the next day, then she'd have another night at her disposal, and she had already formed a plan, weak as it was, for how she might actually get off the island. But she needed to make it to tomorrow night for that to happen. She needed a hole to hide in.

She recognized the back deck of her own bunk, decided to try the bunk directly next to it, then changed her mind.

No one would think she'd return to her own bunk, would they?

29

Maybe her own bunk was the best place to be. And then she remembered the closet, the one that Bruce was using, and the extra space toward the side, the alcove with the shelving. She climbed the three steps to the deck and opened the door. It was dark, but she knew the layout. Even so, she stood for a moment, getting used to the blackness, listening to make sure she was alone. Before hiding she thought it would be a good idea to use the bathroom, and maybe to get some water. She peed first, the sound of it thunderous in her own ears, then forced herself to flush. Afterward, she stood in the bathroom, waiting to see if the sound had given her away. But no one came. No alarm went off. No spotlight flooded the bunk.

She went to the wall that hid the refrigerator and debated whether it was worth it to slide it open and grab a bottle of water. No one had heard the flushing of the toilet, but it was far more likely that someone might see light from inside the bunk, especially since all the bunks were so dark. She decided not to risk it and went to the closet instead.

She pulled the door closed behind her and slid into the large alcove off to one side. It was an even better hiding place than she'd remembered, about three feet of empty space with shelving built into it to hold extra linens and pillows. But underneath the shelving there was enough space that she could push herself back into the corner, even sit up a little. With her feet tucked under her, the only way she could be spotted was if someone peered inside and looked directly into the corner. It was risky, she knew, but she was counting on the fact that everyone would assume she had gone into the woods to try to escape. Would they look for her here? They might, but not immediately. Not until they'd convinced themselves she wasn't hiding in the woods.

She pulled a pillow from the shelf and settled herself into the pitch-black corner. She thought of eating some cheese and an apple, but she wasn't hungry. She stowed the food and the knife below the pillow and leaned back, closing her eyes. She didn't think for a moment that she'd be able to sleep, but she must have dozed off, because she was woken by the sound of movement in the bunk. She braced herself. Were they searching for her, or had Bruce come back to the bunk to sleep?

There was the flush of the toilet, then water running, then there was silence for a long time, broken by the sound of three quick coughs. Bruce's coughs, easily identifiable.

She slid the knife out from behind the pillow. If he did step into the closet in order to search it, she'd have the jump on him. She could strike out with the knife, maybe slash at his Achilles tendon.

She listened some more. Nothing, and then there was the faint rumbling of snoring. She relaxed. He was a deep sleeper, and she knew that once he began to snore, waking him was extraordinarily difficult.

Go kill him.

She ignored that voice in her head, loosened her grip on the knife.

It would be easy, though, sneaking out of the closet, plunging the knife into his chest while he slept. But how would that help her?

He tortured you.

And it would feel good.

It wouldn't help her get off this island.

One less person looking for you.

She loosened her grip on the knife, stretched the muscles in her neck.

Imagine how it would feel.

So she let herself imagine it. Standing above the bed, Bruce on his back, the way he usually slept, one hand touching the side of his face. She'd have a choice: either the exposed neck, or straight to the heart. But it wasn't what she wanted to do. Her goal right now was to survive. To tell her story. Tell people what they'd done to her, and what had happened to Jill.

She settled herself back onto the pillow, then realized she was hungry. She ate half the cheese, almost passed on eating an apple because of how loud it would be, but then did it anyway, chewing quietly and making sure she could hear Bruce's snores while she was doing it.

She wrapped all the food back up, hoping that the smell of the cheddar cheese in the small space would dissipate, then closed her eyes again, drifting in and out of sleep until she heard a loud knock on the bunk door.

"You found her?" came Bruce's querulous voice, muffled but clear. Abigail could hear the hope in his question. He was out of bed and at the door.

There was a response, but she couldn't make out the words, then Bruce said, "You searched the girls' camp?"

Again, she couldn't hear whoever he was talking to. "Fine, I'll be right up," Bruce said, and then there was the sound of the door closing. He moved about the bunk, using the bathroom, grabbing some food from the kitchen. She thought maybe she was going to be spared the terror of his going through the closet, but he swung open the door, quickly rattled through some of his hanging clothes, grabbed something, and left, leaving the door open. She held her breath, then listened as he opened the front door and shut it behind him.

Abigail stayed crouched, barely moving, in the closet for what felt like an hour but was probably only fifteen minutes. Bruce had been headed to the main lodge, probably to discuss strategies for finding her. It was possible that he'd be back, but she doubted it. The search was the most important thing, and if they didn't consider it a possibility that she was back in her own bunk, then she was safe, at least for a while.

It suddenly occurred to her that Bruce had opened the closet in order to get some clothing. She wondered if after she'd been subdued at the airfield he'd come back to the bunk and unpacked again. Or had he never packed in the first place, simply bringing along his empty suitcase as a ruse? And where was her suitcase now? Somewhere in this bunk, or in the lodge? She'd been thinking so much of the nightmare by the firepit that she'd almost forgotten that horrible moment at the airfield when she realized that she was simply a pawn in a cruel game. A bunch of men wanting to humiliate a woman. Or two women. Her and Jill. First play with them, then humiliate them, then make them think they were about to die. Abigail briefly thought about that moment, the fake knife, the certainty that her life was about to end, and the cold helplessness she had felt. And then she pushed it from her mind. What she needed to think about was how to get off this island. She wondered if she could play a waiting game of sorts. Hadn't Chip said that a bunch of guests were due soon? No, that was most likely a lie. Even though this place probably had genuine guests, the real purpose of this island was as a place for a bunch of rich, sadistic men to toy with women. It was off the grid. No doubt the staff had to sign nondisclosure agreements. She would need to get off the island, one way or another.

Why had she not figured it all out earlier? Why had she not been immediately alarmed by the fact that the island was almost entirely populated by one gender? She remembered a story from childhood, a frog getting boiled alive in water that was slowly getting hotter and hotter, so slowly that he didn't notice. Maybe that was her excuse. There were signs, but they were little ones. And now the water was boiling.

What movie am I in? she asked herself. She was hiding in a dark closet, and that made her think of *Halloween*, but that wasn't right. She wasn't being hunted by one psychopath, but by a group of them. In truth, it felt as though she were in a zombie movie, except the horde chasing her weren't zombies. But that's what it felt like. She was in a bad dream being chased through the dark.

As terrified as she was, there was a part of her that felt strangely alive. The fact that Bruce had spent the night just twenty feet from where she was hiding gave her a giddy sense of elation. She'd outsmarted them. It might be temporary, but she'd come this far, and, more than anything, she wanted to get off this island. It was her only purpose. Survival. Then revenge. And it was a purpose that she didn't feel as though she was only trying on, like a new dress, or a new job, or a new boyfriend. This purpose fit her. She felt, right now, like all her life had been leading to this moment, crouched in the dark, a knife in her hand.

She crawled from the closet, then stood up, her knees clicking and her muscles stiff. The curtains at the front of the bunk were half pulled, but it was dawn outside, early morning light filtering through. She stretched her back and her legs, then used the bathroom. Peering out through a crack in the curtain nearest the unmade bed, she spotted someone crossing the lawn, dressed in jeans and a hooded sweatshirt. He was too far away for Abigail to see who he was, or decide if he'd been one of the men who'd tortured her the night before. Even if he wasn't, though, what difference did it make? Mellie hadn't helped her and that meant no one would. She needed to wait until nighttime again. Her job right now was to survive the day, get some food and water inside of her. She was in the best place for that. If Bruce, or someone else, did decide to search the bunk, then she'd most likely be found, but not before she could do some damage with the kitchen knife.

She grabbed the apples and the cheese from the closet and brought them to the refrigerator, shoving the bag way in the back of the vegetable crisper. Even wrapped in cellophane the cheese smelled too sharp and it was too much of a risk to keep it in the closet. She drank a bottle of water, then ate a yogurt, hiding both containers at the bottom of the trash. In one of the cabinets in the kitchen she found an opened bag of smoked almonds and ate two handfuls, then took a risk and opened a package of some all-natural salmon jerky, eating about three pieces, then shoving the package toward the back of the cabinet. Chewing the smoky fish, she was suddenly struck with how good it tasted, amazed that she was finding pleasure in the food, and then just as suddenly she remembered what was happening to her and how slim her chances of survival were.

Saliva pooled under her tongue, and the food started to come back up. She bolted toward the bathroom, but once she was kneeling in front of the toilet the feeling passed and she wasn't sick.

She returned to the closet to wait, curling herself into a ball as though she were a hibernating animal. Something hard pressed against her hip bone and she dug into the front pocket of her jeans and pulled out the small stone that she'd kept from the beach when she'd been building that pile of stones. She rubbed her thumb on the stone's smooth surface. It was too dark for her to look at it, but she remembered the stone well. An almost lucid white with a light red ring that went all the way around it. She curled up again, this time with the stone gripped tightly in her hand.

30

Abigail slept intermittently throughout the day, at times allowing herself to stretch out along the closet floor.

In the afternoon she was hungry again and forced herself to make a brief foray into the cabin's kitchen area for some more food, plus another bathroom break. It took her all of about five minutes, but her heart never stopped speeding the whole time.

When she wasn't sleeping she tried to keep her thoughts ordered, following her father's system and breaking down her problems into pieces, forming lists. Still, she kept imagining what they were going to do to her if they caught her. And she kept seeing Jill, her skull broken, her leg spasming, dying by the light of the fire. The image of it went through her mind on repeat, like a catchy scrap of music, and eventually she stopped trying to block the bad thoughts from coming. Along with terrifying her, they also provided motivation. If she could somehow survive this . . . this thing that was happening to her, then she'd tell her story, make sure these men were locked away, so that it would never happen again.

Her other motivation was her parents, their faces flashing through her mind at odd intervals. She kept thinking of what their lives would be like when they learned that their only daughter had died on her honeymoon. It filled her with a terrible grief. They had already lost each other, not completely, of course, but partly. She knew that her death would be a final blow to them both. They would grow old with no one to take care of them, and that thought alone made her determined to make it off this island, to survive.

Another persistent thought—or was it a dream?—was that her death on this island would mean the death of her own children, children who didn't exist yet. She could almost picture them, almost feel the desperate, scary love that they would arouse in her. They were teetering in the ether right now, as was she, as were her parents, all subject to a crazed, entitled coven of men. *Survive*, she told herself, *survive*.

She didn't know the exact time that Bruce returned at night, but she thought it was about eight o'clock. It had been dark inside the bunk for about three hours. He entered and slammed the door behind him. At first she wasn't one hundred percent sure it was him, but then he coughed and she recognized his sharp hack. She was squeezed into the closet gripping the knife and taking some satisfaction in the fact that she had managed to hide out for an entire day, and that no one had thought to look inside the bunk.

Bruce, after rustling around in what she thought was the kitchen, came briefly to the closet, pulling out his suitcase. She wondered if he was packing, but he didn't grab any of his clothes from their hangers. He did, however, shut the closet door.

He went out again, and about two hours passed. At one point, Abigail thought she heard the distant roar of an airplane overhead. Was it possible that Mellie had done the right thing and alerted the authorities? It gave her a brief feeling of hope, but it was short-lived. Mellie hadn't called anyone. If anything Mellie was probably helping them look for her. That airplane above was probably just passing by, and if it was stopping on the island it would probably be bringing reinforcements, more people to search for her.

She told herself not to speculate, that it wouldn't help her. She concentrated instead on remembering exactly how to get down to the boathouse at the edge of the pond, and from there how to get to the rocky cove where she'd walked with Bruce just a few days earlier. Even though she'd been following him, she could remember the direction they took, up through the woods onto the bluff, then east along the edge of the island to the embankment that led down to the cove. She remembered the entire walk taking twenty minutes, thirty at the longest, and she thought she could do it at night, especially if the moon was out.

When Bruce returned, she listened as he went straight to bed. Snores began almost immediately, and Abigail told herself to wait thirty minutes just to make sure he was truly and deeply asleep.

A part of her wanted to stay another day in the bunk. It felt safe here, and maybe, just maybe, help would eventually come. But she knew that she needed to make her break tonight, that another day inside would make her pursuers decide to search *everywhere*, including inside all the bunks. And then she heard a sound, unidentifiable at first—she almost thought it was an engine catching—but then, unmistakably, she realized it was the sound of a dog barking. A faraway sound, probably from the lodge. And then it stopped.

So maybe a plane actually had landed on the island, bringing a dog. Or, more likely, several dogs. She only hoped that they wouldn't deploy them until morning, that they'd given up hunting for her for the rest of the night. It was time to make her move.

She crawled out from under the shelf in the alcove and stood up in the closet. She held the knife in her right hand and pressed her ear against the closet door. The snores coming from Bruce were deep and regular. Even so, she turned the doorknob as slowly as possible and swung the door open, worried it might creak, but nothing creaked here at Quoddy Resort, all its hinges well oiled. The interior of the bunk was dark, but less so than the closet, and she could see Bruce's shape under the blankets on the bed. There was silvery light coming through the windows where the curtains didn't meet, and she thought that that boded well for a clear night.

After taking two steps toward the back door, she

doubled back in order to close the closet, worried that Bruce might wake up and notice that the door he'd closed was now open. She pushed it slowly shut until she heard a click. She was making her way toward the door again when she realized that Bruce was no longer snoring; she turned back to look at him. He was standing at the edge of the bed, his face obscured by the darkness.

"Hi, Bruce," she said.

He shook his head once and came after her in a rush, bent low and making a strange humming sound in his throat. Even though she had the knife in her hand, she froze, and he was on her fast, grabbing her around the throat and pushing her, her head snapping back into the closet door. He squeezed her throat, and she opened her mouth wide like a fish out of water, gasping for oxygen. Darkness crept into the edge of her vision, weakness flooding her limbs, but she remembered the knife in her hand. Tightening her grip, she swung it in a low arc, hitting Bruce in the rib cage. He jerked backward, swatting at her hand as though he'd just been stung by a bee. She brought the knife back by her side, then swung it a second time, this time in an upward motion, hoping to hit him somewhere in the ribs again, but he was taking another step backward and the blade hit his chin instead. Abigail felt the knife jolt in her hand when it struck bone. Bruce brought a hand up to his chin, where a flap of skin now hung, dripping blood. His face contorted in pain, and Abigail realized he was about to scream. She jabbed at his throat with the point of the blade and it sank in, only about an inch, but when she pulled it away a spray of blood immediately pumped from the wound, going in a high arc over her right shoulder. Bruce dropped to his knees, then fell over onto his side. She sucked in a long, ragged breath.

Even though she was married to him and had made love to him just three nights earlier, Abigail, watching Bruce die, felt as though she were watching a stranger.

No, not a stranger, but something worse. An animal that had to be put down.

She watched the blood pool under his head, spreading rapidly, seeping into the cracks in the floor. The raw coppery smell was filling her nostrils, and she cupped her hand over her face and turned away.

She thought about changing out of her bloodied clothes and went to her bureau, pulling open a drawer just as she realized that she'd already packed her clothes, back when she thought she was going to catch a flight off the island. She quickly looked around the bunk, not seeing her rolling duffel bag anywhere. She was about to give up when she crouched and checked under the bed, and there it was, shoved there by Bruce. She pulled it out and opened it. She decided not to change, but took her phone from the outside pocket and a hooded windbreaker that lay on top of her folded clothes. She figured it would be cold on the open ocean. Before heading out she patted her pockets, a longtime habit, and felt the stone she'd kept in her front pocket. She was not a superstitious person, but she knew that that particular stone would help her get off the island.

Once she was outside, she was glad for the extra layer. It was a clear night, but the temperature had dropped since the day before, her breath billowing. She felt oddly calm, breathing in the night air, and wondered if she was in shock.

She was about to step off the back deck when she noticed a bow leaning up against the railing, maybe left there by Bruce. She wondered if he'd had it with him while he'd been searching for her, as though he really were a hunter and she was his prey. Next to the bow was a quiver of arrows. She lifted the bow by its handgrip to see how it felt, then pulled the string back as far as she could. She'd used a bow once before, at a Renaissance fair she'd gone to with Zoe back when they'd been in high school. Zoe had shot once, missed the target, then quit. Abigail had stayed at the archery tent and fired about twenty arrows, determined to hit the bull's-eye, which she eventually did. The overattentive man in charge had shown Abigail how to stand, how to position her arms, how to release the arrow cleanly. The memory came back now in crushing clarity, a reminder of a life in which she wasn't being hunted. She took the bow and arrows with her.

It was relatively easy to find the path that led down to the pond, and once she was on it, she broke into a slow jog, wanting to move fast but not wanting to make any unnecessary noise. She ran through a copse of trees, the world darkening, and had to slow down to look where she was going. The woods whispered around her, black trees converging, and she felt the bubble of fear in her chest expand into a balloon. Her lungs shriveled, and her heart jackhammered. Something snapped up ahead of her—a twig breaking, a pinecone dropping from a tree—and she instinctively stepped off the path into the dark shadows, standing as still as possible, willing herself not to make a sound. The child in her remembered that if you stayed quiet, the woods would absorb you. The fear went briefly away but was replaced by a kind of grief. When she'd been a young girl hiding in the woods behind her house, she'd been in a world of her own making, but one that she could leave at any time. Her parents had been in the house less than a hundred yards away. Her father probably had been puttering around his study, her mother either in the garden or in her favorite reading nook in the sunroom off the kitchen. Here, now, she was all alone. She might as well be on an island floating in the coldest reaches of space. And the woods were filled with psychotic men, intent on killing her.

But not Bruce, she thought. He had bled out on the floor of their honeymoon cabin. Her mind flashed back to the way she'd slipped the point of the knife in and out of his throat as easily as popping a balloon. And the way the blood had sprung from his body. What had it reminded her of? Something in the distant past. And she thought of the tires she'd slashed all those years ago on Kaitlyn Austin's car after Kaitlyn had said those awful things about Abigail's parents. She remembered it all clearly, the pilfered kitchen knife slicing through the rubber, the instant deflation, her own body relaxing. And she thought of Bruce, enraged, choking her, and then a few jabs from her knife and he was on the floor, leaking blood instead of air.

Abigail told herself to stop thinking about what had happened and listen to her surroundings. There had been no other sounds since that single, horrible snap of a twig, and she steeled herself to step back out onto the path. She moved as quietly as possible, holding her breath, planting her heel on the path, then rolling forward onto her toes. The darkness was both comforting and dreadful. But then the path broke right, and the pond was in front of her, iridescent in the moonlight.

Abigail stopped and crouched, letting her breath return to normal and watching the boathouse for any sign of activity. There was enough light for her to see the canoes lined up along the shore, and also the kayaks she'd seen earlier that week. Each kayak was for one person, made from fiberglass, and Abigail knew from experience that it probably weighed only about fifty pounds. When she'd been thinking about how to get off the island, she kept going back to the fact that there were no boats here, but of course there *were* boats, sailboats and kayaks and canoes, but they were on the pond, not on the ocean's shore. Abigail was pretty sure she could drag, or carry, the kayak to the ocean and paddle to the mainland. What she worried about right now was whether they'd thought of that, too. Would there be a guard? And if so, where was he?

The boathouse was a simple building, more of a shell, really, with unpainted wood sides and a green plastic roof. The side of the building that faced the pond was completely open, and Abigail imagined that if there was a guard, he'd be sitting in the boathouse, waiting, maybe even dozing.

She put her bow down on the ground, alongside the kitchen knife she'd used to kill Bruce, and ran her hands through the fallen leaves and needles till she found a stone about the size of a golf ball. She stood and threw the stone as far as she could, past the boathouse. It skittered along the rocky shore of the pond, and almost immediately a figure emerged from the boathouse, running after the sound, his head swiveling. He was too far away for Abigail to make out who he might be, but she could tell that he carried a rifle with him. The sight of the gun was shocking; maybe the plane she thought she'd heard earlier had brought guns as well as dogs.

Abigail picked up the bow, notched one arrow into the string, and ran quietly down to the boathouse, pressing up against its back wall, then moving to its edge, peering around at the man, who was still scouring the area. She suddenly felt stupid with the bow, remembering how long it had taken her at the Renaissance fair to get in one decent shot. What made her think that she'd be able to hit this man on her first try, before he turned and simply shot her? She should have brought the knife and charged him while his back was turned. At least then she might have had a fighting chance. She decided to wait in the shadow of the boathouse until he gave up wondering what had made the sound, then go back and get her knife and try to get the drop on him.

Just then she heard a sound, a brief snippet of static, and saw that he was on his walkie-talkie, probably calling for reinforcements. Without thinking, she took a step away from the boathouse, squared her feet, and pulled the arrow back. He must have heard the creak of the bow, because he turned and looked at her, and she fired, the string smacking against the windbreaker on the inside of her arm, but the arrow flying straight, striking the man below his left shoulder. He stepped backward, lost his balance, and went down. Abigail ran over and knelt above him. It was the island detective—Bob something—instantly recognizable by his white hair. He looked up at her with fear in his eyes, then yelled, "She's here." Another staticky squawk came from the walkie-talkie, still in his hand. Abigail picked up the rifle and, holding it by its barrel, smacked the other end down toward his forehead, but hit his nose instead, breaking it, blood pooling into his mouth. He squealed, an almost purely animal sound, and she hit him again, this time in the head, and he was quiet.

She ran to the kayaks and examined the nearest one. It had a convenient handle on its bow, a plastic grip attached to two inches of synthetic rope. She stowed the rifle inside the kayak, then went in search of a paddle, finding several lined up against the interior wall of the boathouse. She picked the shortest one. On the way out of the boathouse she smelled coffee and spotted an open thermos next to a lawn chair. She picked up the thermos and took a long pull, the coffee hot and milky and sweet. And there was a sharp undertaste of alcohol, probably whiskey. She spotted the thermos's lid, on top of a paperback novel splayed open on the floor, and twisted it back onto the thermos, deciding to bring it with her. She didn't know how long it would take her to kayak from the island back to the coast of Maine, but it couldn't hurt to have some fuel with her.

With the rifle, the thermos, and the paddle all stowed, she grabbed the handle and began to pull the kayak along the shore.

31

She was on the bluff when she heard the dogs.

Two distinct howls followed by the sound of barking.

She didn't know exactly how long it had been since she'd taken the kayak from the edge of the pond, but she thought it was at least an hour. The hardest part had been along the shore, the boat scraping over the rocks, her heels banging against the bow. Then she'd remembered that there was a better way to move across land with a kayak. She even remembered the word—portaging—something her father had taught her many years ago. She bent her knees, then slid an arm through the rim of the kayak's cockpit and lifted, settling the kayak on her shoulder. She tilted it slightly so that the paddle and the rifle wouldn't fall through the opening. Once she was upright the kayak didn't seem too heavy, and she quickly reached the path through the woods. She had to climb an embankment, the path covered with mossy rocks and occasional patches of weeds, and she was terrified of slipping. But she kept going and, ignoring a painful stitch in her side, little by little made her way through the woods.

When the path evened out, she began to smell the

ocean in the breeze, and when she reached the edge of the bluff the sky, anchored by a nearly full moon, was an expanse that arched above her. Her lungs ached and the muscles in her legs were cramping, but she felt an almost alarming sense of hope. She could see the ocean, placid in the light of the moon.

She walked slowly over the bluff, saving some energy, cutting diagonally across to where the path began along the cliff edge. Halfway there was when she heard the dogs, the distant howls and the barking. They'd be out in force now looking for her. She wondered, also, if there was a guard near the cove where she was headed. It was one of the few places where it would be relatively easy to launch a boat. But she couldn't worry about that now. She needed to pick up speed. The dogs would be following her scent.

She turned left at the cliff and began down the path, the rim of the kayak's opening biting into her shoulder. Another bark reached her, this time much closer. She looked back and saw what she thought was the faint glimmer of a flashlight emerging from the dark line of woods on the other side of the bluff. She peered over the edge of the cliff, wondering if it was worth throwing the kayak off and jumping after it. It looked like about a twenty-yard drop, but the brief line of shore below was covered with black jagged rocks. She kept moving.

The cramp in her side got worse and the roof of her mouth ached, saliva pooling under her tongue. She bent over, resting the bow of the kayak on the ground, and was briefly sick, tasting only the coffee that she'd drunk back in the boathouse. Then she began to run, her shoulder screaming at her, her legs rubbery.

She heard a human voice, a shout that sounded like the words "This way," and she glanced back again. Flashlights were now visible not too far back and she could make out the dark figure of a dog bounding ahead of the men.

If she hadn't seen where the path ahead dipped down toward the shore, she would have thrown the kayak off the cliff right there and jumped after it. But the cove was close—thirty feet away—and she picked up speed, reaching the edge and peering over.

There was a man on the beach below, pointing a rifle up at her.

"Hold it," he said, and she recognized him as Eric Newman. Without hesitating, she dropped the kayak over the edge and watched as it bumped and skidded down toward where he was standing. He tried to step out of its way, but the kayak hit him just below the knees, then bounced off and kept sliding along the seaweed-slicked rocks. He was on his back, gripping his leg, the rifle to his side. Abigail followed the path down as fast as she could, reaching Eric just as she heard the grunting sound of a dog right behind her. She picked up the rifle, spun, and the dog, a dark brown hound, merely bumped up against her, its tail wagging, sniffing at her, obviously pleased to have done its job. Eric grabbed a handful of her windbreaker, but she easily broke free, spun, and pointed the gun at him.

"Abigail, don't," he said, and held up his hands. "I was going to let you go. That's why I asked to guard this beach." The dog barked twice beside her.

"Bullshit," she said, and placed the butt of the rifle against her shoulder.

"Listen to me. Don't do this. No one was supposed to get hurt. We're going to take care of Alec. He'll pay for what he did."

She imagined a bullet ripping through his skull, shutting this man up forever, but she pointed the gun toward where he was cradling his damaged leg and pulled the trigger. He jerked his hand away, but his leg bucked back, blood pumping from his destroyed knee. The dog whimpered, then scrambled away.

As he screamed, Abigail turned and took three steps to the kayak, pushing it with her foot out past the rocks and into the cresting surf. She dove onto the hull as she heard gunshots behind and above her. Holding on to the crisscrossed cording at the stern of the boat, she got her feet through the opening of the cockpit, then slid inside, dropping into the seat. She got her body as low as possible. More shots rang out, but Abigail had begun to paddle, digging deep with each stroke and keeping her head low. The kayak bucked up against a series of waves, and then it was moving steadily along the calm surface, picking up speed. She heard a few more shots, and then there was silence, and then she heard the low howl of the dog, sounding distant and lonely.

When she was far enough away from the island, she pulled her cell phone out from her jeans. It turned on, showing that it had three percent battery power. She checked for service but there was none, then opened her compass app, held it flat in her hand, and adjusted her direction so that she was heading exactly due west.

She'd kayaked plenty in her life, along the Connecticut River and at a pond one town over from Boxgrove, and she easily got back into the rhythm. She was exhausted and cold, but her arm muscles felt good, and her feet had found the footholds up under the bow.

Trying to remain calm, she worked at a steady pace, occasionally glancing down at the phone she'd placed on the floor of the kayak, making sure she was still moving in the right direction.

The night was quiet, and a steady but slight breeze ruffled the surface of the ocean. She kept imagining the guttural thrum of a small airplane coming to find her, but there were no sounds except for the paddle slapping against the water and her own labored breathing. She felt the stitch in her side acting up again, like a hot needle had been slipped between her ribs. She took a quick break, checking the compass to make sure she was still going in the right direction, then finishing the whiskey-laced coffee, its warmth spreading down her center, making her realize how cold the rest of her body had become. She dumped the thermos overboard, somehow imagining that it would significantly lighten the boat, then began to paddle, harder now that blisters were opening up on both of her palms. She thought of Jill again, lying dead on the cold floor of the forest.

Something streaked in the sky, and she stopped paddling for a moment, searching the glittering expanse above her. Then another shooting star caught her eye, a brief line of light. She repositioned her stinging hands on the paddle, then instinctively looked over her shoulder, her neck creaking. There was no sign of the island she had left, just a black stretch of ocean. And there was nothing in front of her, either. She reached down to touch the screen of her phone, and nothing happened. It was out of power. She was out in the open, and for a moment she felt not just scared but overcome with horror that seemed to empty her out, that squeezed at her lungs. She told herself to keep going, that there would be time in the future for her to have a breakdown.

Wiping her hands on her thighs, then getting a new grip on her paddle, she began to steer in the direction she'd been heading, keeping her eyes on the stars above her, recognizing three in a row that made up Orion's belt. The constellation was slightly to her left, and she focused on keeping it there as she paddled as hard as she could. The faster she went, the less chance that she would veer off course.

Twenty minutes later she spotted a lighthouse, a dim sweeping beam of light. Its appearance ratcheted up her dread of hearing the sound of a plane, or of another boat, but none came, and the lighthouse got closer, close enough that she could make out its shape against the purple sky. It was built on an outcropping of rock, barely an island, so she kept going. She thought she was in Casco Bay; she could see shoreline now, and another lighthouse. Her muscles burning, she picked up the pace, dipping the paddle deep into the water, gritting her teeth. Soon she could see scattered lights along the shoreline, even the sweep of what looked like a car's headlights. Everything was blurry, and she realized that her eyes were watering in the cold wind, tears streaming down her cheeks. She kept paddling toward the lighthouse.

Just as she neared the shore, she saw a faint glimmer of dawn light on the horizon, the sky lightening to gray. The lighthouse was like something from a postcard. White with a black top, below it a lightkeepers' house, painted red. And in front of the house she could make out a lone car, its lights off, along the edge of what was probably a visitors' parking lot. Was someone waiting for her? She turned south and began paddling as hard as she could. She was hoping to spot a better place to come onto shore, less rocky, and not someplace where she might be spotted.

The kayak was moving slowly, a rip current working against her, but soon she spotted a tree-shrouded cove, a strip of sand visible in the dawn light. She pointed the kayak toward the shore, slapping against a flat rock just under the water, then the bow of the kayak slid up onto the beach. She stood, lost her balance, and fell out of the kayak into three inches of icy water. Her elbow hit something sharp and her arm went numb. She grunted, then quickly stood, pulling the kayak a little farther up on the beach.

The sky was now a pearly white, and the air was filled with dawn mist.

A man stepped out of the tree line about ten yards from her, a long rifle in the crook of his arm.

32

Abigail reached inside the kayak, trying to get hold of her own gun with numb fingers.

"Can I help you?" the man said. His voice, the calmness of it, was startling.

"Stay right there." Abigail found the gun and pulled it out, pointing it at the man. He was heavyset, wearing a fleece hoodie with a camouflage pattern.

"Shit," he said, and dropped his own gun, which had been pointing at the ground, then put his hands up.

Abigail had begun to shiver, but she kept her finger on the trigger and kept the gun pointed at the man. "Step back," she said, and he did. She let her eyes flick toward the ground in front of him and saw that it wasn't a rifle he had dropped but a metal detector, an elaborate handle on one end, a flat disc on the other.

"What are you doing here?" she said.

"I was here yesterday. My wife and I were fishing, and she lost her wedding band. I'm here to look for it." His voice trembled. Abigail believed him, but she didn't want to take a chance and kept the rifle pointed in his direction.

"Do you have a phone?" she said.

"Yeah. It's in my front pocket."

"Reach in slowly, okay? And pull it out."

He did as he was told, pulling out a flat black phone from the front of his baggy jeans.

"Toss it to me."

He threw the phone in a low arc and it landed three feet in front of Abigail on the sand. "Sit on the ground, okay, and keep your arms above your head."

"Okay," he said, and awkwardly lowered himself onto a hump of grass at the edge of the beach. Once he was settled, Abigail picked up the phone. The screen was asking for a four-digit passcode, but on the lower left was the word EMERGENCY, and when she pressed it, the phone dialed 911.

"Where are we?" Abigail said quickly to the man, once she heard the ring in her ear.

"What?" he said.

"What location are we at? What street?"

Before he could answer, she heard a click, then a female voice. "Nine-one-one. What's your emergency?"

"I've just kayaked from Heart Pond Island," Abigail said into the phone. "There are men there, they were trying to kill me. I'm at . . ."

She looked over at the man, who was sitting cross-legged, his arms still above him, and he said, "Hannaford Point on Cape Elizabeth."

She repeated the information to the woman on the other end of the line, then answered more questions, the dispatcher assuring her that a patrol car was on its way.

After Abigail ended the call, the man said, "You kayaked here from Heart Pond Island?"

"Uh-huh. You know it?"

"I did some work out there a few years ago. I'm an electrician."

"For Chip Ramsay?"

"I don't remember. Maybe. What happened to you?"

"Bad marriage," she said, then laughed, realizing that she sounded a little hysterical.

"Can I put my arms down now?"

"What's your name?"

"James Pelletier."

"Go ahead and put your hands on your knees. I don't really trust you yet, James."

He lowered his hands slowly and placed them on his knees. Abigail, without thinking, lowered herself to the damp sand, but kept the rifle pointed in the man's general direction. "Where will the police car come from?" she said.

"The road's right behind that line of trees. There's a little dirt parking lot. We'll see it coming."

Sitting down had been a mistake. Abigail could feel the exhaustion flooding through her limbs, and she wondered for a moment if she'd be able to stand up again.

"I really thought you were going to shoot me," James said, shaking his head.

She looked at him, still waiting for his hand to move swiftly into the pocket of his hoodie, whip out a gun, and put a bullet through her head. She didn't think it was going to happen, but why wouldn't it?

"Ever heard of a green man?" she said.

"A green man?"

"Yeah, what does it mean to you?" She studied him, and suddenly he looked fearful again.

"I don't know," he said.

"What about Silvanus? That mean anything?"

He shook his head.

Flashing lights suddenly penetrated the hazy gray of dawn, and Abigail could make out the cruiser pulling into the parking lot. James turned his head.

Holding on to the rifle, Abigail planted a hand by her side to push herself upright again, and she felt something embedded in the sand under her palm. Cold metal. She picked at it with her fingers, realized it was a ring, and glanced down at it. Holding it up for him to see, she said, "Your wife's ring."

"Ha," James Pelletier said, smiling.

For the first time in a long time, she thought she might actually live.

She was shaking uncontrollably in the interrogation room when they wrapped her in a blanket and told her to wait for one minute. There had been a brief discussion when she'd been brought in through the reception area over whether she should go directly to the hospital, but Abigail was able to convince the desk sergeant that she was fine, and that she wanted to report a murder, that she'd go to a hospital right after she filed her report. It was clear they thought that she was on drugs, at least that the patrol officer who drove her from the shore to the police station thought so. He asked her several times what substances she'd taken in the previous twenty-four hours. He'd asked in a purposefully calm voice that had made Abigail want to scream at him.

When at last a plainclothes policeman came into the interrogation room, he held two cups of coffee and handed one to her. He was wearing a blue suit and a maroon tie, and when he sat down his stomach pushed out against his button-up shirt so that Abigail could see the T-shirt he wore underneath. He introduced himself as Detective Mando, then indicated a camera in the corner of the room and told Abigail that she was being recorded.

"There's been a murder on Heart Pond Island," Abigail said. "Jill Greenly was murdered by her husband two nights ago."

"Okay," he said, flipping open his notebook. "What's your name, ma'am? Your full name, please."

"It's Abigail Elliot Baskin. I married Bruce Lamb last week and he brought me to Heart Pond Island for my honeymoon. He's dead, too."

"You're going to have to slow down. Tell me how you wound up out at Hannaford Point."

"I kayaked from the island."

He nodded, and she watched him write the words *Heart Pond Island*, *Abigail Baskin*, then *Bruce Lamb*.

"Are you sending someone there?" she said. "They're probably covering it up right now."

"Officers are on the way already," he said. "Don't worry. Whatever happened to you, we're going to sort it, okay? In the meantime, I need you to tell me exactly what happened."

Unable to stop herself, Abigail brought her hand up and pressed a finger and a thumb against her eyelids. She cried solidly for about two minutes while Detective Mando waited. There was nothing she could do to stop it from coming out of her. She'd been wound so tight for so long and now everything was unspooling, her body out of her control.

When she eventually stopped crying, he pushed a box of tissues across the table toward her and said, "Okay. Let's start at the beginning."

EPILOGUE

Abigail received the email on Friday afternoon, but didn't open it until Sunday, after she'd brought her laptop onto her back patio. It was a beautiful late April morning, one of those rare warm spring days in Massachusetts. All the remnants of that winter's numerous snowstorms were gone, and crocuses and daffodils had just started to appear. The email was from the wedding photographer.

Dear Abigail, I didn't know if I should send you these pictures, but then I figured that that was your decision, and not mine. I was very sorry to hear about what happened after the wedding. I hope you are doing as well as can be. For what it's worth, it was great getting to know you and your family and friends a little bit over that weekend in October. The attached link will allow you to look at all of the photographs (almost 500!), if you choose. If you do end up wanting higher res versions of any of these, please let me know. But other than that, no need to respond. All the best and take care, Natalie Ramirez

She remembered the photographer, a woman so tiny that eventually you almost didn't see her, wending her way around the various wedding events with a camera that looked enormous in her hands.

Abigail wondered what Natalie had thought when she first heard about the events on Heart Pond Island. The initial news reports had been somewhat vague. "Police Investigating Multiple Suspicious Deaths on Honeymoon Island." Then, later, "Inside the Alleged 'Cult' That Punished Wives for Infidelities." At that point it was a federal case, and the story had broken nationally, leading to a deluge of reporters descending on Boxgrove, where Abigail was now living. She hadn't returned to New York City after what had happened on the island. She'd returned home, sleeping in her mother's bed for a while, then in her childhood bedroom. A month earlier she'd moved half a block away to a small rental house, already furnished. Her parents thought it was silly for her to get her own place, but her own place made her feel she was moving in the right direction.

It had been more than six months of talking. To her parents, to Zoe, to a succession of therapists. And, of course, constant interrogations, some under oath, with both federal agents and a slew of attorneys. In the midst of all this she'd somehow managed to work on her novel, about the twins in New York. She knew it was less than stellar but didn't mind. Involving herself in that fictional world, no matter how dark that world was, was preferable to thinking about what had happened in her actual life.

Two months earlier, Charles "Chip" Ramsay III had been arrested in Mexico, where he'd fled after his indictment. Eric Newman, last Abigail had heard, was cooperating with the federal investigation into what was now being called the Silvanus Cult, a small group of men with ties to other men's rights groups, and with a history of testing their girlfriends and wives for fidelity. Some of the wealthier members, such as Bruce, were also partners in a limited liability corporation set up by Chip Ramsay called Silvanus Incorporated, named after the Roman god of the woods and of wild nature. That corporation had purchased Heart Pond Island and the defunct summer camps on it, as well as a similar island in the Puget Sound, the place where Bruce had gone for his bachelor weekend. Once the floodgates had been opened, a surprising number of current and ex-employees of both these places had stepped forward to give testimony, along with multiple women, all with stories about being elaborately punished for their transgressions. Chip Ramsay's own wife had disappeared two years earlier, and that disappearance was now being treated as a potential homicide.

Mellie, whose full name was Melanie Nadeau, had turned herself in as a cooperating witness, claiming that she had been coerced against her will by Chip Ramsay to work on Heart Pond Island. Porter Conyers, the man from Bermuda who had once been involved with Jill

Greenly, had somehow managed to entirely disappear. Jill's husband, Alec Greenly, the producer, had committed suicide in his jail cell in February by hanging himself with a bathroom towel.

Abigail was a star witness in the wide-ranging investigation. She was hoping it would never go to court, but she was also willing to do whatever it took to make sure the various members of Silvanus paid for what they'd done.

Eric Newman had tried to get in touch with her, sending an email to the same address he'd used way back when, before the wedding. He said that he didn't expect her to ever forgive him, but that he'd like to explain his role in what had happened. She imagined that he wanted to talk about how Chip Ramsay was a charismatic figure, that he'd been seduced like other damaged men during one of Chip's seminars in San Diego, a weekend event called "Men Finding Their Voice" or something like that—that was most likely where both Eric and Bruce had been recruited years earlier. She never replied to Eric Newman's email.

She was about to open the photographer's link when movement in her small backyard caught her eye. It was the black feral cat that sometimes lived in the attached garage. The owners, before renting to Abigail, had informed her about the cat they'd named Bonnie, wanting to ensure that Abigail would keep an eye out for her and occasionally put food and water out, especially if there was bad weather. Abigail had agreed, but she'd rarely spotted Bonnie since she'd moved in.

Abigail watched the cat move stealthily across the lawn, keeping low, stalking a lone sparrow on a fence post that marked the boundary of the property. Bonnie got about three feet from the bird before it sprang into the air and landed on a low branch of a tall maple tree. The cat stretched her spine and nonchalantly circled back, as though she hadn't been that interested in the bird in the first place. Abigail watched the sparrow, now arcing its way toward a small shrubby tree. Did it know how close it had come to being eaten?

She finished her coffee, went back inside to get a second cup, and made toast for herself. Her father had called and left her a message wanting to know if she'd like to go see an afternoon movie, and Zoe had sent a text to see if she wanted to get lunch. She decided she wasn't quite ready to make decisions regarding her day and took her second cup of coffee back outside to the patio, putting it down on the coffee table next to the small white stone with the red ring that she'd kept from Heart Pond Island. She touched a finger to the stone before leaning back, gathering her laptop, and clicking on the link that brought her to the wedding photographs.

There were hundreds of them, as the photographer had promised, laid out in a grid that loaded surprisingly fast. Most were in black-and-white, but a few were in color, and the images unspooled on the page like cards being turned over. Abigail had been prepared for a tidal wave of emotions but, oddly, maybe because she was expecting that, she felt relatively unmoved by all the pictures. She remembered the day well—getting dressed with the bridesmaids while sharing champagne, the official photographs on the hill with the Hudson River in the background, the walk down the aisle, the vows they'd written themselves, the cocktail party, dinner and dancing. She actually found herself enjoying some of the pictures, getting to see her friends and family dressed up again, having fun. The pictures that showed Bruce were harder to look at. Not because she grieved for him or missed him in any way, but because she found herself studying his face in the pictures, trying to see if there was any moment when he gave himself away, when he showed his true nature. She couldn't see it. In the posed pictures he looked stiff at times, his smile a little too wide, but that could mean anything. In the candid shots, he mostly looked relaxed and at ease with himself. There were even shots where he was looking at Abigail, and it looked as if there was love in his eyes. How had she been so fooled?

It was one of the questions she found herself asking a lot these days. How had she not recognized Bruce's true nature? Had she been blinded by his romantic gestures? Or by his money and his success? Or had he just seemed so different from Ben Perez that she'd fallen for him regardless? She wasn't sure she'd ever know.

But she did think there was maybe a clue in the wedding pictures. Maybe he looked as though he was in love with her because he really was, in some perverted and strange way? Even though he knew what lay ahead, that he would get his revenge for her infidelity, he still felt love for her, or an approximation of love? And maybe she was reading too much into it? The most logical explanation was that Bruce was a psychopath, a psychopath who had gone to a seminar that told him what he always believed down deep, ever since his mother had abandoned his family: women weren't to be trusted.

And the reason he'd looked genuinely in love in the photographs was because he was good at faking it.

Abigail was almost done looking at the album when something caught her eye in one of the last pictures. It was a photo of the last dance, she and Bruce looking tired and happy at the center of the dance floor. She remembered it well. Her stinging feet, the jazzy version of "Every Breath You Take," making jokes with Bruce. In the photograph they are out of focus while the onlookers, the wedding stragglers on the edge of the dance floor, are shown in sharp detail. There are her parents, standing next to each other, her mother looking sleepy, her father beaming, probably a little drunk. Behind the onlookers is the wide-open door of the barn, its white-painted trim strung with garlands of flowers. A man stood just inside the door, edged by light, probably from the headlights from a departing car. Abigail zoomed in on the man. He was heavily pixelated, but she knew without a doubt that it was Eric Newman.

She remembered thinking she'd spotted him on her

walk back down the carriageway that night. Not spotting him so much as smelling the French cigarette that he was smoking. It was strange to think he really had been there. She wondered if Bruce had snuck off at some point to talk with him, maybe even chat about the game they were about to play on Heart Pond Island.

She closed her laptop. She'd seen enough of the photographs and didn't think she'd ever need to look at them again.

A cloud had gone over the sun, and the day had dimmed. The line of woods along the property was dark, and she looked for the sparrow but didn't see her. She didn't see the cat, either. A phrase entered her head: *The woods are lovely, dark and deep*. She'd said those words to Bruce on the island. Remembering that moment, she didn't feel awful; she didn't feel anything, actually. Most importantly, her mind didn't automatically go flipping through that catalogue of terrible images she'd carried with her for six months. Men in masks. Alec Greenly battering his wife to death by the fire. The feel of sliding a knife into Bruce's throat, and watching an arc of blood leave his body. Instead, she thought about the day ahead, and what she might want to do with it.

Beasts had come for her. And she was still alive.

ACKNOWLEDGMENTS

Margaret Atwood (for a quote I didn't use, but thought of many times), Danielle Bartlett, Angus Cargill, Caspian Dennis, Bianca Flores, Joel Gotler, John Grindrod, Kaitlin Harri, David Headley, Sara Henry, David Highfill, Tessa James, Emily Langner (for telling me the Margaret Atwood quote), Ira Levin, Kristen Pini, Sophie Portas, Josh Smith, Nat Sobel, Virginia Stanley, Gordon Sumner, Sandy Violette, Judith Weber, Ben Wheatley, Dave Woodhouse, Adia Wright, and Charlene Sawyer.

COMING SOON
from Peter Swanson

NINE LIVES

Matthew Beaumont

Jay Coates

Ethan Dart

Caroline Geddes

Frank Hopkins

Alison Horne

Arthur Kruse

Jack Radebaugh

Jessica Winslow

'I loved this, Swanson's sharp and insightful characterization brought to life a fascinating premise, beautifully worked out.' Ann Cleeves

'With economical strokes of his pen, Peter Swanson presents us with a clever homage to the Golden Age of Mystery which keeps you guessing right to the end.' Peter May

3 March 2022
Available in hardback, ebook and audio

WEDNESDAY, SEPTEMBER 14, 5:13 p.m.

Jonathan Grant, unless he let her know ahead of time that he couldn't make it, always visited on Wednesday evening. His wife had a standing "girls' night out" on Wednesdays—occasionally in the city, but usually in New Jersey—so Jonathan would leave the office by five and be at Alison's one-bedroom apartment in Gramercy Park by five-thirty at the latest.

Alison Horne was ready when the doorman buzzed up to let her know Jonathan was on his way.

She met him at the door, and he presented her with a bottle of Sancerre, a Bulgari scarf she didn't think she'd ever wear, and that day's mail that he'd picked up from the doorman. She started to flip through the mail, but he stopped her and led her to the bedroom. She was in a white satin robe—it was how he liked to be greeted—and she slid back onto her bed while he undressed. He looked great for a man in his early seventies, full head of hair, fairly trim, but the muscles in his chest and arms were beginning to sag. He slid next to her on the bed, already erect, and with the red mottled skin on his face and neck that was a telltale sign he'd taken some kind of ED pill as soon as he left the office. Sometimes he took it just after he arrived, in which case they'd drink the bottle of wine first while the pill kicked in.

Afterward, while Jonathan dozed, Alison took her second shower of the day, then dressed as though they were going to go out for dinner later, although that hadn't been confirmed. She opened the wine and poured herself a glass, then looked through her mail. Two catalogues, an Amex bill, and an envelope with no return address. She opened it, curious, and pulled out a single folded sheet of paper, and stared at a list of names.

Matthew Beaumont
Jay Coates
Ethan Dart
Caroline Geddes
Frank Hopkins
Alison Horne
Arthur Kruse
Jack Radebaugh
Jessica Winslow

She frowned and pressed the sheet of paper flat onto the coffee table, telling herself that she'd show it to Jonathan. A shiver went over her skin, and she shook out her limbs to make it stop. There was something vaguely threatening about receiving a list of names with no explanation. It occurred to her that it just might have something to do with Jonathan, currently dozing in her bedroom. Although she knew relatively little about him, considering the time they spent together, she did know that he had a lot of money. And people who have money usually have enemies. It made her wonder if he would recognize any of the names on the list, besides hers.

He emerged from the bedroom fully dressed, accepted a glass of wine, then looked at the sheet of paper Alison handed to him. "This mean anything to you?" she asked.

He shook his head. "What is it?"

"I just got it, in the mail."

"Was this all?"

"Yeah. Strange, huh?"

"Strange."

He handed the list back to Alison. She asked: "We going to dinner?"

"I would if I could, but I got roped into dinner uptown with some hedge fund guys. Sorry, Al."

She shrugged. When they'd first begun this relationship—a year and a half ago—she used to make a fuss when he had to leave her. She did it for him, mostly, till she realized that he didn't need those kinds of reassurances. He was in it for the sex and the company, and she was in it for the money, and, she supposed, the sex. Before he left, he gave her a prepaid Visa card, telling her it was an anniversary gift, in case she didn't like the scarf.

"How much is on it?" she asked. Again, something she

would never have asked when they were first together.

"I'll let you be surprised. Don't try to buy a car with it, though."

After he left, Alison Horne called her best friend, Doug, and asked if he'd like to have dinner that night. On her.